MASSACRE
OF EAGLES

RvG

MASSACRE
OF EAGLES

William W. Johnstone
with J. A. Johnstone

PINNACLE BOOKS
Kensington Publishing Corp.
www.kensingtonbooks.com

PINNACLE BOOKS are published by

Kensington Publishing Corp.
119 West 40th Street
New York, NY 10018

PUBLISHER'S NOTE
Following the death of William W. Johnstone, the Johnstone family is working with a carefully selected writer to organize and complete Mr. Johnstone's outlines and many unfinished manuscripts to create additional novels in all of his series like The Last Gunfighter, Mountain Man, and Eagles, among others. This novel was inspired by Mr. Johnstone's superb storytelling.

All Kensington titles, imprints, and distributed lines are available at special quantity discounts for bulk purchases for sales promotions, premiums, fund-raising, educational, or institutional use. Special book excerpts or customized printings can also be created to fit specific needs. For details, write or phone the office of the Kensington special sales manager: Kensington Publishing Corp., 119 West 40th Street, New York, NY 10018, attn: Special Sales Department; phone 1-800-221-2647.

ISBN-13: 978-0-7860-2349-3
ISBN-10: 0-7860-2349-X

First printing: August 2011

10 9 8 7 6 5 4 3

Printed in the United States of America

Following the Custer fight at Little Big Horn, the Northern Cheyenne were sent to Oklahoma, then known as Indian Territory. The Cheyenne were not accustomed to the hot conditions of Oklahoma and they began dying in great numbers. In desperation, a small band left the reservation and headed north, settling in the Tongue River watershed in Montana Territory. Here, they established homesteads in the northern edge of the Big Horn River Basin, which they considered their natural home. And, because their settlement was peaceful, President Arthur, by executive order, established the Tongue River Reservation, making it legal for them to stay there.

PROLOGUE

Tongue River Reservation, Montana Territory

One of the residents of the Tongue Reservation was Mean to His Horses, a member of the Crooked Lance Warrior's Society, and a nephew of the most notable of all Cheyenne warriors, Roman Nose. Mean to His Horses was but a youth when he saw his uncle killed at Beecher Island in September of 1868. Later, Mean to His Horses had been by the side of Crazy Horse in the fight against Custer. Crazy Horse was killed September 5, 1877, at Fort Robinson, Nebraska. He had been told that he was going to a meeting with the white officials to correct a misunderstanding. The misunderstanding was the result of a deliberate misrepresentation of his words by a translator during an earlier conference. Instead Crazy Horse was arrested, and as they attempted to put him into a guard house, he resisted. During the altercation, Crazy Horse was stabbed and killed.

Mean to His Horses was thinking about this when he entered the sweat lodge. Though he was alone, he observed the etiquette that would have been required had there been others in the lodge. He smudged his face with sage, he loaded his sacred pipe with tobacco, he turned in a clockwise circle at the door, then he crawled in through the opening, saying the sacred words *Mitakuye Oyasin* (All My Relations). Crawling in a clockwise direction, he completely circumnavigated the tipi, then he poured water over the seven hot stones to produce the steam.

He did not know how long he had been in the sweat lodge when it began. He heard singing and drums, but he had built the sweat lodge far from the village, so he knew there were neither drums nor singing to hear. He could see, in the clouds of steam, a great battle between Cheyenne and white soldiers, and he saw that the Cheyenne were winning because all the soldiers were falling from their horses.

Then the scene of the battle went away, and the drums and the singing stopped, and it was so quiet that he could hear his own blood flowing through his veins. That is when a new vision came to him.

The vision was of a man with long curly hair, not too tall and with a somewhat rounded face. His hair hung to his waist, braided with beaver-pelt covering and with two eagle feathers hanging down on the left. This could be only one person, and yet Mean to His Horses knew this could not be.

He challenged the apparition.

"Are you Crazy Horse?" Mean to His Horses asked. He asked the words with his heart, since speaking aloud would be inappropriate.

"Look," the apparition said, putting his finger to his left jaw. "What do you see here?"

There, Mean to His Horses saw a scar on the apparition's left jaw near his mouth and nose. The scar, Mean to His Horses knew, was from a bullet wound where No

Water shot him for being with Black Buffalo Woman, who had been No Water's wife at the time.

"It is you!" Mean to His Horses said.

"Listen, and I will tell you of a new thing," Crazy Horse said.

Mean to His Horses listened, and learned of the new thing: *Wagi Wanagi* or Spirit Talking.

"If all Indian people will do Spirit Talking, the Great Spirit who guides our lives will be pleased, and he will send the whites away so that all the land and the water and the game will return to the Indian people," Mean to His Horses was told. "You have been chosen to teach this thing to all Indian people."

"And if the white man objects and there is war?" Mean to His Horses asked.

"You are a war leader," Mean to His Horses was told. "If there is to be war, the people will follow you."

"I will lead them," Mean to His Horses said.

"From this day forward, you must wear the sacred paint," Crazy Horse said. The right side of your face, you will paint red. That is for the blood of the whites that must be spilled. The left side of your face you will paint white. That is so that our people will no longer be in darkness. Do these things and you cannot fail."

Upon leaving the sweat lodge, Mean to His Horses obeyed the commands of Crazy Horse. He painted the right side of his face red and the left side of his face white.

No one asked why he had done this.

Broken Bar K Ranch, near Virginia City,
Montana Territory

It was late morning and Len Kennedy and his two oldest boys, Len Jr. and Luther, were working in the field. Len's wife Mary had just called her family in to lunch when they saw Indians approaching. They thought nothing of it. All the neighboring Indians were friendly.

There were ten Indians in the party, and they rode right up to the back of the house.

Len was still not concerned because the Indians, while hunting, often came by the house for water, and sometimes for food. Just as often, the Indians left some of their game with Len. He recognized the leader of the group.

"Mean to His Horses," Len said. He chuckled. "Why do you have your face all painted up like that?"

Suddenly, and without so much as a word, the Indians attacked, sending an arrow through the senior Len's torso.

"Pa!" Len Jr. shouted.

The Indians shot Len Jr. and then they shot Luther as he tried to climb over the fence.

Mary Kennedy, hearing her son call out, then hearing the sound of a gunshot, came out onto the back porch.

"Mean to His Horses! What are you doing?" she screamed in fear and anger.

Mean to His Horses signaled to some of his men, and they grabbed Mrs. Kennedy and the three youngest children. Then his warriors went inside and ransacked the house, taking the money box and whatever else they thought might be useful.

Back outside, they planned to take Mary and her three youngest children with them as they left, but as they started to tie the boy, Toby, to a mule, Mary and Toby began crying and screaming.

Mean to His Horses shot Mary several times and ran a lance through Toby's neck. Then, leaving seven-year-old Tamara with her five-year-old brother Donnie and their dead mother, father, and brothers, the Indians rode off. Tamara stayed with Donnie and the dead members of her family until nightfall. Then she led Donnie back into the house.

The next morning, three passing freight wagons stopped by to visit and to see if they could get water for themselves and their team.

"Whoa," Doodle Priday said, as he halted his team. "Len! Len, where are you? I know you seen us coming, you thick-headed Irishman. How come you ain't out here to meet us the way you always are? I got that tobacco you wanted. Len! Len, where the hell are you?"

"Doodle, they's somethin' that don't feel right here," Arthur said. Arthur, sitting on the seat beside him, was the shotgun guard.

"Yeah, it does seem awful quiet, don't it? Len! Len, where are you?" This time Doodle's call was more insistent, and more worried.

"Doodle!" the driver of the second wagon called up to him. "Look over there. On the fence!"

Looking toward the fence, Doodle saw Luther's arrow-riddled body, draped across the top rung.

"Damn!" Doodle said.

"Ain't that Len, over there?" Arthur said.

"What the hell happened here?" Doodle asked. He set the brake on the wagon and climbed down. By now, the other two drivers had seen the bodies as well, not only Luther and Len, but Len Jr. All three, in addition to bullet wounds, had several arrows protruding from their bodies.

"Oh, sweet Jesus, Doodle, look over there!" one of the other drivers said.

The driver was pointing to the bodies of Mary and Toby.

"God in heaven," Doodle said. "Have the Injuns gone mad?"

After determining that none of the ones they found outside were alive, the drivers and shotgun guards went into the house.

"Is anyone alive here?" Doodle called.

Getting no answer, he called again.

"Hello! Is anyone here!"

"Me and Donnie are here," Tamara answered.

The young girl's frightened voice came from behind a hutch.

"Tamara? Tamara, child, come out here."

Tamara and her younger brother crawled out from behind the hutch.

"We were hiding in case the Indians came back," Tamara said.

"That was a wise thing to do."

"Are they all dead?" she asked.

Doodle was amazed at how calm the young girl was, and he was sure it was the result of her being totally overcome by the events.

"I'm afraid they are, darlin'," he said.

"I thought they were."

"I expect you had better come with us, child," Doodle said.

"Not until mama and daddy and my brothers are buried," Tamara said. Overnight, she had aged from a seven-year-old girl to a responsible young woman.

CHAPTER ONE

From the *New York Register Journal:*

Indian Depredations

GHASTLY RAIDS AGAINST INNOCENT FAMILIES

"Spirit Talking" the Cause

CHICAGO—Recent savage attacks by Plains Indians have given General Nelson Miles, Commanding General of the Department of the Missouri, cause to be concerned about a possible new Indian war. To this end he has ordered all commanders in the field to be alert for any further savageries. His concern is animated by intelligence from the West which suggests that the recent horrors perpetrated by various nations of the Sioux, the same tribe of heathens who so foully massacred Custer and all his brave men, may be the harbinger of renewed war against the white race. The cause of the unrest is thought to be something called Spirit Talking, a quasi-religion espoused by various shamans in which they are told that if all tenets of the strange heresy are followed, the white man will leave the cities and settlements of the West, and the land will be returned to the Indians.

The Indian who started this movement and is its most vocal spokesman is Mean to His Horses, a leader of the Crooked Lance Warrior Society of the Cheyenne. Mean to His Horses was a relative of Roman Nose, the ferocious Cheyenne warrior who led more attacks against the white man than any other Indian. He was also a follower and protégé of Crazy Horse. It is said that the Indians believe that Mean to His Horses is able to communicate with Crazy Horse through the means of Spirit Talking, and that has given him much medicine.

Buffalo Bill's Wild West Exhibition Playing to Packed House

NEW YORK—The Buffalo Bill Wild West Exhibition has performed before the crowned heads of Europe, delighting the royals and their subjects with a view of life in America's Great West. Now that same show is in New York and should a citizen of this fair city wish to be enlightened about the true nature of the Wild West, they need only to apply at the ticket office at Madison Square Garden where daily performances are being given.

Madison Square Garden, New York, New York

By the use of clever stage props, dirt, horses, cattle, cowboys and Indians, Madison Square Garden was transformed into a part of the American West. Falcon MacCallister and his brother and sister, the twins Andrew and Rosanna, were among the many spectators enjoying the Buffalo Bill Wild West Exhibition. So far the show had portrayed Pony Express mail carriers galloping to deliver the mail, leaping off one horse and instantly mounting another to continue at breakneck speed around the arena; Indians setting fire to and attacking a burning cabin from which heroic settlers would escape just in the nick of time; and stagecoach robbers who were fought off by the bravery of the shotgun guard and armed passengers.

They also had cowboys bringing a cattle stampede under control, and it was during the stampede that something went wrong. A bull broke out of the thundering herd to come rushing toward the audience.

"Oh, isn't it wonderful how they have trained the bull to do that?" Rosanna said, her voice tinged with excitement.

When the bull first broke loose from the herd, Falcon, like Rosanna and everyone else in the audience, believed it to be a part of the show. But looking around, he saw that there was no cowboy in position to be able to stop the runaway, and the reaction of the nearest cowboys to the bull clearly indicated that this was unplanned. There was a mounted New York policeman nearby but he was for crowd control only, and Falcon could tell by the expression on his face that he also thought the runaway bull was part of the show.

With no time to spare, Falcon got up from his seat, climbed onto the railing and, pushing the policeman out of the saddle, leaped onto his horse. He wished he was on Lightning, but he had no choice. This police horse was all he had. He raced across the arena toward the bull.

Behind him the policeman blew his whistle in anger. "Stop that man! Stop him! He stole my horse!"

The crowd, still believing that it was all part of the show, cheered in approval and applauded as Falcon, bent low over the horse's neck, urged the animal into what was, without doubt, the fastest it had ever run. Falcon measured the distance between the bull and the crowd and between himself and the bull, and realized that if he was going to catch up with it, it would be at the last possible second.

As he drew alongside the bull, he could smell its pungent odor and see the fear, confusion, and anger in the bull's eyes. Falcon leaned over the bull, then leaped from the saddle, grabbing the bull by the horns as he did so. He dug his heels into the ground as he twisted the bull's neck, throwing the animal over onto its side.

With the bull safely on the ground, Falcon quickly regained his feet, then swung back into the saddle of the horse that had stopped running and was now waiting for him. The bull, its initial charge stopped, got back to its feet, shook its head and snorted a few times. By now a couple of the cowboys from the show had come over and herded the bull, docile now, back to rejoin the others.

Buffalo Bill himself rode up to Falcon's side and, reaching over, grabbed Falcon's hand and lifted it up into the air.

"Ladies and gentlemen!" he shouted. "The cowboy

who performed this thrilling rescue for your viewing pleasure is Falcon MacCallister!"

The crowd gave Falcon a thundering ovation.

"You are acting as if you had planned that," Falcon said quietly.

"Why not?" Cody replied, still smiling and speaking without moving his lips. "It was a great act."

Falcon laughed, shook his head, then rode the horse back to the policeman who, while angered by the "theft" a few minutes earlier, had now joined the crowd in applauding him.

Falcon swung down from the saddle and handed the reins to the police officer.

"Thank you for the loan of the horse," he said.

"Well, I didn't exactly lend the horse to you," the policeman replied with a big smile. "But I'm glad Harry was here for you."

"Harry, is it?" Falcon asked. He rubbed Harry behind one of his ears. "You did well, Harry."

"I'll say he did. I never knew he had that in him."

"Treat him well."

"He'll get an extra ration of oats tonight," the policeman promised.

"He's a good horse," Falcon said.

"And you are a good man," the policeman responded. He stuck his hand out and Falcon shook it.

Delmonico's, New York

The waiters at Delmonico's Restaurant on Number Two William Street vied for the opportunity to serve the handsome assemblage of guests in the private dining room on the upper floor. All the diners were well known personalities. There was Buffalo Bill Cody, easily recognizable by his flowing blond hair and his neatly trimmed moustache and goatee. In addition there were the MacCallister twins, Andrew and Rosanna, who were famous show business personalities. Andrew had what the newspapers called "rugged good looks," handsome enough to play the most romantic lead, but manly enough to play the most gallant hero. Of Rosanna it was said that she had discovered the fountain of youth, for her skin was smooth and flawless, her dark hair luxuriant, and her eyes ablaze with still-youthful beauty.

The fourth diner was Falcon MacCallister, brother to the show-business twins. Falcon was over six feet tall with wide shoulders, a flat stomach, and powerful arms. Someone once described his face as "not weathered, but cured." It bore a permanent tan, and his eyes had the suggestion of a squint as if he were outside in the sun. Unlike Buffalo Bill, Falcon wore his hair, which was the color of sun-ripened wheat, cut short.

The four were here at Delmonico's because after the performance Buffalo Bill had insisted they be his guests. There was an empty chair available and when Rosanna asked who it was for, Cody was rather circumspect. Then, about fifteen minutes later, the mysterious guest arrived.

Cody's guest was shorter than any of the other three men present, slender of build, with dark, piercing eyes and a sweeping moustache, but no beard.

"Friends, may I present Colonel Prentiss Ingraham? At least, that is the name he is going by today. He has also been called, at various times in his life, Dr. Noel Dunbar, Dangerfield Burr, and Colonel Leon Laffite. Of course, you can understand that, when you realize what an unsavory life he has lived. While training for the noble profession of medicine, Ingraham left school to become a soldier for the South. He was wounded and captured at Fort Hudson, but escaped only to be wounded for a second time at the Battle of Franklin, Tennessee.

"Then after the war ended, Ingraham, not content to return to civilized life, traveled the world to find another war to fight. He served under Juarez in the Mexican rebels' revolution against Maximillian, then went to Europe to fight against the Turks, was in the Austrian army during the Austro-Prussian War, and was in Egypt with the Khedive's army, then was a colonel in the Cuban army, and if that isn't enough, he was also a captain in the Cuban navy. While fighting for the Cubans against Spain, he was captured and sentenced to death. But as they say, only the good die young, so once again he escaped."

"Why, thank you, Cody. Never have I received a more eloquently delivered introduction," Ingraham said, speaking in a soft Southern accent.

"But, surely, none of that can be true?" Rosanna said. "Have you really lived such a dangerous life?"

"I have had a terrible case of wanderlust for my entire life," Ingraham said. "But I'm afraid my friend, Bill Cody, is making it sound much more romantic than it really is."

"Romantic? Not a word of it," Cody said with a scoffing sound. "Seedy you are, and seedy I report. And why, you may ask, would I be friends with such a seamy character?" Cody asked.

"Are you really going to tell them, Cody?" Ingraham asked. "I think they could accept a rebel, a soldier of fortune, and an escaped convict. But if you tell them the worst of my sins, they will rise as one and walk away from here."

Rosanna laughed. "Surely it can't be that bad. What sin is it?"

"Will you tell them, Ingraham, or shall I?" Cody asked.

Ingraham made a courtly bow, then held his hand out toward Cody. "I defer to my esteemed and famous friend, Buffalo Bill Cody."

"I am famous," Cody said, "because this gentleman made me famous. Indeed it was he who coined the moniker Buffalo Bill." Cody looked at Falcon. "He made you famous as well, my friend. Because, to date, he has written over three hundred literary master-pieces," Cody said, then he chuckled. "At least, that is how he refers to them, though the rest of the world considers them dime novels."

"Wait a minute," Falcon said. "You mean I have you to thank for those awful dime novels about me?"

"You may call them awful, Mr. MacCallister," Ingra-ham said. "But the rest of the world calls them heroic." He began to recite as if on stage. "*With the reins of his horse held tightly in his teeth, a flaming six-gun in each hand dispensing death to the desperados, our hero hurled a chal-lenge that brought fear to the heart of the evildoer. 'Dangerous Dan, your day is done!'*" Ingraham smiled. "I particularly like the alliteration of the letter 'D.' Do you recognize that passage?"

"Do I recognize it? No, should I?" Falcon asked.

Ingraham chuckled. "No, I suppose not. I seriously doubt that anyone with your sterling qualities would ever be impressed by, or even read, stories that glorify your name. But what I just quoted came directly from that stirring novel of derring-do: *Falcon MacCallister and the Robbers of the Deadwood Stage.*"

"If he had the reins of his horse clenched between his teeth, how could he yell?" Andrew asked.

Ingraham stopped to think about it for a moment, then he burst out laughing.

"An excellent point, my good man," Ingraham said. "A most excellent point indeed."

"You were at the Wild West Exhibition today, Ingraham. What did you think of the thrilling new act that I added? Did you see the way Falcon, who for all intents and purposes was naught but a spectator, suddenly appeared from the crowd to wrestle to the ground a runaway bull?"

Ingraham laughed. "You may have had it planned, Cody, but something tells me that Falcon was not in on the plan."

"Maybe not," Cody agreed. "But knowing Falcon as well as I do, I knew that were I but to present him an opportunity to be heroic he would react exactly as he did."

"Surely you aren't saying that you arranged for the bull to break away, are you?" Rosanna asked.

Cody held up his finger. "That, my dear, will forever be a closely guarded secret. But, what about it, Falcon? Would you care to join my exhibition?"

"Thank you, Cody, but I'll pass. Andrew and Rosanna are the two show-business luminaries in the MacCallister family."

"And luminaries they are," Cody agreed. He glanced over toward Falcon's siblings. "I loved your performance in *The Lady and the Soldier*."

"Thank you," Andrew said.

"No, not you, Andrew, I was talking to Rosanna," Cody said, and all laughed.

"Cody, what is the latest on your town?" Ingraham asked.

"Your town? What town?" Andrew asked.

"Haven't you heard?" Ingraham asked. "There is to be a town in Wyoming Territory named Buffalo Bill."

"Really?" Rosanna asked. "My, how wonderful!"

"It isn't to be called Buffalo Bill," Cody said. "It is to be called Cody, if it comes about."

"It will happen," Ingraham said. "Thornton Beck is behind it, and he is a man who accomplishes what he starts."

"Thornton Beck, the financier in Wyoming Territory?" Falcon asked.

"Yes. He has already developed three towns in Wyoming Territory: Sheridan, Buffalo, and Beckton. He wants to develop a town in the Bighorn Basin, along the Stinking Water River between Heart Mountain and Cedar Mountain, very near Yellowstone. Do you know the area there?"

"Yes, I know the area quite well," Falcon replied.

"I suppose some people might think it a bit vain of me to be interested in a town that bears my name, but I'm sure you understand the attraction, as you have a town named after you."

"Actually, MacCallister is named after my father, not me," Falcon said.

"Mr. Cody?" a young man called, stepping into the room then.

Looking toward the visitor, they saw that he was wearing a cap with a shield stating that he was an employee of Western Union.

"Yes, I am Bill Cody," Cody said.

The young man smiled. "I know you, Buffalo Bill. I would recognize you anywhere," he said. "I've seen your Wild West Show."

"It is an exhibition, my good man," Cody said. "It

is not a show. A show is make-believe, whereas an exhibition is real."

"Yes, sir, well, it's real all right. Oh, I have a telegram for you."

Cody took the telegram, and tipped the young man a dollar.

"Gee, thanks, Buffalo Bill!" the young man said, his smile growing even broader at the large tip.

Cody opened the telegram and took a moment to read it. "It is from General Miles," he said. "He wants me to come to Chicago."

"Why?" Falcon asked.

"Here, you read it," Cody replied, handing the telegram to Falcon. "You may read it aloud, if you wish."

Falcon began to read.

"There is a movement among the Indians that they call Spirit Talking. This is a dangerous new development and should it get out of hand, I am concerned that another Indian war might be in the offing. It is also my belief that Sitting Bull is behind the unrest. As you are familiar with the badlands and have befriended Sitting Bull, request you visit me soonest at my headquarters in Chicago. Respectfully, Nelson Miles, General, Commanding Department of the Missouri."

"My," Ingraham said. "That certainly sounds like an invitation to adventure."

Falcon handed the telegram back to Cody. "Are you going to see him?" Falcon asked.

"I don't know," Cody said. "He said he wants to see me as soon as possible, but I have one more week of the show remaining in New York. What do you think, Falcon? Have you ever heard of this Spirit Talking movement the general mentions?"

"I have heard of it, yes," Falcon said.

"Do you think, as General Miles does, that there may be an Indian uprising because of it?"

"A general uprising? No, I don't think so," Falcon said. "There are some renegades causing problems, but nothing on the order of a full-scale Indian war."

"I think you are right," Cody said. "And even if were true, Sitting Bull wouldn't have anything to do with it. As you well know, Sitting Bull was, for a short time, a member of my Wild West Exhibition. I got to know him very well, and I have a great deal of respect and admiration for him. He told me that it came to him in a spirit dream that the Indians and the White Men must live in peace, and that it is the responsibility of the Indians to adapt to our ways."

"Do you believe that?" Andrew asked.

"The real question is, does he believe that?" Cody replied. "And because it came to him in a spirit dream, I think yes, he does believe it. From what I know of Sitting Bull, he gives great credence to the power of visions and dreams."

"Yes, and it may well be that is exactly what has Miles worried," Falcon said. "As you say, Sitting Bull is known to be a person who believes in talking with spirits, and as this new movement is called Spirit Talking, it is easy to see how General Miles may have made the connection."

"But it's not the same thing," Cody said.

"No, it is not the same thing. However, once something like this gets started, it tends to develop a life of its own, so it is important to get it stopped before it gets started," Falcon said. "I know you haven't asked for my opinion, but I think you should suspend the show for now, and go see General Miles just as quickly as you can pack your clothes and catch the next train."

"All right, I'll do that if you will come with me," Cody said. "General Miles holds you in high regard. I know he would like to see you, and I would like you with me when I meet with him."

"I'll come with you. I was about to start back anyway, and it has been a while since I've seen General Miles, so it would be nice to see him again."

"So you are saying there is absolutely no possibility that there will be any Indian trouble?" Ingraham asked.

"I wouldn't say absolutely," Falcon said. "There will always be a few Indians who, for excitement or some perceived injustice, are willing to go off the reservation and cause trouble."

"I hope so."

"You hope so? What a strange thing for you to say," Rosanna said, and she and the others looked at Ingraham with equal surprise.

"Oh, don't get me wrong," Ingraham said. "I certainly would not want another incident like what happened to Custer. But a little excitement would be welcome and, as you know, I live for excitement."

CHAPTER TWO

A Crow village on the Meeteetsee River,
Wyoming Territory

It was just after sunup and Running Elk left his tipi to walk out onto an overlook where he could view the mountains around him. Though it was late spring, the higher peaks were still covered with snow. Interspersed with the snow-covered peaks were the slab-sided cliffs rising a thousand feet or more into the sky. At the lower ranges were the sage-covered mountains that lay in ridges and rolls, marked here and there by patches of light and shadow from the early morning sun. On the lower elevations of the treeless mountains, elk were grazing.

Down in the valley he could see, sparkling silver in the sun, the Meeteetsee River. Alongside the river was a small herd of antelope, and sneaking up on them, a wolf was hunting his morning meal.

Today, Gray Antelope and Howling Wolf were going hunting. Running Elk would have gone with them had they asked, but they did not. He had not been hunting since returning from the white man's school, and he missed it, but he knew it was not his place to invite himself.

When Running Elk was back East attending Carlisle Indian School, they changed his name from Running Elk to Steve Barr, and they told him and the other students that the Indian ways were bad. They said he must get civilized and be like the white man. While he was there he wore white man's clothes, cut his hair as a white man, ate white man's food, went to the white man's church, and spoke the language of the white man. If any of the students were ever overheard speaking their native tongue, they were severely punished.

The books Running Elk learned to read told how bad the Indians had been to the white men. They made no distinctions among the Indians as to what tribes were friendly and supportive of the white man and what tribes were enemies. Running Elk was Absaroka. The Absaroka were called Crow by the white man, and though most of the Crow were in Montana, many had settled in the Big Horn Basin just outside the newly designated Yellowstone National Park. The Crow were a Siouan language tribe, but they maintained an identity beyond that of the Hunkpapa, Lakota, Oglala, Mineconjou, Brule, Blackfeet, and Cheyenne, who were their traditional enemies. Because of this natural enmity, the Crow had been allies with the U.S. Army during their fight with the Sioux.

Running Elk had been gone for four years, and when he first returned to his tribal home, he was treated as a stranger because of the ways and habits he had acquired while away. It took a while for the rest of the tribe to accept him, but Quiet Stream had greeted him warmly from the first day he was back. Quiet Stream was a young woman who had caught

Running Elk's eye even before he left for school. Now he was thinking about marrying her, but in order to do so, he would have to present gifts that would satisfy her father, Stone Eagle, and convince him that he was worthy of his daughter.

"Could it be that the others are right, and you have lost your Indian ways? Had you not gone to the white man's school I would not have been able to sneak up on you."

Turning toward the sound of the voice, Running Elk saw Quiet Stream, smiling at the trick she had just played on him.

"You did not sneak up on me. I heard you."

"Oh? And has the white man also taught you to lie?"

Running Elk laughed. "You are right, I did not hear you. But that is because you cross the ground like a butterfly."

"Ah ha, another lie you learned from the white man," Quiet Stream said. "But this lie, I like."

Running Elk saw Grey Antelope and Howling Wolf mount their horses as they left for their hunting trip. Quiet Stream read, in his eyes, his disappointment at not having been invited to go with them.

"You should have gone with them," Quiet Stream said.

"No."

"Do you not wish to hunt with Running Elk and Grey Antelope? I think you do. I think I can see this in your face."

"They did not ask me."

"Perhaps they did not know you wished to go. You should have asked them."

"One should be invited, one should not ask," Running Elk said.

"Have you not asked my father for me?" Quiet Stream asked. "Or has only White Bull asked?"

"White Bull has asked?" Running Elk replied, surprised by Quiet Stream's announcement.

"Last night, he came to our tipi and asked my father if he could marry me."

"What did Big Hand say?"

"He said another has asked, and that he must think on this."

"What do you say?" Running Elk asked.

"It is you I prefer," Quiet Stream said. She smiled. "And I will say this to my father. Do not worry, he will listen to me."

White Bull and Running Elk were friends, and had been friends since both were young, but Running Elk had gone to the white man's school and White Bull had not. It wasn't a matter of Running Elk choosing to go; in fact, he had had no choice in the matter at all. He had been chosen by the Indian agent and told that he would go.

Since Running Elk had returned, the relationship between him and his old friend had changed. There was no animosity between them, but neither was there the closeness there once was. And now, with both young men interested in the same woman, the situation could only worsen.

Grand Central Terminal, New York

Buffalo Bill was in the main concourse surrounded by a dozen or more newspaper reporters and photographers. Falcon was several feet away, standing with Andrew and Rosanna, both of whom had come to see him off on his trip.

"I see that Mr. Cody is surrounded by his adoring press," Andrew said.

Rosanna laughed. "My, brother, do I detect a twinge of jealousy?"

"Jealousy?"

"The press is around Mr. Cody, but not around you?"

"You know better than that, Rosanna. I abhor the press."

"I know, dear. So I wouldn't call attention to it if I were you. No doubt they would be over here as well, if they knew that you were here."

"If they knew that *we* were here," Andrew said, emphasizing the "we." "For they would not come to see me, alone."

"They are calling our train," Falcon said.

Just inside the gate leading to track number thirty-one, a man appeared with a megaphone. Holding the megaphone to his mouth he called out loudly, his words clearly audible.

"Train for Philadelphia, Harrisburg, Cleveland, and Chicago, now boarding on track thirty-one! All passengers proceed to the train now!"

Rosanna hugged Falcon. "You are the only one in the family who ever comes to see us," she said. "Is it any wonder that you are my favorite brother?"

"He's your favorite brother?" Andrew said. "What about me?"

"Oh, don't be silly, Andrew. Falcon is my brother, you are my twin. And you are my favorite twin."

"All right then, that's better, that's . . . ," he paused, realizing then what she had said. Falcon and Rosanna both laughed, then Andrew laughed with them. He reached out to take Falcon's hand.

"I agree with her," he said. "You are also my favorite brother."

As Falcon and Cody started toward the gate, Falcon heard one of the reporters behind him call out.

"Hey! Look there! Aren't those the MacCallisters? Yes, that's Andrew and Rosanna, the famous actors."

"What are you two doing here?" another asked and, glancing back over his shoulder, Falcon saw that the entire press corps had hurried to their side. He saw, too, that his siblings were handling it with their usual aplomb.

"It's Buffalo Bill Cody!" a passenger said as Falcon and Cody stepped into the palace car of the train. Almost instantly the other passengers crowded around him and, obligingly, Cody began signing autographs. Smiling and shaking his head, Falcon found a seat at the rear of the car and watched with bemusement.

"Do you know Buffalo Bill?" one of the other passengers asked Falcon.

"Yes."

"Is he a real man of the West? Or is he merely a showman?"

"Trust me, Buffalo Bill is a real man of the West," Falcon said. "He was a Pony Express rider, a buffalo hunter, a soldier, and a scout for the U.S. Cavalry. He is also a recipient of the Medal of Honor."

"I thought that was all hokum, just to promote his show," the passenger said.

"It isn't hokum," Falcon said. "And I'll correct something else you said. He isn't *merely* a showman; he is a showman of the first order."

"Is that so? Maybe I have made a mistake in my judgment of him," the passenger said. "I wonder if I could get his autograph. For my children, of course."

"Of course," Falcon said. "If you ask for it, I am sure

he will give you his autograph. I have found him to be
most generous in such things."

That night, as Falcon lay in his berth, feeling
the gentle rocking motion of the train and hearing the
sound of steel wheels rolling on steel track, he recalled
the last time he had been with Buffalo Bill. The
memory was so strong and so real that he didn't know
if it was a memory or a dream.

It was a time before the Buffalo Bill Wild West Exhibition, when he was still known as Bill Cody. Falcon
had been wandering through the West with no particular reason or destination when he found himself in
Hayes City, Kansas. He met Bill Cody in the saloon, and
because Cody had once ridden with the Pony Express,
as had a close friend of Falcon's, the two discovered a
mutual connection.

The two men were enjoying each other's company,
exchanging stories and gossip, when they learned that
a local rancher and his wife had been killed and their
eighteen-year-old daughter raped, leaving a soul-
scarred shell of the vibrant young girl she had been.

The man who had perpetrated the crime was Drew
Lightfoot, a well known desperado who had boasted
that he would never be taken alive. Already a wanted
robber and murderer, Lightfoot had committed crimes
against one of the leading families of the county, and
the reward for his apprehension had doubled. He was
now worth two thousand dollars, dead or alive.

"And he says he'll never be taken alive?" Falcon
asked the man who had brought the news to the saloon.

"That's what he says, all right."

Falcon finished his beer, then stood up.

"Where are you going?" Cody asked.

"I'm going to see what I can do about granting that fella's wish that he not be taken alive," Falcon said.

Cody stood up as well. "Do you want company?" he asked.

"A good friend is always welcome company," Falcon replied.

Soon after they got onto Lightfoot's trail, they learned that he wasn't traveling alone, but had five others with him, and was riding as the head of a gang of robbers and cutthroats. If that made Lightfoot more formidable, it also made him easier to track, for the Lightfoot gang was leaving a path of murder and robbery all across western Kansas and eastern Colorado.

They caught up with him in Puxico, Colorado. Passed up by the railroads, Puxico wasn't even on most maps. Falcon surveyed the town as he rode in. He had seen hundreds of towns like this one, a street faced by false-fronted shanties, a few sod buildings, and even a handful of tents, straggling along for nearly a quarter of a mile. Then, just as abruptly as the town started, it quit.

In the winter and spring the single street would be a muddy mire, worked by horses' hooves and mixed with their droppings, so that it became a stinking, sucking pool of ooze. In the summer it was baked hard as a rock. It was summer now, early afternoon, and the sun was yellow and hot.

The saloon wasn't hard to find. It was the biggest and grandest building in the entire town, and Cody pointed to it.

"I'd say our best bet would be to start there," Cody said.

"I'd say you are right."

Loosening their pistols in their holsters, the two men walked inside.

Anytime Falcon entered a strange saloon he was on the alert. As he surveyed the place, he did so with such calmness that the average person would think it no more than a glance of idle curiosity. In reality it was a very thorough appraisal of the room. He checked out who was armed, what type of weapons they were carrying, and whether they were wearing their guns in a way that showed they knew how to use them. There were five men sitting together in the back of the room, and they were surveying Falcon and Cody as carefully as Falcon was surveying them. Falcon knew it wasn't idle curiosity that had drawn their attention, and he was certain they were the men he and Cody were after.

"Cody," he said quietly.

"I see them," Cody answered just as quietly.

The bartender stood at the end of the bar, wiping used glasses with his stained apron, then setting them among the unused glasses. When he saw Falcon and Cody step up to the bar, he moved down toward them.

"Two beers," Falcon said.

The bartender had seen the way Falcon and Cody had examined the five men in the back, and he had seen the way the five men had studied them. He poured the drinks with shaking hands, and Falcon knew that they had found their men.

"Do you know why we are here?" Falcon asked quietly.

"I reckon I do," the bartender replied, his voice strained with fear.

"I'm told there are six of them. I see only five sitting back there."

The bartender raised his head and looked toward the stairs at the back of the room, but he said nothing.

"Would the one upstairs be Lightfoot?" Falcon asked.

Again, the bartender said nothing, but he answered in the affirmative with a slight nod of his head.

"Thanks," Falcon said. He finished the drink then looked toward the flight of wooden stairs that led upstairs to an enclosed loft.

"You go after him," Cody said. "I'll take care of these galoots."

"All right."

Falcon pulled his gun as he started up the stairs. The five in the back, seeing that, stood up as one, pulling their pistols as they did so.

"Hold it!" Cody called, pointing his gun at the five. "Drop your guns, all of you!"

"The hell you say!" one of the five men shouted, and they turned toward Cody.

Seeing that Cody was now in danger, Falcon called to them from the stairs. "Do what he says!" Falcon shouted.

One of the five men fired toward Cody and another fired toward Falcon. Even though the five men outnumbered Falcon and Cody, they were at a disadvantage because they were bunched into one big target, whereas their targets were separated.

Guns roared as they all began firing. Smoke billowed from the barrels of the guns, filling the saloon with a thick, acrid cloud. When the smoke moved away, the five were lying on the floor. Then, from the room at the head of the stairs, Lightfoot emerged, gun in hand. He fired at Falcon, and a hole the size of a man's thumb and the height of a man's chest appeared in the wall right beside Falcon as the heavy .44 caliber slug tore into the wood.

Both Falcon and Cody returned fire at the same time and Lightfoot, struck by two bullets, tumbled over the banister and, turning in midair, landed on his back on the very table around which his five confederates had been sitting.

An unexpected roughness in the track jarred Falcon from his sleep and he lay in his berth for a moment, halfway between dream and wake as the scenes of that event, so long ago, gradually faded away. He heard the sound of the train whistle as he drifted back to sleep.

CHAPTER THREE

Chicago, Illinois

When Falcon and Cody stepped down from the train in Chicago they were met by a young army lieutenant, accompanied by two enlisted men. Stepping up to Cody, the lieutenant saluted.

"Colonel Cody, I am Lieutenant Vaughan. If you will come with me, sir, I have a carriage waiting that will take you to your meeting with General Miles."

"Thank you, Lieutenant, that is most kind of you," Cody said. "This is Falcon MacCallister. I have brought him with me to meet with the general."

"Sir, I don't mean to be particular, but General Miles said nothing about anyone named Mr. MacCallister. I was told to meet you and provide you with transportation to the general's headquarters."

"I assume, Lieutenant, that the carriage you have brought is large enough to accommodate all of us?"

"Yes, sir."

"Then I suggest that you let me handle the general."

"Very good sir," Lieutenant Vaughan replied. "If you

will give these two privates your claim tickets, they will secure your luggage."

"Thank you," Cody said as he and Falcon turned over their claim checks.

Lieutenant Vaughan led Falcon and Cody through the crowded station, then out to the front where an army carriage and an army buckboard stood. The carriage was being driven by an army sergeant, who stepped down to salute as the three men approached.

"If you gentlemen wish to proceed, we will go on ahead," the lieutenant said. "Cooper and Dagan will come along behind us in the buckboard with your luggage."

"That'll be fine, Lieutenant," Cody said, as he and Falcon got into the carriage. They rode on the back seat facing forward, while the lieutenant rode in the front seat facing to the rear. The driver climbed onto his seat, snapped his whip, and they started forward. The team moved out at a trot, pulling the carriage at a rapid pace, but the carriage had good springs, so the ride was smooth and pleasant.

General Miles stood when Lieutenant Vaughan brought the two men into his office. A tall, slender man, General Miles looked very much at ease in the uniform of an army general, though, unlike most of the other generals in the army, Miles was not a graduate of West Point. In fact, he had been a clerk in a crockery factory when the Civil War began and he had volunteered his services as a private. He was commissioned a second lieutenant shortly after he enlisted, and rose quickly through the ranks, attaining the brevet rank of Major General at the very young age of twenty-six. After the war he was appointed colonel and given command of the Fifth Cavalry. It was there that he met Buffalo Bill Cody, though then Cody was not known as Buffalo Bill and there was no Wild West Exhibition. Then it was simply William Cody, army scout. Now Cody was a world famous show business personality, and Nelson Miles was commandant of the Department of the Missouri, again wearing the rank and uniform of a Major General.

"Colonel Cody, it was good of you to come," Miles said. "Please, come over to the nest and have a seat."

The "nest" General Miles was referring to was a collection of sofas and chairs in the corner of his commodious office. It was here that he held meetings with his subordinates when he wanted to make them feel comfortable. He was well known among his officers as a no-nonsense general who never invited anyone to the nest on routine matters—nor did he if they had done something to evoke his displeasure.

"General, I hope you don't mind," Cody said, "but as you can see, I have brought someone with me."

"Falcon MacCallister," General Miles said, extending his hand for a hearty handshake. "I didn't expect to see you here. It's been a long time."

"That it has, General," Falcon said. "I hope you don't mind that I came with Cody."

"Mind? No, of course I don't mind. But tell me, are you a member of the Buffalo Bill Wild West Exhibition now?"

"He sure is," Cody said, speaking up quickly. "You should have seen him the other day. He raced after a runaway bull and leaped from the saddle to grab the critter by its horns and bring him down. And, I might add, he did this just in the nick of time, because the creature was hell-bent to dash into the audience to work its mayhem."

"Isn't that a dangerous act to be putting into your show?" General Miles asked, concerned about what Cody had just told him. Then he smiled. "Or is that just part of your spiel?"

"It's true, all right," Falcon said. "But believe me, it wasn't a part of the act. The bull just got away."

General Miles laughed. "Buffalo Bill Cody," he said. "P.T. Barnum has nothing on Buffalo Bill. Our friend, here, is, without doubt the greatest self-promoter on earth."

"Tell me, General, what is the emergency? Why did you send for me?" Cody asked.

"I am sure you have heard of the recent disturbances coming from some of our Western Territories," General Miles said. "There was an incident where a farmer named Kennedy was killed, along with practically his entire family. They were massacred by Indians. A stagecoach was attacked and two whites were killed. There have been some prospectors killed, and a freight wagon train was attacked."

"I have heard of some of it, yes," Cody said. "The newspapers have carried the reports, though I am always of the belief that the newspapers tend to exaggerate the events to make a better story."

"Believe me, there is no exaggeration, these events have occurred. And now we have been getting some disturbing reports from some of the more friendly Indians suggesting that these may not be isolated events, that there may be something afoot among the Sioux. We are also hearing that Sitting Bull himself may be behind it. I know he was with your show for a while."

"Yes, he was, but he was only with us for about four

months," Cody replied. "I paid him fifty dollars a week to ride around the ring one time. He was quite a box office attraction, and he wound up making even more money by selling his autograph."

"Is it true that he yelled curses at the audience in Lakota?" General Miles asked.

Cody laughed. "Well, since he was the only member of the show who could speak the language, that is something that only Sitting Bull knows."

"Be that as it may, the task I have for you is a simple one, if you will agree to take it. I want you to go to Standing Rock to visit Sitting Bull. Well, it isn't Standing Rock anymore. Now it is Fort Yates, but most people still call it Standing Rock. Anyway, I want you to speak to him while you are there and determine, if you can, if there is another Indian uprising in the making. And if there is, I want you to find out if he is a part of it. Though I have no doubt but that he will say he isn't."

"I'm sure he will say that he isn't a part of it, General, and he will be telling the truth," Cody said. "I do not believe for one moment that he is instigating another Indian uprising."

"General, are you talking about *Wagi Wanagi?*" Falcon asked.

"*Wagi Wanagi?*"

"Spirit Talking."

"Yes, Spirit Talking, that's it," General Miles said. "I'm told it has all the Indians in a frenzy."

"The Indian behind Spirit Talking is Mean to His Horses, not Sitting Bull," Falcon said.

"Falcon is right, General. I think you are making a mistake," Cody said. "I am absolutely positive that Sitting Bull has nothing to do with this."

General Miles stroked his moustache as he looked at Cody and Falcon. "Have I chosen the wrong man for the job, Colonel Cody? Have you become so enamored of him that you will believe anything he tells you?"

"General, if you will allow me, I have a suggestion," Falcon said.

"By all means, Falcon, if you have any ideas please share them with me. This is too important to let something pass without exploring every avenue."

"With your permission I will accompany Colonel Cody," Falcon said. "Although I have no doubt but that the colonel is capable of determining whether or not Sitting Bull will be telling the truth—it is also possible that the two of us will sharpen the perception."

General Miles nodded. "Yes, an excellent idea, Colonel MacCallister."

"Colonel MacCallister?" Falcon replied.

"Bill Cody is already a colonel in the Army Scouts, and, for the duration of this assignment, I am appointing you as well. Both of you will be paid accordingly, though," he looked at Cody and chuckled, "as much money as you make with your Wild West Exhibition, I'm afraid any army pay you draw would be an insult."

"I will serve for the honor of service, General, not for the money," Cody said. "And one can never be insulted by honor."

"Indeed, one cannot," General Miles said. "Falcon, if you will raise your right hand, I will administer the oath of your service."

Raising his right hand, Falcon took the oath, repeating it word-for-word after General Miles.

"I, Falcon MacCallister, do solemnly swear that I will support and defend the Constitution of the United States against all enemies, foreign or domestic; that I will bear true faith and allegiance to the same; that I take this obligation freely, without any mental reservation or purpose of evasion; and that I will well and faithfully discharge the duties of the office on which I am about to enter. So help me God."

"Gentlemen, as of now you are both on the payroll of the United States Army. And I hereby grant you authority to act upon your own and to use, when necessary, the power of your rank to thoroughly investigate the matter pertaining to Indian unrest and possible uprising."

Both Falcon and Cody saluted General Miles and, as they left, Lieutenant Vaughan saluted them. "Sirs, I have made reservations for the two of you at the Palmer Hotel," he said. He smiled. "And I put it on the army's tab."

"You are a good man, Lieutenant," Falcon said.

When they reached the Palmer Hotel they were surprised to see Prentiss Ingraham waiting for them in the lobby.

"Ingraham!" Cody said. "What a surprise! And what a coincidence seeing you here in the same hotel!"

"Isn't it, though?" Ingraham said.

"Why do I have a feeling it is not a coincidence?" Falcon asked.

"Perhaps because you are an astute man," Ingraham replied.

"So, it isn't a coincidence?" Cody asked.

"Not exactly."

"Not exactly?" Falcon challenged.

"All right, it isn't at all a coincidence," Ingraham admitted.

"Then my question is, how did you know we would be staying here at the Palmer Hotel?" Cody asked.

"That part was easy. The Palmer is the best hotel in Chicago, and knowing you as I do, I knew that you would stay in no less a place."

Cody laughed. "You guessed right, but it wasn't I who made the choice. The hotel was chosen by the army."

"When you say that the army chose the hotel, would you be talking about Lieutenant Vaughan?" Ingraham asked.

"Yes, how did you know?"

"I have a confession to make," Ingraham said. "I went to the Headquarters of the Department of the Missouri, and there met the young officer who bears the responsibility of looking out for you. I suggested that you would be satisfied with no less an accommodation than the Palmer, and he agreed. So you have me to thank for these superb lodgings."

"I do thank you," Cody said.

"The one unanswered question now is, why are you here?" Falcon asked.

"I am here to research my next book."

"You're going to write a novel about Chicago?" Cody asked.

"No," Falcon said. "He isn't writing about Chicago. He is writing about you."

"You're too smart for me, Falcon," Ingraham said. "Except it isn't going to be a novel. I will be writing a nonfiction tome."

"Evidently, he is too smart for me as well," Cody said. "Because I don't have any idea what you are talking about."

"My dear boy," Ingraham said. "Whatever mission General Miles has assigned you will be the subject of my book. I am going with you."

"No, you aren't," Cody said.

"Oh, I'm afraid you can't prevent it," Ingraham said.

"We'll see about that. I'm going to General Miles tomorrow."

Ingraham chuckled. "I'm afraid that won't do you any good."

"What do you mean it won't do me any good? If General Miles says you can't go with us, you can't go with us."

"Not even General Miles can prevent me from going with you," Ingraham said.

"What makes you say such a thing?"

"Cody, I believe Mr. Ingraham is holding an ace up his sleeve," Falcon said.

"An ace up his sleeve?"

"In a manner of speaking," Falcon said. "What is it, Ingraham? What are you not telling us?"

"On the night I learned that Buffalo Bill was to come here on a mission for General Miles, I sent a telegram to Washington, D.C., where I have some, shall we say, friends in high places? I now have authority to accompany him from no less a dignitary than General Sherman himself, Commanding General of the United States Army."

"Do you know that Colonel MacCallister is going with me?" Cody asked.

A broad smile spread across Ingraham's face. "No! Really? Why, that is wonderful!"

"What is so wonderful about it?" Falcon asked.

"Well, think about it, Colonel MacCallister. I have written novels about Buffalo Bill, and I have written novels about Falcon MacCallister. Now, I will be able to write a nonfiction book that will include both of you."

CHAPTER FOUR

Big Horn Basin, Wyoming Territory

Don Kelly and his brother Al were knee-deep in the rapid-running stream of Thoroughfare Creek. The water was white foam where it broke over the rocks, but otherwise crystal clear, and they could see all the way to the bottom as they dipped their pans into the rocks and sand. Slowly sloshing the water around, they gradually emptied the pan of the water, sand, and lighter gravel. Then they studied the residue remaining in the bottom of the pan. They had been doing this for the better part of an hour when Al suddenly let out a whoop of joy.

"Don! Don, get over here! Look at this!"

Al turned his pan slightly, and Don could see, in the bottom of the pan, bright flashes.

"That's gold!" Al said. "There's bound to be more here."

"All right!" Don said. "Now we're getting somewhere!"

Don joined his brother in the part of the river he

was working, and with his very first pan came up with gold of his own.

"If we keep this up, we'll take seventy-five to a hundred dollars out of here just today," Al said.

As the two men continued to pan the river, they spread out a cloth on the bank and piled their gold there. Some of the gold was coming in nuggets as large as kernels of corn, and within two hours they had accumulated several ounces.

"Seventy-five dollars my hind leg," Don said. "We've got two, maybe three hundred dollars here if we have a dime."

Mountain Saloon, DeMaris Springs, Wyoming Territory

The town of DeMaris Springs was in the shadows of Cedar Mountain, bordered on the south by Stinking Water River, and on the north by the hot springs that gave the town its name. The Mountain Saloon was made of rip-sawed wide, unpainted boards, though it did have a false front with the name of the saloon rendered in black outlined in red. It was the center of activity in a little town of under two hundred people, and it had the distinction of having one of only two pianos in the town, the other being in Mme. Mouchette's House for Discriminating Gentlemen.

Excitement was keen in the saloon because Don and Al Kelly had just come in with news of their gold find.

"There ain't no tellin' how much gold there is up there," Don said, holding court among all the other saloon patrons.

"Where'd you find it?"

"Huh, uh, I ain't a-goin' to tell you that," Don said.

"You're goin' to have to look for yourself to find your own gold."

"But it's up there," Al said. "If we was able to find what we did, why my guess is that it's all over the valley."

"I'm goin' up there," someone said.

"Yeah, me too!" another added, and within moments, nearly every patron in the saloon had stated his intention to go up into the Big Horn Basin to try his luck at gold hunting.

Two of the patrons of the saloon were Sam Davis and Lee Regret.

Davis was a man of medium height and size. Clean-shaven, his most distinguishing feature was a pock-marked face and a drooping left eye. The droop was the result of an old wound, suffered in a knife fight the first time Davis was ever in jail.

Regret was relatively small and so dark that he was often mistaken for a Mexican. He had a full beard that was as dark as his long black hair.

Unlike the others, Davis and Regret weren't crowding around the two brothers trying to get more information. They already had the information they needed.

"Bellefontaine ain't goin' to like this," Regret said. "They's too many prospectors up there already, this is just goin' to bring a lot more."

"No, he ain't goin' to like it at all," Davis agreed.

"We're goin' to have to tell him," Regret said.

"Not yet."

"What do you mean, not yet? He's goin' to find out sooner or later, then he'll be mad at us for not tellin' him."

"We're goin' to tell him," Davis said. "But not until after we have took care of the problem."

"Took care of the problem? How we goin' to do that?"

"You'll see."

When Don and Al left the Mountain Saloon, they were so excited by their discovery that they didn't notice the two men following them. Their only thought was to get back to the creek where they had first made their discovery, and start panning again. It took two hours of riding before they returned to the spot where they had discovered gold, and within a few moments after they started panning, they were bringing up more color.

Sam Davis and Lee Regret watched the two men for a few moments, and saw with their own eyes the success the Kelly brothers were having.

"They wasn't lyin'," Davis said. "They really did discover gold. They just got started, and look at the gold they done got piled up alongside 'em there."

"Yeah," Regret said. "I see it."

"That sure is somethin'," Davis said.

"What are we goin' to do now?" Regret asked.

"Like I said when we started out, we're goin' to take care of the problem," Davis replied. He pulled his pistol, and Regret pulled his as well.

With pistols in hand, the two rode up to the gold-panning brothers. Not until they were right upon the two brothers did Don notice them.

"What are you doing here? What did you do, follow us?" Don asked. "We told you people back in town to find your own place. This is ours."

Davis and Regret aimed their pistols at the two brothers.

"What? No, wait!" Don said. "You don't need no guns, you can have this spot! Me 'n my brother will find someplace else."

"There is no place else for you," Davis said. "This whole valley belongs to Mr. Bellefontaine."

"Bellefontaine? He might own the town, but he don't own this valley," Al said. "This is public land!"

"No it ain't public land. This land and ever' thing on it belongs to Mr. Bellefontaine," Davis said. "So, what I'm going to ask you to do is hand over the gold, pack up your belongings, and leave."

"Hand over the gold? Are you crazy, Mister?" Al replied. "Me 'n my brother been workin' out here for near a month and this here is the first color we've turned up, so we ain't givin' it away. Besides which, there ain't nobody said nothin' to us 'bout this bein' private property. Seein' as you got guns and are makin' us do it, we'll go somewhere else, but we ain't handin' over the gold we done found here."

"I'm sorry you feel that way," Davis said. He pulled the trigger and his bullet plowed into Al's chest.

"Al!" Don called, shocked at seeing his brother shot before his very eyes. "You bastard! You shot my brother!" Don shouted angrily at Davis. Grabbing a pickaxe from the ground, he started toward Davis.

"Yeah, I did, didn't I?" Davis said. He fired again, this bullet hitting Don in the stomach.

Don went down as well, and now both brothers were lying facedown in the water. Swirls of blood, caught up by the swift current, began flowing downstream.

Davis got down from his horse and, drawing his knife, proceeded to scalp both of the prospectors.

"Get the gold, Regret," Davis said calmly as he went about the grizzly process of lifting the two scalps.

Regret dismounted, then walked over to fold the cloth over and scoop up the gold.

"We goin' to tell Bellfontaine about the gold?" Regret asked.

"We got to," Davis replied as he stuck his hands into the swiftly flowing water to wash away the blood.

"Why? How's anyone goin' to find out?"

"What would we do with the gold, even if we did keep it?" Davis asked. "Bellefontaine owns the bank. Soon as we tried to cash it, he'd find out. Then we'd be in a lot of trouble. We got easy jobs that pay good, why get greedy just over a few dollars in gold?"

"Yeah," Regret said. "I reckon you're right."

DeMaris Springs

Pierre Bellefontaine owned Bellefontaine Mineral Asset Development Company, a large mining company operating in the public land area throughout the Big Horn Basin. One of the largest mining operations of its kind, it employed prospectors, geologists, engineers, and miners, men who willingly gave up the uncertainty of merely looking for gold for the certainty of a pay-check by working for someone else who was willing to take the risk.

Bellefontaine was willing to take risks because he could afford them. In addition to the Bellefontaine Mineral Asset Development Company, he also owned the Bank of DeMaris Springs, the DeMaris Springs Mercantile, the Bellefontaine Freight Line, and the stagecoach line that connected DeMaris Springs with Sheridan, Wyoming Territory, and Billings, Montana

Territory, Billings being the closest railhead. Bellefontaine often made the remark, and with some justification, that he owned the town of DeMaris Springs.
Located in the Stinking Water Valley, DeMaris Springs
was the only town between Green River, Wyoming Territory and Virginia City, Montana Territory, and between Buffalo, Wyoming Territory, and Yellowstone
National Park.

He also knew what many others did not know. The
"real" gold of the Big Horn Basin wasn't gold at all. It
was coal. The gold finds had been few and far between,
but his mining engineers had told him that there was a
vein of coal that rivaled that of any other coal-producing
area in the entire country. And with steam engines
transitioning from wood to coal, this find would be
worth a fortune.

But he had two problems. One problem was the
number of gold prospectors who continued to work
the valley in their quest of the yellow metal, and the
other was the increasing number of ranchers and farmers who were moving into and settling the valley. In
order for his dream of a coal empire to work, he would
need uninhibited access to the entire valley.

At the moment, Bellefontaine was dealing with two
of his employees, Lee Regret and Sam Davis. They had
brought him information about their encounter with
the Kelly brothers, and Bellefontaine drummed his fingers on his desk as he examined the map that was
spread out before him.

"And you say they found gold here?" he asked, placing his finger on a place alongside Stinking Water River.

"Yes, sir. And they told the other folks about it as
well," Davis said. "Like as not, there are twenty or thirty
more people out there now than there was yesterday."

"Are you sure they found gold? Or were they just talking?"

"No, sir, they found gold all right. This gold," Davis said, pulling the little cloth-wrapped package from his pocket. He put the package on the desk in front of Bellefontaine, and Bellefontaine examined it more closely, moving the small nuggets around with his finger.

"How is it that you did not keep this gold for yourselves?" Bellefontaine asked, looking up at the two men.

"Well, sir, it's like you said," Davis replied. "The land and ever' thing in it belongs to you. Wouldn't be right for us to be runnin' the other folks out of there by tellin' 'em ever' thing out there belongs to you, then us be keepin' this gold they found. Most especial since we are workin' for you," Davis said.

Bellefontaine laughed. "Wouldn't be right? Or you knew you would be caught?"

"Maybe both," Davis admitted.

Bellefontaine laughed again, then, once more turned his attention to the map.

"How many people do you think are in this area?" he asked, making a small circle over a portion of the map.

"Don't nobody know for sure. Could be a hunnert or more," Davis said. "All of 'em prospectin'."

"Other than this, are they finding anything?" Bellefontaine asked, pointing to the little pile of gold on his desk.

"Don't nobody know that neither," Regret said. "But if them two that was in the saloon come up with gold, then it would be a safe bet to say that others is goin' to do it too. Especially, like I said, since they come into the saloon mouthin' off about it. That couldn't of done nothin' but start a little gold rush."

Bellefontaine stroked his chin as he continued to study the map. "I would try and buy all of them out, but if there are a hundred in there, and they all wanted a thousand dollars, it would about break me," he said. "Especially with all the money I've already got in mining equipment. It wouldn't do any good anyway unless every one of them agreed to a buyout, and I don't think they are going to do that, do you?"

"No, sir," Davis said. "I sure don't."

"You said you—uh—took care of the two men who panned this gold?"

"Yes sir."

"Where are they now?"

"Where are they? They're still lyin' there as far as I know," Davis replied, somewhat confused by the question.

"Good. If some of the other prospectors come across them, it may not be a bad thing if they get the idea that it's dangerous out there."

"Yes, sir, that's sort of what we was thinkin'," Davis said. "That's why I scalped 'em."

"You what? You scalped them?"

"Yes, sir. I figured it would make it look like the Injuns done it."

"Yes, that's probably a pretty good idea. But I'm afraid that two scalped prospectors won't be enough to get everyone out of there. And getting everyone out of there is what we need to do."

"If you're really wantin' all them folks out of there, me 'n Regret have come up with this idea."

"What idea is that?"

"Well, you might mind, Mr. Bellefontaine, that me 'n Regret was oncet soldiers. Members of the Sixth Cavalry we was, out of Fort Keogh."

"Yes, I know that."

"Well, sir, we still keep in touch with some of our old pards, and they've been tellin' us about Injuns attackin' prospectors, ranchers, farmers and the like up in Montana. And they been talkin' 'bout somethin' new that's goin' on with all the Injuns now."

"Something new? What are you talking about?"

"It's called Spirit Talkin'," Davis said.

"Spirit Talking? What's so new about that? Indians are always talking to spirits."

"Not like this. Like I said, this here is somethin' new. Seems like a chief by the name of Mean to His Horses has been sayin' that the spirits is tellin' him that all the white men are goin' to leave, and all the land is goin' to be give back to the Injuns."

"And they actually believe that?" Bellefontaine asked.

"A whole lot of 'em do, and, like I said, they been sorta helpin' it along up there in Montana, attackin' citizens and all. And it's got the army all worried," Davis said. "They're lookin' for an uprisin' among the Injuns."

"Mean to His Horses is Crow, is he?"

"No, sir, he is Cheyenne."

"That's all very interesting, but what has that got to do with our problem?" Bellefontaine asked. "All the Indians we have around here are Crow."

"Well, that's just the thing, you see. It ain't just the Cheyenne that's been doin' this Spirit Talkin'," Davis said. "It's spread all over the Sioux nation: Lakota, Oglala, Brule, Miniconjou, Hunkpapa, and even some among the Shoshone and the Crow. So, what if we was to sort of give the Injuns a little poke, so to speak, and prod 'em in to goin' onto the warpath, why it would wind up running all the squatters off," Davis said.

"What good would that do me?" Bellefontaine asked. "If the Indians run everyone out of the valley, I won't be able to be in there either."

"Sure you will," Davis explained. "What will happen is this. Once the Injuns go on the warpath, why the army will come in and move 'em out, not only from the public land, but more than likely run 'em off their own reservation as well. And once that happens, it will leave the whole valley open. At least from here all the way to the Yellowstone."

"Do you think you could do that? Get the Indians to attack the prospectors?"

"Oh, yes, I think me 'n Regret could do that just real easy," Davis said. Bellefontaine stared at Davis for a long moment. Then a huge smile spread across his face, and he hit his hand on the desk.

"By damn!" he said. "You two boys come up with that idea, did you?"

"Yes, sir, me 'n Regret."

"Well, let me tell you, that is one hell of a good idea! How soon can you get started?"

CHAPTER FIVE

On the Northern Pacific Railroad
in Dakota Territory

Angus Ebersole had seven men with him. In truth, it made his gang a little unwieldy by having so many, but it also made him formidable. There were few posses that were this large, and no target he ever selected would have as many guards as he had men.

He was waiting now with his men along the Northern Pacific Railroad for the train that would be coming through in about half an hour. The train, he knew, would be carrying the payrolls for Fort Lincoln, Fort Rice, and Fort Harrison. The payrolls for three army posts would be a considerable amount, enough money so that, even divided eight ways, it would make this operation a very profitable one.

"Dewey, Hawkins, do you have the wood laid out on the track?"

"Yeah, it's all there. Think we ought to light it yet?"

"Not yet, we don't want it to burn down too much before the train gets here."

"Hey, Taylor, what are you going to do with your money?" Peters asked.

"I'm goin' down to Arizona where the weather is warm and the Mexican girls is hot," Taylor replied. "I'm goin' to get me a room, a case of tequila, and have me a different señorita ever' night."

"Ha! Well, that sounds good enough for me. What about you, Smitty?"

"I'm goin' to find me a poker game," Smitty said. "And I'll win ever' hand 'cause I'll buy the pots. I'll bet so much that the suckers won't be able to match me."

"Nothin' like spendin' your money before you got it," Dewey said.

"Hush," Ebersole said, holding his hand up. "I think I hear it."

Straining, the men could hear a distant whistle.

"Yeah, that's it," Hawkins said. "Hadn't we better light the fire?"

"All right. Go ahead, get it started," Ebersole ordered.

Augmented by kerosene, the fire took quickly, and was blazing brightly when they first saw the train. From this distance, against the great panorama of the surrounding mountains, the train seemed quite small.

Now they could hear the train easily, the sound of its puffing engine carrying to them across the wide valley, echoing back from the towering mountains. When they heard the steam valve close and the train begin braking, Ebersole knew that the engineer had spotted the fire and was going to stop. Squealing, squeaking, and clanging, the train ground to a reluctant halt, its stack puffing black smoke, its driver wheels wreathed in tendrils of white steam drifting off into the night.

The engineer's face appeared in the window, backlit by the orange glow of the cab.

"What's up?" the engineer asked. "What's the fire for? Is there track out ahead?"

"Get your hands up," Ebersole said.

"What? Good God man, are you telling me this is a train robbery?"

"Yeah, that's what I'm tellin' you. Taylor, climb up there on the coal tender and keep your eyes on the two of 'em."

Falcon was sound asleep when the train came to a sudden, screeching halt in the middle of the night. The stop was so abrupt that it woke him up, and he slid the curtains apart just long enough to look out into the aisle of the sleeper car. He saw a porter.

"Porter, what happened?" he asked. "Why did we stop?"

"I don't know, sir," the porter answered. "I was sleepin' in the back of the car my ownself. I thought I might take a peek outside and see if I can find out what it is."

Falcon saw Cody sticking his head through the curtains of the top bunk just across the aisle from him, and Ingraham was looking out from the bottom bunk.

"You have any idea what's going on?" Cody asked.

"No, but I don't like it," Falcon said. "I think I'll have a look around."

"I'll join you," Cody said.

Slipping back into the bunk, Falcon pulled on his trousers and boots. Then, picking up his gun belt, he stepped out into the aisle as he strapped it on. By now, several others were looking out from the bunks: women, children, and men of all ages. Many of them were talking back and forth, wondering why the train had made such an abrupt stop in the middle of the night.

Cody stepped out into the aisle with Falcon and, like Falcon, had put on his gun belt. Ingraham stepped out as well, though, unlike Falcon and Cody, he was unarmed. When Falcon and Cody started toward the front of the car, Ingraham went with them.

"Where are you going?" Cody asked.

"With you two."

"You stay here. We don't know what's out there."

"I know," Ingraham said, his eyes flashing with excitement. "That's why I'm going with you."

When the three men stepped out of the train they could see the steam drifting away from the engine, so white against the dark night that it was almost luminescent. The only light to be seen was that cast through the windows of the coaches. A few of the windows were open and heads were poked through, looking toward the front.

"You folks best keep your heads inside, we don't know what this is all about yet," Falcon said as the three men passed by the coaches on their walk to the front of the train.

When they got close enough to the front to see what was going on, they saw at least eight men, four mounted and four dismounted. One of the dismounted men was on top of the tender, pointing his gun toward the cab of the engine. The other three were standing on the ground just outside the express car.

"You may as well open the door," one of the men yelled. "Because we have dynamite, and if you don't open it we'll blow this car all to hell."

"Gentlemen!" Ingraham shouted. "You have chosen

the wrong train to rob. The two men with me or none other than Falcon MacCallister and Buffalo Bill Cody!"

"Ingraham, what are you doing?" Cody asked.

"I am helping these gentlemen understand that they have made a big mistake," Ingraham said.

The three men on the ground turned toward Falcon, Cody, and Ingraham and began firing, lighting the night up with the bright flares of their muzzle flashes. Falcon and Cody returned fire and all three went down.

"Damn, did you see that?" one of the mounted men said. "Let's get out of here!"

"Bring me my horse!" the man on the coal-tender shouted, but the four riders who had been holding the horses of the four who had dismounted rode away without responding to his call.

"You no-count bastards!" the man on the tender shouted. He pointed his gun at the retreating robbers, but didn't fire. Instead, realizing that Falcon and Cody were quickly closing on him, he threw his pistol down, then put his hands up.

"I give up, I give up!" he shouted. "Don't shoot! I ain't makin' no fight of it!"

"Climb down," Falcon ordered, and, meekly, the man did as ordered.

By now the train conductor, who had been monitoring events from a safe place, came hurrying up.

"Mr. MacCallister, Mr. Cody, the Northern Pacific owes the two of you a big thank you for saving the train," the conductor said.

"MacCallister? Cody?" the outlaw said. "You mean this here fella wasn't lyin'? You really are Falcon Mac-Callister and Buffalo Bill Cody?"

"They are indeed," Ingraham said. "You need not feel shame over being bested in your failed endeavor, for you have been taken by the most famous and skilled shootists in the world."

"Who are you?"

"I sir, am merely a simple purveyor of tales, a scribe who records the heroic deeds of such men as these. I am sure you have heard of me. I am Prentiss Ingraham."

"Prentiss Ingraham?" The would-be train robber shook his head. "No, can't say as I have heard of you."

Ingraham was visibly crestfallen.

Because the would-be robbers had stopped the train by building a fire on the track, for the next several moments the crew and men passengers of the train worked feverishly to clear the path. They had to hurry, because another train would be coming behind them within the next hour.

"That's no problem," Ingraham said. "Won't the train engineer have his light on? He'll just stop when he sees us."

"It won't matter whether he has his headlamp on or not," Falcon replied.

"What do you mean it won't matter? Of course it will matter. If his headlamp is on, he will see us."

"Even if the engineer did see us, it would be too late," Falcon explained. "The purpose of the headlamp is so people can see the train and get out of the way. Once the train's headlamp picks up something, it is already too late. The train is so fast and so heavy that it is impossible for it to stop within the limits of the headlamp."

"So what you are saying is that if a train approaches us, it will plow right into the back of us?" Ingraham asked.

"That's what I'm saying," Falcon replied.

"Let's get busy then," Ingraham said, and he began working with renewed effort to clear the track.

Angus Ebersole, Clay Hawkins, Ike Peters, and Jim

Dewey rode hard for the first mile, then stopped atop a hill and looked back down at the track as the passengers and train crew worked to clear it.

"I thought you said this would be easy," Hawkins complained.

"I didn't say it would be easy, I said it would pay off well," Ebersole replied. "That train is carrying army payrolls for three forts. There's no tellin' how much money is there."

"Yeah, that's the thing," Hawkins said. "The money is there, it ain't here."

"How was I to know that Falcon MacCallister and Buffalo Bill would both be on that train?" Ebersole asked. "There just ain't no way of findin' out about stuff like that."

"You think that was really them?" Dewey asked.

"You seen how easy they cut down Smitty, Hunt, and Collins, didn't you?" Ebersole answered. "Yeah, I think it was really them."

"I didn't know they was real," Peters said.

"What do you mean you didn't think they was real? You seen 'em, didn't you?"

"Yeah, I seen 'em. But like I said, I didn't think there was really any such people. I thought they was like Santa Claus, I thought they was just somethin' someone made up to tell stories about."

"They are real, all right," Ebersole said.

"What if we was to go back down there now, catch 'em while they're workin'?" Dewey said. "We might be able to surprise 'em."

"The rest of us might also get kilt," Ebersole said.

"Damn, and I 'bout had that money spent," Hawkins said.

"I reckon ole Billy Taylor won't be havin' hisself none of them Mexican gals," Dewey said.

"Won't none of us be doin' nothin'," Peters said.

"Let's get out of here," Ebersole said, turning his horse away from the track.

Bismarck, Dakota Territory

It was mid-morning when the train rolled into Bismarck, Dakota Territory, where it was met by Mr. I.W. Emmons, the station agent. Behind them the train, temporarily at rest from its long run, wasn't quiet. Because the engineer kept the steam up, the valve continued to open and close in great, heaving sighs. Overheated wheel bearings and gearboxes popped and snapped as tortured metal cooled. On the platform all around them, there was a discordant chorus of squeals, laughter, shouts, and animated conversation as people were getting on and off the train.

Told of the attempted robbery, the station agent summoned Sheriff Walter Merrell, who took the prisoner into custody. Within fifteen minutes of the arrival of the train the entire town was aware of the attempted train robbery. They also knew that the robbery was prevented by Falcon MacCallister and Buffalo Bill Cody, two of the nation's most storied Western personalities.

The three would-be robbers who had tried to gain access to the express car had succeeded, but only in death. They had ridden the distance between the holdup attempt and Bismarck in the express car. Now their bodies were removed and laid out on the depot platform, waiting for the undertaker to call for them.

As they lay there, scores of people passed by to stare down at them in morbid curiosity. Though only two men had been shooting at them, all three had multiple bullet wounds in their torsos, and one had a bullet wound in his forehead.

"Look at that. That was some good shootin'," one man said.

"Well, yeah, when you consider who it was that shot them, you wouldn't expect anything but good shooting."

"Who did you say shot them?" someone asked.

"It was Falcon MacCallister and Buffalo Bill Cody."

"Wow. I sure wish I had been on the train to see that."

"I was on the train," another said. "But it was too dark to see anything but the muzzle flashes."

"It sure would have been something to see."

That same morning, Prentiss Ingraham presented himself to Marshal Jewel, editor of the *Bismarck Tribune*. The *Tribune* had been started by C.A. Lounsberry, and was made famous by its coverage of Custer's last fight at Little Big Horn, but Lounsberry sold the paper in 1884 during his unsuccessful bid to be governor of the territory.

"My good man, I am here to offer you the sum of fifty dollars," Ingraham said.

"Is that a fact? And just what do I have to do for you for that fifty dollars?" Jewel asked.

"Oh, you don't understand, sir," Ingraham said. "It isn't what you are going to do for me, it is what I am going to do for you. I am Prentiss Ingraham, famous author and journalist. It so happens that I was on the train, and was a direct witness to the thrilling events involving Buffalo Bill Cody, Falcon MacCallister, and the would-be train robbers. I am offering you my services in writing the story for you. Normally, I would get seventy-five, even one hundred dollars for the story, but I am going to do it for you for the paltry sum of twenty-five dollars."

"Wait a minute," Jewel said. "I am to give you twenty-five dollars? I thought you were going to give me fifty dollars."

"Oh, but I am, my good man. Consider that, by writing an article for you for the paltry sum of twenty-five dollars, you are to the good in the difference my efforts normally earn."

The editor laughed. "Very well, Mr. Ingraham. I confess that I have heard of you, and it may do my paper well to have a story written by the famous author of so many dime novels."

Borrowing a pen and paper from Jewel, Ingraham sat at a table in the back of the newspaper office and began writing the story. He heard the train whistle announcing that it was about to leave the station, but he was not concerned, for Bismarck would be their last stop as passengers. From here Ingraham, Falcon, and Cody would go by riverboat down the Missouri to Standing Rock Reservation where they would speak with Sitting Bull.

Ingraham composed the story quickly, writing it with large and easily read strokes of the pen.

Daring Train Robbery Foiled

FALCON MACCALLISTER AND BUFFALO BILL CODY THE HEROES

Account Told by Prentiss Ingraham

This scribe is well known throughout the world for penning epic and heroic tales of the valiant and exciting exploits of America's daring and intrepid Western heroes. But rarely has the author of such tales been privileged to be a personal witness to such courageous and audacious action as he was last night when this humble chronicler of bold events was on hand to see, with my own eyes, a performance so daring and so fearless that it made the fictional accounts of the popular Prentiss Ingraham novels pale in comparison.

This writer was on board the Northern Pacific train somewhere east of Bismarck, in company with Buffalo Bill Cody and Falcon MacCallister as part of our remarkable transit across America, when the attack occurred. With the muzzle flashes of their guns lighting up the dark night, eight armed and ferocious robbers attempted a train robbery. Bullets were flying through air as the outlaws went about manifesting their evil deed, and all on board the train were fraught with terror.

All were frightened, that is, except for the fearless duo of Buffalo Bill and Falcon MacCallister. For, unbeknownst to the would-be perpetrators of this dastardly crime, there were, among the passengers, two of America's most storied heroes. Cool and professional in the face of danger, these two intrepid gentlemen, Falcon MacCallister and Buffalo Bill Cody, engaged the road agents in a deadly gunfight. And whereas the missiles launched by the outlaws flew through the night without finding any targets, the bullets fired by the intrepid duo of MacCallister and Cody wrought a terrible effect among the would-be train robbers. Three of the desperadoes were killed outright when struck by the well-aimed balls, and one was captured. The remaining four retreated into the night like the cowards they are.

Buffalo Bill Cody, as readers of this newspaper may know, is the proprietor and chief performer of the world famous Buffalo Bill Cody's Wild West Exhibition.

When Ingraham rejoined Falcon and Cody, he was wearing a pistol.

"That's something new," Cody said.

"I figured if I am going to live in the Wild West, I may as well dress for the part," Ingraham said. "Especially in light of the excitement on board the train last night."

"I won't ask you if you can use that," Cody said. "I'm sure you have been in enough wars by now that you can handle it quite well."

"As well as any of the cowboys in your show, Cody," Ingraham said.

Cody chuckled. "I don't doubt it."

CHAPTER SIX

The last time Falcon had been to Fort Lincoln was in July 1876, having returned to the fort with what remained of the Seventh Cavalry after the disastrous fight at Little Big Horn.* Because the Seventh had moved to Fort Meade, Dakota Territory, none of the Seventh remained at Fort Lincoln. Nevertheless, memories of the post, the events, and the people of Fort Lincoln came flooding back to him. But it wasn't for nostalgia alone that Falcon was visiting. Colonel Sturgis, currently the commanding officer at Fort Lincoln, would be an ideal person to talk to with regard to the Spirit Talking movement, and it was for that reason they had come.

Reporting to the adjutant, Buffalo Bill introduced Falcon and himself.

"Lieutenant, I am Colonel William Cody, this is Colonel Falcon MacCallister, and we would like to speak to your commander."

"You are colonels?" the young lieutenant said.

* *Bloodshed of Eagles*

"I told you that we were," Cody said.

"I'm sorry, sir, but you aren't in uniform, and I can't just let anyone in to see the commander."

"Perhaps this will help," Falcon said, showing the letter of commission given him by General Miles.

The lieutenant looked at the letter for a moment, then stood quickly and saluted sharply.

"I beg your pardon, sir!" he said. "Please forgive me for my behavior."

"There is nothing to forgive, Lieutenant," Buffalo Bill said. "You were just doing your job. Would that I had an adjutant as dedicated to protecting me from unwanted visitors."

"Wait here, sir," the lieutenant said. "I'll be but a moment."

The lieutenant went into the commandant's office, but he left the door open and, though neither Falcon nor Cody could hear what he said to Colonel Sturgis, they certainly heard Sturgis's reply.

"What? Falcon MacCallister and Buffalo Bill Cody are both in my office and you left them cooling their heels outside? Show them in! Show them in at once! No, wait, I'll do it myself!"

Colonel Sturgis left his office before the lieutenant, and with a broad smile and an extended hand, he greeted Falcon and Buffalo Bill. As it turned out, both men knew him, so it was a greeting more than an introduction.

"You are here just in time for lunch," Sturgis said. "Please, be my guests."

"We wouldn't want to put Mrs. Sturgis out any," Cody said.

"Don't be foolish, Cody," Colonel Sturgis said. "She

is the wife of a post commandant. It is her duty, always, to be prepared to feed guests."

Mrs. Sturgis went all out in preparing the lunch, complete with a chicken consommé, roast beef, roast potatoes, lima beans, and an apple pie for dessert.

"Now, gentlemen, what brings you here?" Colonel Sturgis asked.

"Need you ask?" Cody replied as he carved into his roast beef. "We have traveled two thousand miles for this delightful lunch, and it was worth every mile." He smiled at Mrs. Sturgis. "And, madam, may I say that this meal is the equal to any I have had in all the courts of Europe?"

Mrs. Sturgis laughed self-consciously. "I know you are just saying that," she said. "But I am vain enough to appreciate such a comment."

"But there is another reason, is there not?" Colonel Sturgis asked.

"Colonel, have you ever heard of something called Spirit Talking?" Cody asked.

"Yes, Spirit Talking. The Indians call it *Wagi Wanagi*," Colonel Sturgis said.

"Do you think it is likely to cause another Indian War?" Cody asked.

Sturgis stroked his jaw for a moment as he looked back at Falcon and Cody.

"Why do you ask that? Have you heard something that I have not?" he asked.

"We can't answer that until we know what you have heard," Falcon said.

"I know that it has made the Indians a bit more as-sertive, if not aggressive," Sturgis said.

"What do you know of Spirit Talking?" Cody asked.

"The best way to describe it would be to call it a

religion," Sturgis said. "Though it is an unholy religion at best. It was started by Mean to His Horses, who was with Crazy Horse during the battle of Little Big Horn. But he was such an unknown then that nobody had ever heard of him. Now, he has a movement following him, and the movement has cut across the nations; not just the Cheyenne, but all the Sioux nations, and even some Indian tribes beyond the Sioux.

"From what some of the Indians have told me, it is a way of talking to the souls of Indians that have already died. The dead know everything, including the future. And the dead have told them that all the white men will soon be leaving. When that happens, the buffalo will come back and the land will return to the Indians."

"So I will ask again. Do you think this portends war?" Cody asked.

"General Miles thinks that, does he?" Sturgis asked.

"He thinks it is possible, and he thinks that Sitting Bull is behind it."

"As to whether or not this could lead to war, I can't answer," Sturgis said. "As I said, it has made the Indians more assertive. But I believe I can answer as to whether or not Sitting Bull is behind it."

"And what would that answer be?" Cody asked. "Do you think Sitting Bull is behind it?"

"Absolutely not," Sturgis said, emphatically.

"Good," Cody said. "Because I don't believe he is, either."

Near the Big Horn River, in Montana Territory

Since leaving the Cheyenne Reservation, Mean to His Horses had gathered almost four hundred followers, including the women and children who had come with the warriors. There were at least two hundred warriors with him, having joined him not only from his own tribe, but from other tribes: Lakota, Oglala, Brule, and even some Shoshone.

Black Rock, who had been a longtime friend of Mean to His Horses, was sitting with Mean to His Horses and others in council.

"We need more guns," Black Rock said. "Too many of us have only bows and arrows."

"We took two guns from the ranch of Kennedy," Mean to His Horses said. "And we took three guns from the wagons."

"We need many more guns."

"We will get them," Mean to His Horses promised.

"Where will we get them?"

"We will get them," Mean to His Horses repeated, without further clarification.

Near the Meeteetsee River

Nearly one hundred miles away, Pony Face and Red Shield, two Crow hunters, were looking for elk in the open range near the Meeteetsee River. They were off the Crow reservation, but they had no cause for worry. They had a long record of peaceful coexistence with the white man.

Now one band of Crow, under Chief High Hawk, lived on a reservation set aside for them just outside the eastern entrance to Yellowstone Park. And though they had a specific part of the valley set aside for their use, it was understood that they could hunt anywhere in the Valley they wished. In addition, many of the Crow had made friends with farmers and ranchers in the area, often trading with them, sometimes stopping by to visit while on a hunt to take a meal with them, and to leave game for them.

Because of that friendly relationship, when Pony Face and Red Shield saw a couple of white men approaching them, they weren't concerned. Perhaps they were part of the group of white men who were looking for gold. The hunters approached the white men to extend the sign of peace.

"We are Crow," Pony Face said, holding his hand up, palm out to show that he was friendly. "We are friends."

To the surprise of the two Crow hunters, the white men pointed their guns at them.

"We've had enough of you Injuns attacking our homes and killin' our women and children," one of the white men said.

"You speak of Cheyenne. We are not Cheyenne, we are Crow," Red Shield said.

"You're Injuns," the white man replied.

Pony Face and Red Shield were shot down, even as they were protesting.

Sam Davis and Lee Regret stood over the two bodies, holding their still-smoking guns. The sound of the gunshots echoed back from the nearby mountains.

"Think there are any more around here?" Regret asked.

"We haven't seen any more," Davis answered.

"What do we do now?"

"Let's get out of here," Davis said. "I don't think there's any more of 'em around, but there's no need to hang around, just in case."

* * *

The day after the shooting, Grey Antelope and Howling Wolf found the two hunters, and when they brought the bodies back into the camp the entire village turned out. Both Pony Face and Red Shield had wives and children, so the mourning was intense.

High Hawk, the tribal chief, called a council to discuss the killing of the two hunters.

"We should kill two whites," White Bull said.

"The whites already think we have killed two of them," Jumping Elk said. "Two of the men who hunt for gold were found dead and scalped."

"It was not an Indian who scalped them," White Bull said.

"I think they were killed by other white men who hunt for gold," High Hawk said. "But the white men think that they were killed by Crow."

"And I think that Pony Face and Red Shield were also killed by men who hunt for gold," Running Elk said.

"Running Elk, you speak the White Man's tongue, I think you should go to the white man's town and tell them that we have found two of our people killed, and ask if they will find and punish the ones who did this thing."

"I will go," Running Elk said.

No one in the village believed it to be any kind of organized action against the Indians, because the Crow were friendly with the white man. But it was known that white men could be driven crazy when they were searching for gold, so all were cautioned to be very careful while hunting, and to do nothing to anger the white man.

Bismarck

Angus Ebersole, Clay Hawkins, Ike Peters, and Jim Dewey were at a table at the back of Fireman's Exchange Saloon. Ebersole was the biggest of the four men, and though no vote had ever been taken, he was the leader of the group simply because he had assumed leadership. Ebersole was bald, but had a dark handlebar moustache. Hawkins was thin and wiry with a nose that was so flat that it made a whistling noise when he breathed. Peters and Dewey were medium-sized with unremarkable features. The saloon was busy with the usual clientele: miners, ranchers, freighters, and soldiers. There were several bar girls working the room as well, but none had approached the four men.

Ebersole folded the *Tribune* and put it on the table in front of him. He had been reading the article Ingraham wrote about the would-be train holdup.

"Falcon MacCallister and Buffalo Bill Cody," Ebersole said. "They're the sons of bitches that messed up our plans. We'd have money now if it wasn't for them."

"Yeah, I'm so broke I don't have two coins to rub together," Hawkins said.

"Falcon MacCallister and Buffalo Bill," Peters said. "Who would've thought that two men would shoot down Smitty, Hunt, and Collins."

"And Billy," Peters added.

"They didn't kill Billy. Fact is, they got him in jail, right here in town," Dewey said.

"Yes, and we need to get him out of jail," Ebersole said.

"Get him out? Get him out how?" Hawkins asked.

"Break him out," Ebersole said.

"Yeah, I reckon we do owe it to him, seein' as we run off and left him," Dewey said.

"Owin' it to him ain't got nothin' at all to do with why I'm wantin' to break him out," Ebersole said.

"Well then, if you don't think we owe it to him, why are you wantin' to break him out?"

"He was with MacCallister and Cody all the time from where they got him, till they come here. I think he probably knows where they are going."

"Why do we care where they are going?"

"Because soon as we find out where they are goin', we are goin' to track 'em down and kill 'em," Ebersole said.

"Why?"

Ebersole smiled. "Boys, you got 'ny idea how famous we'll be if we do that? There won't be a person in the country who ain't heard of us."

"That's why you want to kill 'em? So we'll be famous?" Dewey asked. "I always sort of thought that in our line of work we didn't exactly want to be famous."

"It depends on what line of work you are talking about," Ebersole said.

"Now, I don't have no idea in hell what it is you are talkin' about," Dewey said.

"There's folks all over the country that needs jobs— special jobs—done," Ebersole said. "If we kill both Mac-Callister and Cody, we'll be known as the kind of people who can do those special jobs. We'll be able to hire out our guns, and we'll make a ton of money from it."

"Yeah," Dewey said. "I guess you have a point there. It ain't somethin' I've ever thought about, though."

"How are we goin' to break him out?" Hawkins asked.

"We'll do it tonight when the town is real quiet," Ebersole said. "Like as not they won't have no more than one man a-watchin' over things at the jail. We'll just go in and force him to let Billy go."

CHAPTER SEVEN

Big Horn Basin, Yellowstone Valley

When he was but fifteen years old, Frank Barlow joined the army to save the Union. Captured at Kennesaw Mountain, he was one of the youngest prisoners of war in the Confederate Prison of War camp at Andersonville, Georgia. He spent just under a year in the prison where over 13,000 died, emerging from his incarceration weighing only ninety-four pounds. When he went back to Indiana he worked on his pa's farm until, learning of land to be had simply by homesteading out West, he got married and moved to Wyoming Territory.

It was a gamble and both his family and his new bride's family had tried to talk him out of it, but he was adamant, and his wife Ann backed him in his resolve. Now the gamble seemed to have paid off, and Frank owned a small but successful ranch. Last year he not only managed to support his family, he actually turned a profit, and he was already thinking about taking on a few hands to help him run the place.

His son Davey, who was eight years old, had just

celebrated his birthday and yesterday he and Ann had thrown a little party for him. He was looking forward to the time when Davey would be old enough to become a full partner in the operation of the ranch.

Frank pumped water into the basin, worked up lather from a bar of lye soap, then washed his hands and face. The cold well-water was bracing, and he reached for a towel and began drying off, thinking about the chicken and dumplings Ann had cooked for their supper. He had worked hard today and the enticing aroma was already causing his stomach to growl.

Barlow had the towel over his face when he thought he felt a presence. Dropping the towel, he was surprised to see two mounted men looking down at him. Where had they come from? He had neither seen nor heard them before this moment.

"Oh, you surprised me," he said. "Can I help you gentlemen?"

The two men unnerved Frank. There was something about them, suddenly appearing as they did, that left him with a troublesome and unsettled feeling in the pit of his stomach.

"Are you Frank Barlow?" one of the men asked.

"Yeah, I'm Barlow."

"Barlow, you've got twenty-four hours to get off this property."

"What are you talking about? Why the hell would I do that?"

"You are occupying land that belongs to the Bellefontaine Mineral Asset Development Company."

"The hell I am," Frank replied angrily. "I homesteaded this land near ten years ago. I have clear title to it."

"Show him the paper, Regret," one of the men said.

The one called Regret dismounted, and took a paper over to show to Frank.

"Can you read?" Regret asked.

"Yes."

"Then read this."

Frank took a folded piece of paper from Regret, then opened it up to read.

UNITED STATES OF AMERICA
DEPARTMENT OF THE INTERIOR

All homestead claims for land located within the boundaries of the area known as the Big Horn Basin, are herein invalidated. Occupants of this land, whether it be Home Site, Ranch, or Farm, are hereby ordered to vacate the property.

Ownership will be transferred to the Bellefontaine Mineral Asset Development Company for the purpose of extracting gold, silver, lead, tin, iron, or any and all such minerals as may be found there.

– Clarence King, Secretary of the Interior

Frank finished reading the document, then looked Regret.

"This ain't no way right," he said.

"What do you think, Davis. He don't believe it."

"Are you questioning the United States government?" Davis asked.

"Why would the government give me this land, then come take it away from me?"

"How many men do you employ on this place of yours?" Davis asked.

"Nobody. There is just me, my wife, and my boy."

"Well, there's the answer for you. Bellefontaine employs near thirty people. We will expect you to be off this property by noon tomorrow," Davis said.

"Mister, I've got a hundred head of cattle," Davis said. "What am I supposed to do with them?"

"This order don't pertain to your cattle, just to your land. You can take your cattle with you."

"Take them where? This is a small ranch. I told you, there is only my wife, my boy and me. And my boy's only eight years old. How are the three of us going to move a hundred head of cows?"

"That ain't my problem, mister. It is your problem," Davis said.

"And if I ain't off tomorrow?" Frank asked.

"You'll be off tomorrow," Davis said, resolutely.

"That's tomorrow," Frank said. "For now, I still own this property, and I'm ordering you off."

Regret laughed. "What do you think, Davis? He ordered us off."

"Now," Frank said. Turning, he walked toward the house without looking around one time.

"Are you hungry?" Ann asked when Frank stepped in through the kitchen door. "Dinner's ready, have a seat and I'll bring you a plate."

Frank didn't say a word to his wife. Instead he got the double-barrel twelve-gauge shotgun down, broke it open, slid two shells into the chamber, then snapped it shut.

"Frank, what is it?" Ann asked when she saw him load the gun. "What are you doing? What's wrong?"

"Stay inside," Frank said.

* * *

Davis knew that Barlow would come back, and he expected him to be armed.

"Get off my land you thieving sons of bitches!" Frank shouted, raising the shotgun to his shoulder.

The shotgun never reached his shoulder. Both Davis and Regret already had their pistols drawn, and they fired as one. The shotgun discharged with a roar, but the gun was pointing down so there was no effect from the double load of buckshot.

"Frank!" a woman screamed. Running out of the house she knelt beside her husband who was already dead. "Frank!" she cried again. She looked up at the two men who were still holding the smoking guns in their hands.

"You killed him!"

Davis pulled the trigger, hitting the woman in the side of her head. Blood, brain, and bits of bone tissue erupted from the entry wound.

"Ma! Pa!" Davey shouted as he ran out of the house. He started toward his parents, but didn't make it. He was shot down even before he stepped off the stoop.

The sound of the shots echoed back from nearby Jim Mountain.

"I didn't think that paper we had printed up would work," Regret said.

"Just 'cause it didn't work this time, don't mean it won't work next time we try to use it," Davis said. He dismounted and drew his knife. "You want the woman or the kid?" he asked.

"Don't make me no never mind," Regret said, as he pulled his own knife and started toward the young boy.

Fort Yates Indian Reservation

The first U.S. Army post at this site was established in 1863 as the Standing Rock Cantonment with the purpose of overseeing the Hunkpapa and Blackfeet bands. Though many still referred to it as Standing Rock, its name was changed in 1878 to honor Captain George Yates who was killed at the Battle of Little Big Horn in 1876, and it was here that Falcon, Cody, and Ingraham came to meet with Sitting Bull.

After the defeat of Custer, public reaction demanded revenge against the Indians, and over the next year thousands of additional military were sent into the area. There, they relentlessly pursued the tribes who had been a part of the battle: the Lakota, Cheyenne and Arapaho. But the Indians were no longer massed as they had been during the battle, and were now split up.

Because the Indian nations had separated, they were unable to withstand the military pressure brought against them, and the military subdued them rather quickly. The other Indian leaders surrendered, but Sitting Bull did not; and in May of 1877, Sitting Bull led his band of Lakota across the border into Canada. When General Terry traveled north to offer him a pardon in exchange for settling on a reservation, Sitting Bull sent him away.

He was unable to continue in Canada though, because unlike the United States, Canada provided no beef or provisions of any kind. And, with the buffalo nearly extinct, Sitting Bull was unable to feed his people. He had no option remaining except to come south to surrender, and this he did on July 19, 1881, whereupon he was sent to Fort Yates.

In 1885 Sitting Bull was allowed to leave the reservation to join Buffalo Bill's Wild West Exhibition. However he was very uncomfortable in white society, so he left the show after only four months. During that time, though, he did shake hands with President Grover Cleveland, which, in his mind, meant that he was still regarded as an important leader of the Sioux.

"Why do you wish to see Sitting Bull?" James McLaughlin asked. McLaughlin was the Indian agent at Fort Yates.

"Because General Miles asked us to," Falcon replied.

"You can understand why I ask, I'm sure," McLaughlin said. "People from all over come here to see Sitting Bull, Senators, Congressmen, Cabinet Members, even foreign royalty."

Cody chuckled. "Yes, he wasn't with my show for very long, but he was immensely popular while he was there."

"It's not good for him to be so uppity," McLaughlin said. "He has the idea that he is still a chief, and the other Indians on the reservation look up to him, even though he can do nothing for them. I am the one in charge. Sitting Bull can do nothing."

"That isn't quite right," Falcon said.

"What do you mean, it isn't quite right?" McLaughlin demanded.

"Sitting Bull can give them dignity."

McLaughlin laughed, a high-pitched cackle. "Dignity?" he said. "You want to see dignity?" He pointed toward a large garden, wherein potatoes, cabbage, cauliflower, eggplant, celery, peppers, cucumbers, and tomatoes were being grown for use on the post. There were several people working in the garden, all women, except for one man who, bent at the waist, was working with a hoe. "There is Sitting Bull. How is that for dignity?"

"Why are you doing that?" Ingraham asked. "Why are you subjecting Sitting Bull to such ignominy?"

"Who are you?" McLaughlin asked.

"My name, sir, is Prentiss Ingraham. I am a writer."

"A writer? You aren't part of General Miles's delegation?"

"He is with us," Cody said. "That makes him part of General Miles's delegation."

"I have heard that you are a vain man, Cody . . ."

"That is Colonel Cody to you, Major," Cody interrupted.

"Colonel Cody," McLaughlin said, correcting himself. "But I had no idea that you were so vain as to have with you your own member of the press."

"He will not only write about me, Major," Cody said. "He will also write about you."

Though subtle, the implied threat hit home, and McLaughlin blinked and swallowed, as he understood the circumstances.

"I, uh, all right, Colonel Cody, what do you want?"

"I told you, we want to speak with Sitting Bull."

"Very well, I will summon him."

"Major McLaughlin," Falcon said. "Do you have a reception room of some sort, a room where visiting dignitaries such as Congressmen and Senators are welcomed as guests?"

"Yes, I have such a room."

Falcon pointed to Cody. "Buffalo Bill Cody is the most famous man in America, if not in the world. He has been the guest of kings and queens the world over, and now he is the guest of Sitting Bull. Please show us to the reception room."

"Just a minute," McLaughlin said. "Are you telling me you want me to bring Sitting Bull to the reception room?"

"Oh, I don't just want it," Falcon said. "I expect it."

"And you might have your cook make some lemonade," Cody added. "Working in the garden as he is, I expect Sitting Bull is thirsty. I also remember from his time with me that he has a fondness for sweets. I'm sure your cook can accommodate us with some sort of treat."

"Look here," McLaughlin said angrily. "I'm in charge here. I'll not be taking orders from visitors."

"You'll take orders from these visitors," Falcon said quietly. It was that—the cold, calculated, quietness of his voice—that persuaded McLaughlin to change his mind.

"I'll bring him to you," he said.

The reception room was quite nice, and, under the circumstances, quite well furnished with sofa and chairs. The walls were decorated with heads of game, and a huge buffalo skin was on the floor. A few minutes after they went into the room, two Indian women came into the room, one of them carrying a large carafe of lemonade and the other a platter of cookies.

Cody walked over to take one of the cookies. "They must have already had some baked," he said. "They couldn't have made a new batch this fast. Would you like one, Ingraham?"

"No, thank you," Ingraham answered. He was sitting off to one side, writing furiously on his tablet.

It was at least half an hour before McLaughlin returned with Sitting Bull. "In there," he said, gruffly. Then to the others, McLaughlin said, "Sorry it took so long, but he insisted upon changing clothes before he met with you."

"We don't mind the wait, and I am sure it made him more comfortable," Cody said.

Sitting Bull's face was expressionless until after McLaughlin left. Then, with a smile, he extended his hand to Cody.

"Ho, Cody," he said. "It is a good day to see you again."

"Hello, Sitting Bull, you old war horse," Cody said. "It is a good day to see you as well. This is my friend Falcon MacCallister."

"You were with Custer," Sitting Bull said.

"Yes."

"That is past," Sitting Bull said. He offered his hand to Falcon. "Now, we can be friends." Sitting Bull looked over at Ingraham, and though he said nothing, the expression on his face asked the question.

"This is Prentiss Ingraham," Cody said. "He is a writer."

"You mean he does paper words," Sitting Bull said.

"Yes," Cody answered. "How are you doing, Sitting Bull?"

"I have food and shelter," Sitting Bull replied. "My wives, Four Robes and Seen by the Nation have food and shelter and do not complain."

"I see McLaughlin has you working in the field. That is not right for a chief like you."

"If it is right for my people to work in the field, then it is right for me as well," Sitting Bull said.

"But can you keep their respect?"

Sitting Bull was quiet for a moment. "It does not matter," he said. "They will kill me anyway."

"Who will kill you?" Falcon asked.

"My people will kill me," Sitting Bull said. "In a vision, I saw a meadowlark land beside me. I approached him, and I was surprised when he did not fly away. 'Why do you not fly away?' I asked the bird. 'Do you not fear me?' The bird answered me. 'Your own people, the Lakota, will kill you.' And because I heard this with my own ears, this I believe."

"Your people love you," Cody said. "They will not kill you."

"Was there not a great chief of the whites, loved by all, who was killed by a white man?"

"You are talking about Abraham Lincoln," Falcon said.

"Yes. Was he killed by an Indian?"

"No. He was killed by John Wilkes Booth, a white man," Falcon said.

"One of his people."

"Not exactly," Cody said. "Booth was a Southern sympathizer."

"One of his people," Sitting Bull repeated.

"If you put it that way, yes."

"I, too, will be killed by my own people."

"Sitting Bull, what do you know of the *Wagi Wanagi?*" Falcon asked.

"*Wagi Wanagi?* You wish to know of *Wagi Wanagi?* You have come to the wrong person. *Wagi Wanagi* is a religion, started by Mean to His Horses," Sitting Bull said.

"Do you follow this religion of Spirit Talking?" Cody asked.

"Many have heard and some believe," Sitting Bull replied. "Many do not believe."

"That is not what I asked, Sitting Bull," Cody said. "Do you follow this religion?"

"I do not follow this religion, but I have honor for

this religion. I do not follow the Jesus religion of the white man, but also, I have honor for that religion."

"Do you think it will be a danger to the white man? Do you think it will start a war?"

"I think it will be a danger only to the Indian," Sitting Bull said. "For it is a religion that says the white man will leave and all the land will be returned to the people."

"You don't believe that, do you?" Cody asked.

"I do not believe that," Sitting Bull said. "But my people do not understand. They think the only white people are those that they see—the soldiers, the Indian agents, the ranchers, farmers, and those in the towns. They have not seen what I have seen; they do not know what I know. I know how large is the village of the white man, I know that on the train, going much faster than the swiftest horse, it takes many days to cross the white man's land. I have seen, gathered to see one show, more white people than there are in all the nations of the Sioux. Another war can only mean the end of my people."

"Will you do all that you can to prevent another war?" Cody asked.

Sitting Bull raised his hand to point to the garden. "I can tell the women who work in the garden with me that there should not be another war. But the women do not want war anyway. I can tell the old men who come to gather their rations that there should not be another war, but they are old and they have seen war and do not want to see another. I can tell the young men that there should not be another war, but in many, their blood is hot with anger and distrust for the white man, so I do not think they will listen to me."

* * *

After his meeting with Sitting Bull, Cody went to the Army Signal Center where he composed a telegram to be sent to General Miles.

AS PER YOUR INSTRUCTIONS, I HAVE
INTERVIEWED SITTING BULL. IT IS MY BELIEF
THAT HE HAS NO CONNECTION WITH THE
SPIRIT TALKING MOVEMENT. THE ONE BEHIND
THE MOVEMENT IS MEAN TO HIS HORSES A
CHEYENNE. I BELIEVE THAT IF THERE IS TO BE
ANY INDIAN TROUBLE IT WILL COME FROM A
MIXED BAG OF RENEGADES AND NOT A
COORDINATED WAR LAUNCHED BY ANY
PARTICULAR TRIBE. WILLIAM CODY.

After sending the telegram, Cody, Falcon, and Ingraham took their lunch at the Officers' Open Mess at Fort Yates.

"I thank you for coming with me, Falcon," Cody said.

"I didn't mind. As I said, I was coming back home, anyway."

"Before you return to Colorado, I wonder if you would like to stay with me a little longer," Cody invited. "You may find the next part of my trip interesting."

"What do you have in mind?"

"First, I'm going to DeMaris Springs, Wyoming Territory," Cody said. "The site where my town is to be is very close to there. I thought I might look it over and show it to you and Ingraham. From there, we will take a turn through Yellowstone Park. Have you ever been there?"

"Yes, I have."

"There are some fascinating things to see there," Cody said. "Then, from Yellowstone, I am going up to Cinnabar, where I will be holding an audition."

"An audition?"

"Yes, I will be looking for new cowboys. Where do you think I get the people for my exhibition?"

"I don't know," Falcon replied. "I guess I've never really thought about it."

"Well I think about it, all the time. I have to think about it. And believe me, I can't get cowboys from Brooklyn. They have to be authentic, or the people who come to my shows will see it in a second. And to be honest, I would like to have you help me pick out the ones I can use."

Falcon chuckled. "All right," he said. "I've never thought of myself as a talent scout, but I suppose I could do that."

"I suppose you are coming too, Ingraham?" Cody said.

"Of course. There is still a chance that something exciting may happen that I can write about," Ingraham replied.

Prentiss Ingraham's notes from his book in progress:

> *He is a small man, and physically most unprepossessing, though he struts and frets his hour upon the stage as if the entire nation weighed heavily upon his shoulders, and not merely the administration of a small Indian agency. His name is Major James McLaughlin, and a more unpleasant gentleman you are unlikely to meet during your appointed years on earth.*
>
> *McLaughlin is in charge of none other than Sitting Bull, unquestionably the most famous of all America's Indians. Perhaps intimidated by the bearing*

*and dignity of the celebrated chief, McLaughlin has
done all in his power to demean and discomfit the
noble Sioux leader. Despite his ignoble efforts, Sitting
Bull has maintained all the dignity and élan of one
of his station. During his audience with Buffalo Bill
Cody and Falcon MacCallister, he was straight
forward and completely in command of himself. The
result of the meeting was just as Buffalo Bill
expected. Sitting Bull is not a part of the Spirit
Talking movement which has so animated the
Indians of late.*

Bismarck

It was just after midnight in Bismarck, and by now
even the saloons were quiet. The Missouri river
gleamed silver in the moonlight as Angus Ebersole,
Clay Hawkins, Ike Peters, and Jim Dewey walked quietly down 4th Street, heading for the jail, from which a
light was shining, dimly.

Looking around to make certain they weren't being
watched, the four men stepped up onto the porch of
the jail. Ebersole tried the door, but it didn't open.

"Damn, it's locked," he said.

"It's supposed to be locked," Hawkins said. "It's
a jail."

"Yeah, but jails are supposed to lock people in, not
lock 'em out," Ebersole said.

"I got an idea," Dewey said. "Knock on the door."

"Ain't much chance of surprisin' him by knockin'
on the door," Ebersole said.

"I'm goin' to pretend to be drunk," Dewey said.
"Knock on the door, when the deputy opens it, tell him
you want to put me in jail to keep me out of trouble."

"That might work," Hawkins said.

"May as well try it," Peters added.

Ebersole nodded, then knocked loudly on the door. "Marshal!" he called. "Marshal, you in there?"

He knocked again.

The door opened and a young man, wearing the badge of a deputy, stepped back from the open door. He was holding a double-barrel shotgun in his hands.

"What do you want?" the deputy asked.

"Our pard here is drunk," Ebersole said.

"I ain't no more drunk than you are, you lyin' sumbitch!" Dewey said, slurring his words.

"What does that mean to me, that he is drunk?" the deputy asked.

"Well, we want you to lock him up tonight so's he don't get in no trouble."

"Just take 'im somewhere and let 'im sleep it off," the deputy said. "I don't have any authority to lock someone up."

"What do you mean you don't have any authority? You're a deputy, ain't you?" Ebersole said.

"I can't lock someone up just for being drunk. If I did that, the jail would be full every night."

"See, I tole' you I wasn't goin' to spen' no night in jail," Dewey said. He made a drunken lurch toward the deputy. "You're a good man, dep'y," he said as he reached him. "Yes, sir, you're a good man."

The deputy tried to back away from him, but it was too late. Dewey grabbed his shotgun and pointed it straight up, then jerked it away from him.

"What the hell?" the deputy yelled, but before he could say anything else, Ebersole brought his pistol down, sharply, on the deputy's head. He fell unconscious to the floor.

"Billy?" Ebersole shouted. "Billy boy, are you back there!"

"Yeah, I'm here," Billy answered.

"Hold on a second. We're gettin' you out of here."

Ebersole got the key from a hook on the wall, then went into the back of the jail. The cell door was held closed by a hasp and padlock. He tried three keys before he found the right one. The padlock clicked open, then Ebersole removed it and opened the cell door.

"I know'd you boys wasn't goin' to leave me here," Billy Taylor said with a wide smile spread across his face. Taylor was the youngest of the group, and at first glance most women found him good looking, but upon further examination there was something in his eyes that put them off. One woman said that he was like fine crystal, but with a flaw in its casting. "Yes, sir, I know'd you boys was goin' to get me out of here, one way or the other."

"Come on," Ebersole said. "Let's get out of here before anyone comes."

CHAPTER EIGHT

DeMaris Springs

It was not unusual for Running Elk to ride into the small town of DeMaris Springs but there was something going on today that was unusual. As he rode down Center Street he saw several people gathered around the front of a hardware store. Curious as to what was attracting so much interest, he guided his pony over to see. There, in front of the hardware store and strapped to boards so they could be stood up, were the bodies of a man, woman, and child. All three had been scalped, and a sign posted over the top of the three bodies read:

Frank, Ann, And Davey Barlow

MURDERED BY INDIANS

Running Elk was mounted, and was behind the crowd of people so at first, no one saw him. Then, a woman happened to turn and seeing Running Elk, screamed. Her scream caused the others to turn, then all saw Running Elk.

"There's one of the savages now!" a man shouted.

"Get him! String him up!"

Running Elk spoke excellent English, and he was certain he could convince them that they were wrong.

"We did not do this terrible thing!" Running Elk shouted. "We are Crow! We are friends with the white man!"

"Get him! Get the heathen!"

Fortunately for Running Elk, none of the townspeople who gathered around the hardware store were armed. Neither were they mounted, so as they surged toward him, it was easy for Running Elk to slap his legs against the sides of his pony and gallop away.

Big Horn Basin, Yellowstone Valley

Before Running Elk could get back home to warn the others, Many Buffalo, an older Crow who was very friendly with the whites, decided to take a wagon into town. He was accompanied by his granddaughter White Deer, her husband One Feather, their two children, and Quiet Stream, who was One Feather's sister. Quiet Stream was riding into town in order to sell her blankets. One Feather was mounted on his pony, and he rode alongside the wagon, carrying on banter with his wife and children.

Suddenly a shot rang out, and Many Buffalo fell out of the wagon, dead. White Deer jumped down and tried to run away, but she was shot as well.

"Quiet Stream! Turn the wagon! Drive back to the village!" One Feather shouted.

Picking up the loose reins, Quiet Stream turned the

wagon around, then drove away as rapidly as possible. Several white men came over the crest of a hill and began chasing her, but One Feather, who had stayed behind, was able to hold them off long enough to give Quiet Stream a head start.

After running the team for at least ten minutes at full speed, Quiet Stream looked back and, seeing no one, slowed the team to a walk. Then she saw a house ahead, and decided she would stop there for shelter. But as she approached, she was fired at by people within the house, so she knew she had no choice but to continue to run. The children, who were very young, were frightened, and worried about their mother and father.

Quiet Stream and her two small nephews made it safely back to the reservation only because her brother, One Feather, had succeeded in holding off the white men.

Back at the point of the initial attack, White Deer, who was shot twice, was lying helpless on the ground when she saw two of the men who had attacked them walk over to Many Buffalo and look down at the old Indian's body.

She lay very quietly, pretending to be dead.

Though she didn't know them by name, it was Sam Davis and Lee Regret who were leading the posse that had been constituted after the slaughter of the Barlow family.

"Look at the old son of a bitch," Davis said, pointing to Many Buffalo's body. "You know in his life he's taken a few white scalps."

"Yeah, I believe it," Regret said.

"I don't feel all that good 'bout killin' the woman though," one of the other riders said.

White Deer knew they were talking about her, and she lay very still, lest they realize that she was still alive.

"Why not? The Injuns didn't mind killin' the Barlow woman and her kid," Davis said.

"Yeah, I guess you're right."

"So, what are we going to do now?" one of the other riders asked.

"We're goin' to leave the Injuns a message," Davis said.

"Yeah, I reckon this will leave them a message."

"No, I mean a real message. We're goin' to leave a note. I want the Injuns to know who done this, and why."

"What note?"

"This note. I already got it wrote, and all we have to do is leave it pinned on 'em so's the Injuns will find it."

"How we goin' to pin it on 'em?"

The first man chuckled, then kneeling down he pulled Many Buffalo's hunting knife from its sheath.

"You want to see how I pin the note on? Watch," he said.

He drove the knife through the note, pinning it to Many Buffalo's chest.

"Haw!" the second man said. "I don't reckon that note's goin' to blow away."

White Deer knew that her father was already dead, but it was all she could do to keep from crying out when she saw the knife plunged into his chest.

"What about the squaw?"

"What about her?"

"We just goin' to leave her there?"

"What do you want to do, bury her?

"No, nothin' like that. I was just wonderin'."

"Leave her. When they find her, the old man, and the buck we killed, they'll know we mean business."

"Yeah. If this don't teach 'em a lesson, nothin' will."

"Let's go."

White Deer continued to lie unmoving for a long moment after they left, still terrified that they would come back. She waited until the sound of hoofbeats could no longer be heard before she raised her head. The first thing she saw was the pony of her husband. When she saw the pony of One Feather, she knew that if the pony was without a rider, One Feather must have been killed as well. She also knew that Quiet Stream had driven the wagon away with her children and she could only hope that they were still alive.

Painfully, laboriously, saddened by the deaths of her father and husband and worried about her children, White Deer managed to mount the pony and ride away. After a ride of well over an hour, she reached the house of Chris Dumey, a settler that she knew, and experienced a great sense of relief at her salvation.

She stopped in front of the house and stayed on the pony by a great effort because she was still losing blood.

"Help!" she called. "Please, I have been shot! Mr. Dumey, please help me!"

The door to the house opened just a crack, and a man thrust a shotgun through the opening.

"Get out of here Injun," he said, his voice a low growl.

"Mr. Dumey, it is me, White Deer! I have been shot. I need help," White Deer said.

"If you don't get now, you're goin' to get shot again," Dumey said. "Now get!" He shouted the last two words, and thrust the gun forward dramatically.

Somehow the fear helped her overcome the dizziness and White Deer slapped her legs against the side of the pony and raced out of the farmer's yard.

She passed at least three other settlers' homes on

her way back to the village, and even though she also knew the people who lived in those houses, she gave them a wide berth.

It was dark by the time she returned to the village, and because Quiet Stream had already made it back safely with word of the attack, the entire village was in an uproar.

"We thought you were dead," High Hawk said.

"Where is One Feather?" Big Hand, the father of Quiet Stream and One Feather asked.

"He is dead," White Deer said. "So is my father. I don't know where my children are. I don't know where Quiet Stream is."

"I am here, White Deer," Quiet Stream said. "Your children are safe."

Although she had managed to stay conscious during her long arduous ride back home, knowing now that her children were safe, White Deer quit hanging on. She passed out from her wounds, and she was picked up and carried into her tipi where the bullets were removed from her body, and a poultice put over each of the two bullet wounds.

Big Horn Basin

It was two hunters from the Crow village who found the bodies of Many Buffalo and One Feather the next day. Constructing a travois, they brought the four back to the village. They had found a piece of paper on Many Buffalo's body, pinned to him by his own knife.

The rest of the village wept and shouted in anger at the brutal slaying.

"Here are some paper words," one of the two Indians said.

"Show the paper words to Running Elk," one of the villagers said. "He has been to the white man's school, he can read the paper words."

Running Elk was as angry and aggrieved as all the other villagers, but he was pleased that he had been chosen to read the paper words. He read the words aloud, in English.

"*We kilt these Injuns because they did not stay where they belonged. We will kill all Injuns who do not stay where they belong.*"

Because not everyone understood him when he read the note in English, Running Elk translated it for them.

Now the people became painfully aware of the situation. The paper words made it clear that the earlier murders, like these, were not merely the isolated incident of one or two whites. It was an organized movement, designed, no doubt, to run the Indians away from their land so that the whites could look for gold anywhere they wanted.

"The whites are devils!" White Bull shouted.

"We should kill them all!" another yelled.

"Mean to His Horses is right. There can be no peace until the white man knows we are men and not animals to be hunted!" White Bull said.

"White Bull, do not let the heat of your heart rule the reason of your mind," High Hawk said. "Mean to His Horses is Cheyenne. The Cheyenne are our ancient enemies. We are friends with the white men. Our warriors have fought at the side of the Long Knives. We have learned many things from our white brothers."

"We have learned to be cowards," White Bull said scornfully. "But I will not be a coward. I will join Mean to His Horses."

"I will join him as well," Running Elk said.

"Running Elk, no," High Hawk said. "You have been educated by the white man. You are the future of our people."

"If the white people kill us all, we have no future," Running Elk said. "White Bull speaks for me."

"And for me," another said.

"All who are brave of heart, come with me!" White Bull shouted. "We will go to Mean to His Horses and ask him to lead us!"

Trooper's Saloon, Miles City, Montana Territory

Though the saloon didn't cater exclusively to the army, its proximity to Fort Keogh meant that soldiers made up the bulk of its customers. Today was payday for the army, and on this evening the saloon was full. One of the centerpieces of the saloon was its recent acquisition of a lithograph of "Custer's Last Fight."

Sergeant Patrick Connelly was sitting at a table with Sergeant Lucas Depro and several other soldiers. All were asking him about the fight because the Irishman had been with Custer on that fateful scout, taking part in the hilltop fight with Reno and Benteen, where he was wounded. Connelly was pointing to figures in the painting.

"That lad there is m' friend Edward Connor, like me, Irish born," Connelly said. "And Patrick Downing and Charles Graham, Irish born too. And there's himself, Captain Myles Keogh, as fine an officer as ever drew a breath. Irish he was, like the others."

"You were with Benteen, were you?" Depro asked.

"Aye, though I was with Reno when first we split up. Benteen, you know, came up to join us."

"What do you think of Benteen?" Depro asked.

"Sure now, 'n why do you ask? Would you be wantin' me to speak unkindly of an officer who shared the dangers of the hilltop fight with myself? For I'm tellin' you, that I'll not do."

"You know he is here at Fort Keogh in command of the colored troops, don't you?"

"Aye, and how is it that I would not know, being as I am on the same post and I've known the man for more than ten years now," Sergeant Connelly said.

"Maybe what I should have asked is what kind of white man would let himself be stuck with a bunch of colored men?"

"Don't you be makin' the mistake now of thinkin' that the coloreds don't make good soldiers, Depro," Connelly said. "They are good soldiers, the lot of them."

"I've nothin' good to say about Coletrain," Depro said.

"I know the two of you are workin' together now," Connelly said. "'Twas thinkin' I was, that mayhap the two of you would be gettin' on just fine."

"We ain't workin' together," Depro said. "We're in the same buildin', but he's supply sergeant for the Ninth, and I'm supply sergeant for the Sixth."

"But 'tis the same army, is it not?"

"Not to me, it ain't. The Ninth is all colored soldiers, the Sixth is all white."

"Sergeant Depro, 'tis Irish born I am, but since takin' the oath to wear this uniform and defend the flag of the United States, I'm more American than I am Irish. Seems to me you could do the same."

"Maybe the Irish and the colored are the same," Depro said. "But don't include me with you."

"Hello, Sarge, can I speak with you for a moment?"

Looking up toward the speaker, Depro recognized

Sam Davis. Davis had been a trooper in his platoon but got out when his enlistment expired.

"Want to join up again, do you, Davis?" Depro asked.

"No, nothin' like that. This is somethin' else," Davis said.

"Well, speak up."

Davis shook his head. "I'd rather talk to you in private. I'll buy you a beer."

Depro chuckled. "Well, bein' as you are a rich civilian now, I reckon I can let you buy me a beer all right. You boys carry on without me," he said to the other troopers at his table.

Davis followed Depro through the crowd of loud-talking, often laughing soldiers to a table in the far back corner where another civilian was sitting. When the civilian looked up toward them, Depro recognized Lee Regret. Like Davis, Regret had once served in Depro's platoon.

"Now if you're plannin' on tellin' me that Regret wants to re-enlist, you can just forget about it," Depro said.

"Nah, he don't want to enlist neither," Davis said. "But he's in on what I got to talk to you about."

"Hello, Sarge," Regret said.

"Regret," Depro replied.

"Regret, how about get us another beer? And get one for the sarge," Davis said.

Regret nodded, then got up from the table and headed toward the bar.

"Regret is your dog-robber now, is he?" Depro asked.

"I know you and Regret never got along, but he's a good man," Davis said.

A moment later Regret returned with three beers and passed them around.

Depro took a swallow, then wiped the foam from his

moustache. "All right," he said. "What is it you want
to talk about?"

"Money," Davis said.

"What about money?"

"I know how you can make some," Davis said.

"You know how I can make some money?"

"A lot of money," Davis replied.

Fort Keogh, Wyoming Territory

Established in August 1876, Fort Keogh was located
on the right bank of the Yellowstone River, just west of
Miles City and two miles above the mouth of the
Tongue River. Established by Colonel Nelson A. Miles,
by order of Brigadier General Alfred Terry, it was in-
tended to serve as a base of supply and operations
against the Sioux Indians. Construction of permanent
buildings commenced in 1877. Originally called "New
Post on the Yellowstone," the "Cantonment on Tongue
River," then "Tongue River Barracks," it was finally designated Fort Keogh on November 8, 1878, in honor
of Captain Myles Keogh, Seventh U.S. Cavalry, killed in
the Battle of Little Big Horn on June 25, 1876. The
post was one of several established during this period
for the purpose of subduing the Indians of the northern plains and securing permanent control over them.

The fort was substantial, consisting of several buildings, including quarters for officers and men, barns,
warehouses, and mess halls. Stationed at the fort were
four troops of Buffalo Soldiers, the Ninth Cavalry, with
their headquarters and band, under Major Fredric
Benteen. Here too, were three troops of the Sixth Cavalry, under Lieutenant Colonel Benjamin Whitehead.

As a general rule, the officers did not frequent the

Trooper Saloon in Miles City, because to do so would put them in close social contact with the enlisted men. Close social contact between enlisted and officers was frowned upon, so the officers plied their social intercourse in the Officers' Open Mess on the grounds of the fort. Because there were no black officers, all of the Ninth Cavalry officers were white, and thus, in the mess at least, the officers of the Ninth and the Sixth commingled.

When Major Benteen stepped into the Officers' Open Mess there were several of the officers engaged in a spirited discussion and one of them looked up as Benteen came in.

"Major Benteen was there," a lieutenant said.

"I was where, Lieutenant Purvis?"

"At Little Big Horn."

Benteen sighed in resignation. In the last ten years he had been asked thousands of questions about the fight at Little Big Horn, and he was reasonably certain that there could be no question he had not heard.

"Tell me, Major, why did Custer refuse to take the Gatling guns? Don't you think that if he had had them, the outcome would have been different?"

"Custer refused to take the guns and I concurred," Benteen said.

"But why? That doesn't make sense."

"Think about it, Purvis. The Gatling gun is wheel-mounted, just like a piece of artillery. The topography around Little Big Horn was such that it would have extremely limited mobility. In addition, it is crew-served, which means that two men must be standing upright to fire it, and that exposes them. And finally, they jam up so frequently as to be ineffective, especially in a battle situation as fluid as was the situation at Little Big Horn. One can find a lot of fault with Custer, and God knows I can, because I despised the man. But his decision not to take Gatling guns into the battle was a correct one."

"Major Benteen, you've been fighting Indians for over twenty years now. Tell me, do you think we are about to get into another Indian war?" a Captain named Jones asked.

Benteen who had taken his seat at the table with the others, poured himself a glass of whiskey before he answered.

"What would make you think that?"

"It's this Spirit Talking business," Captain Jones said. "It was started by an Indian who was at Custer's last fight, a chief by the name of . . ."

"Mean to His Horses," Benteen said, interrupting Jones. "He's not a chief, he's a shaman."

"Whatever he is, a lot of Indians are listening to him. And I don't mean just the Cheyenne, either."

"Yes, well, I wouldn't worry about it," Benteen said. "If we do get into another little skirmish, I don't expect it will come to much. I think the Indians are all whipped now. They are tired of fighting."

"Excuse me, Major, but isn't that what Custer thought?" a newly minted second lieutenant asked. "I mean, from what I read and heard while I was in the Academy, the Indians gave Custer, you, and the rest of the Seventh a pretty good whipping."

There was a corporate gasp from the others, and conversation halted in mid-syllable as all stared toward Benteen to see how he would react.

Benteen said nothing. He lifted his glass to his lips

and glared at the young lieutenant. He held the silent glare for a long moment, and as the moment lengthened and the silence stretched out, the lieutenant became visibly shaken.

"Uh, I didn't mean you got the whipping," the lieutenant said. "Everyone knows that you weren't actually with Custer when he went into battle, that you hung back and—uh . . ."

"Lieutenant Simmons, I think you had better quit before you get yourself in any deeper," Colonel Whitehead said. Lieutenant Colonel Whitehead was Benteen's counterpart, the commanding officer of the Sixth.

"Yes, sir. I—uh—told Sergeant Templeton that I would look into something with him. I need to leave."

"But, Lieutenant," Benteen said. "You didn't finish your drink."

"I'm not thirsty, sir," Lieutenant Simpson said as he hurried out of the club, chased by the laughter of all the other officers therein present.

"You're going to have to teach me that stare some time, Benteen," Whitehead said.

"Yes, sir, I would be glad to," Benteen replied.

"But, first, I would be interested in knowing what you think about our current situation. I'll ask you the same question Captain Jones asked. Do you think there is going to be another Indian war?"

"Do you think there will be?" Benteen replied.

"I don't know," Whitehead admitted. "I know that Mean to His Horses has been leading some renegades on a tear. There was that massacre of the Kennedy family up in Montana Territory, then the attack on the freight wagons."

"Yes, but you said it for what it is. It is a group of renegade Cheyenne."

"Not just Cheyenne," Whitehead said. "There was the Barlow family that got murdered, and those two white prospectors found shot and scalped in the Yellowstone Valley. That was down here in Wyoming, and more than likely, it was Crow that did that."

"How many prospectors do we have poking around out there right now?" Benteen asked.

"I don't know for sure. Twenty or thirty I would say," Whitehead said.

"With that many gold hunters out there, don't you think it is just possible that those two got into an argument with some other prospectors, were murdered, then scalped to make it look like Indians did it?"

"As I understand, there were also some Indians killed, no doubt reprisals by the whites who live nearby," Whitehead said.

"At this point I don't see a couple of white men and a few Indians getting killed being enough to get us into a war. Especially with the Crow. I have put my life in the hands of the Crow many times."

"Yes, but that was then, and this is now. Things are different now."

"What is so different?" Benteen asked.

"I'll tell you what is different. It is this Spirit Talking business."

"As long as they are talking to spirits, they aren't fighting the army," Benteen said.

Whitehead chuckled. "Yes, I guess that's true. Still, one wonders. I know for a fact that General Miles is worried about it. He thinks Sitting Bull might be leading the Indians."

"Sitting Bull? Are you talking about the same Sitting Bull who went into show business with Buffalo Bill Cody? That Sitting Bull?"

"Yes, the one who led the Sioux in the fight at Little Big Horn."

Benteen made a dismissive snort. "Sitting Bull remained in his tipi for the entire fight. He couldn't lead a bunch of Holy Rollers to Jesus," he said.

"What if we do get into a fight?" Whitehead said. "Can we count on you?"

"What do you mean, can you count on me?" Benteen snapped back, forgetting military courtesy in his response. "Sonny, I was fighting Indians when your mama was changing your britches!"

"I don't mean you, personally," Whitehead restated, quickly. "I meant can we count on your colored soldiers?"

"Don't you worry about my colored soldiers, Colonel Whitehead," Benteen replied. "They are as good as any soldiers I ever served with."

Whitehead laughed out loud. "They are as good as any you ever served with? That's quite a statement isn't it? I mean, considering that you served with Custer and the Seventh."

"I will say again," Benteen repeated, more slowly and with greater emphasis. "My colored soldiers are as good as any soldier I ever served with."

CHAPTER NINE

After leaving Fort Yates and their rendezvous with Sitting Bull, Falcon, Cody, and Ingraham proceeded farther west by rail, leaving the train at Miles City, Montana Territory.

At Miles City they would take a boat down the Tongue River to Sheridan, Wyoming Territory, but that would not occur for three days. Cody suggested that they pay a visit to Fort Keogh.

"Good idea," Falcon said. "I well remember Myles Keogh. He was a good man, and a good officer."

After the gate guard was shown their commissioning papers, he saluted, then pointed across the quadrangle to the headquarters building. There were several soldiers out in the quadrangle going through various drills. On one side were a group of black soldiers, and on the other a group of white soldiers.

"The Ninth and Sixth Cavalry share the post," Cody explained.

Once inside the headquarters building, the adjutant showed them in to the office of the post commander, who was also the commanding officer of the Sixth Cavalry.

"Buffalo Bill Cody, I can't tell you how pleased we are to have you visiting us," Colonel Whitehead said.

"Thank you, Colonel," Cody replied. "May I introduce my friends? This is Falcon MacCallister, and this is Prentiss Ingraham."

"Falcon MacCallister," Whitehead said. "You were at the fight at Little Big Horn, weren't you?"

"Yes," Falcon said. "I was actually looking for a couple of lost Gatling guns, but wound up with Reno during the fight."

"Ahh, there is someone here you should see," Whitehead said. He held up his finger, as if telling Falcon to wait for a moment, then he stepped to the door and spoke to his adjutant. "Mike, would you have the CO of the Ninth come to my office, please?"

"Yes, sir," the young lieutenant replied.

"We are sort of a forgotten post here," Colonel Whitehead said, continuing the conversation. "We don't get many guests, especially guests of your caliber. How long will you be here?"

"Just long enough to catch a boat down to Sheridan," Cody said.

"Good, that means you will be here for three days at least, for it will be that long until the next boat leaves. Have you a place to stay while you are here?"

"We thought we would get rooms in the hotel," Cody said.

"Ha. Lots of luck with that," Colonel Whitehead replied. "Chances are there won't even be one room available, since the boat passengers stay there until the boat leaves. And even if you could get a room, believe me, it is little better than sleeping in a stable. We can put you up here on the post."

"We don't want to intrude."

"You won't be intruding. We have enough vacant rooms in the bachelor officers' quarters to accommodate all three of you. You are welcome to them."

"Thank you, that is very decent of you."

"Oh! And tomorrow night, we will have a dance in your honor."

"Colonel, please don't go to any trouble on our part," Cody said.

"Trouble? Believe me, Colonel Cody, it's no trouble. It is an honor and a privilege. And I know the ladies have been wanting to hold another dance. This will be the perfect opportunity to do so. This is difficult duty here for all of us, isolated as we are, but it is particularly difficult for the ladies."

There was a knock on the door, and looking toward it, Falcon saw Fred Benteen.

"You sent for me, Colonel?"

"Yes, Major, you have an old friend here I thought you might like to see. Colonel Falcon MacCallister."

Benteen looked over at Falcon. "I thought your colonel's rank was temporary from the State of Colorado."

"It was, then," Falcon said. "Now I have another temporary rank, this time from the U.S. Army. I see you have been promoted to major."

"What are you doing here?"

"We're just passing through," Falcon said.

"But they are going to be here for a few days," Colonel Whitehead said. "I have asked them to stay in the BOQ. The ladies will be planning a dance for tomorrow night, and they will be our special guests."

"I'm sure the ladies will appreciate that," Benteen said. "Colonel, I must get back to my men. I'll see you tomorrow night."

The dance the next evening was held at the Suttler's Store. For twelve officers, there were six wives present, as well as Colonel Whitehead's daughter, who was eighteen. Of the thirty non-commissioned officers assigned to the base, there were thirteen wives present. In addition, there were two unmarried laundresses. That meant that, for the dance, there were forty-five men and twenty women. Every woman's dance card was full.

Falcon danced once with Mrs. Whitehead, once with Elaine, Colonel Whitehead's daughter, and once with the wife of one of the NCOs. Bill Cody and Prentiss Ingraham were much more active, dancing nearly every dance with the ladies who thought it a great thrill to dance with someone as famous as they both were.

For the most part, Falcon sat at a table with Colonel Whitehead, who graciously allowed his wife to dance with all the soldiers, officers and NCOs who did not have wives of their own.

"Did Sitting Bull shed any light on this Spirit Talking business?" Colonel Whitehead asked.

"Nothing that we didn't already know," Falcon said.

"Mean to His Horses is bad news. I suppose you heard about the Kennedy massacre?"

"Yes."

"Roman Nose, Crazy Horse, Tall Bull, none of them were as brutal to civilians as Mean to His Horses has been."

"There is a difference, though," Falcon said. "They

were all part of their established tribes, and it was during a time of war between the Indians and the white man. Mean to His Horses is a renegade, pure and simple."

"That's true," Colonel Whitehead said. "There is another big difference."

"What is that?"

"Roman Nose, Crazy Horse, Tall Bull are all dead. This son of a bitch is still alive."

Benteen was a late arrival at the dance and when he arrived, Whitehead excused himself.

"I need to dance with my own wife or I'm going to hear about it," he said.

"Mrs. Benteen isn't here?" Falcon asked.

"At the moment, she is in St. Louis," Benteen answered.

The two men sat in silence for a moment.

"Well?" Benteen said.

"Well?" Falcon replied, confused by the cryptic comment.

"Aren't you going to join the chorus?"

"What chorus would that be?"

"The chorus that says I betrayed Custer, that if I had brought my battalion up quickly enough, I could have joined him and the outcome would have been different. *'Benteen, big Sioux village come quick, bring packs. P.S. bring packs.'* Is there one person in America now who is not aware of that last message from Custer?"

"Major, you forget. I was with Reno that day," Falcon said. "If you had not come to Reno's aid, I might not be here today."

Benteen was silent for a long moment. Finally he gave a relieved sigh and shook his head.

"I thank you for that, Colonel," he said. "It is good

to hear something from someone who was there, and who knows all the details and nuances. Sometimes I think I am going to be like Judas Iscariot—damned for all eternity because I betrayed Custer.

"I didn't like the man, and I've made no excuses about that, but damn it, I did what I thought was best that day. Custer had the largest battalion, he had competent officers, I had no idea that he was in such dire circumstances. Reno was the most inexperienced officer in the entire regiment, and he had only half as many men with him as Custer had. Given the choice, I thought Reno and his men were in more danger than Custer."

"You made the choice of a battlefield commander," Falcon said. "There are very few men who have ever actually been in that position, which means there are very few who have the slightest idea of what it is like to make life-or-death decisions in the blink of an eye. And, as I told you, your decision to help Reno probably saved my life."

"Poor Marcus," Benteen said. "He has fallen on very hard times, you know. He was cashiered from the army for public drunkenness and lewd behavior, but I have heard from some of the officers who served with him that it was all a put-up deal."

"Where is he now?" Falcon asked.

"He is in Washington, D.C., working as a very low-level clerk. He tried to get a book published about his role in the battle, but it was rejected. I uh," Benteen cleared his throat. "I sent him some money a few months ago. I hated to embarrass him that way, but I knew that he was just barely hanging on."

"I'm sorry to hear that," Falcon said.

"Godfrey, Larned, Varnum, they have all abandoned him," Benteen said.

At that moment, the current dance having ended, Colonel Whitehead returned to the table, breathless and sweating. "I tell you," he said. "I don't know how the ladies are able to dance every dance as they do. One dance is enough to wear me out. Fred, you must put your name on some of the dance cards, I'm sure the ladies would be happy to dance with you."

"Thank you, Colonel, but I'll defer to the younger offices and NCOs. Besides, as none of my men are here, I feel a little out of place."

"Surely, Major, you aren't suggesting that the dance be open to the colored soldiers?" Colonel Whitehead said.

"No, Colonel, not at all," Reno replied. "I just made the comment that, as they cannot participate in the dance, I, as their commanding officer, feel that I should not be here as well."

"Well, I think that is foolish. But, it is certainly your right to make such a decision. Oh, dear me, the sergeant major's wife is headed straight for me with that look in her eyes. I guess I must dance with her."

Colonel Whitehead excused himself and joined the sergeant major's wife as the regimental band swung into the next tune.

"Did you hear about Tom Weir?" Reno asked.

"I know that he died," Falcon said.

"You remember that he wanted to go help Custer, but got no farther than the very next hill. By the time he got there it was too late. It's obvious now that Custer and all his men were already dead, and the Indians were coming hard toward Weir. He barely made it back in time."

"Yes, I remember that."

"Weir resigned his commission almost immediately after we got back to Fort Lincoln. I tried to talk him out of it, but he wouldn't listen. He went back to New York City. I got a letter from one of his friends there who said that he was afraid Tom was losing his mind. He wouldn't eat, he wouldn't leave his apartment. All he did was lay around and drink whiskey. Toward the end, he wouldn't even talk to anyone, nor would he get out of bed. His depression got deeper and deeper, and his drinking got worse and worse, until one day he lay down to take a nap, and he never woke up.

"All that in less than six months," Benteen said. "The young, aggressive, courageous officer who stormed the hill in his attempt to go to the rescue of his commander was, within six months of that date, a helpless, drunken, despondent invalid, dying in bed in a fifth-floor walk-up apartment in New York."

CHAPTER TEN

The next morning as Falcon was shaving in his room at the BOQ he heard a knock at his door. With the towel draped across his shoulder and half his face still lathered, he took the few steps to the door and pulled it open. A tall, muscular black soldier was standing there. The stripes on his arm indicated that he was a sergeant.

"Colonel MacCallister?"

"Yes, I'm MacCallister." Falcon still wasn't all that comfortable with referring to himself as Colonel Mac-Callister.

The black sergeant saluted. "I'm Sergeant Major Coletrain, sir," he said. His voice was deep and resonant. "Major Benteen has assigned me to you, Colonel Cody, and Colonel Ingraham for the day."

"What do you mean he has assigned you?"

"Aren't you three gentlemen catching the boat, goin' down river?" Coletrain asked.

"We are."

"I've got a team connected to the CO's carriage. I'll be driving the three of you to the steamboat dock."

"Thank you, Sergeant."

"No, sir, it's my privilege to thank you," Coletrain said.

"Thank me for what?"

Coletrain chuckled. "I reckon when someone like does a thing, you don't always know all the good that's goin' to come of it. But some time ago you killed an outlaw by the name of Luke Mueller. Down in Arizona, it was."

"I remember," Falcon said.

"I was in Arizona at the time, the Ninth was fightin' Apaches then. I was married to the prettiest young girl you ever did see. She was a laundress at the post.

"Well sir, one day when she was goin' into town, Luke Mueller raped her, and kilt her. When I found out who done it, I was plannin' on desertin' the army to find him and kill him. Only he run across you, and you kilt him instead.

"I wish it had been me that kilt him, but thinkin' back on it, dead is dead, and I never got myself in trouble with the army. So, Colonel MacCallister, as you can see, I do have somethin' to thank you for."

"I'm sorry to hear about your wife," Falcon said.

"Yes, sir, well, what is done is done," Coletrain said. "You can go on outside to the carriage if you want, I'll get the others."

Sergeant Major Coletrain drove the others down to the riverside where the *Queen of the West*, a very shallow-draft riverboat, was tied nose in to the bank. The riverbank was crowded with people who had just arrived, those who were departing, those who were seeing people off or welcoming them. There were also several others there, just for the excitement. The ticket agent was sitting at a table in front of the boat, checking the tickets of those who had already booked passage, and selling tickets to those who had not yet done so.

Falcon, Cody, and Ingraham were among the latter, so they stood in line for a moment until it was their time. Looking up at them, the ticket agent smiled.

"Has anyone ever told you that you look like Buffalo Bill Cody?" the ticket agent asked Cody.

"I get that a lot," Cody said.

"It must make you angry, being compared to that phony," the ticket agent said.

"Oh, sometimes it does," Cody said with a wry smile.

"All right, one ticket to Sheridan," the ticket agent said. "Your name, sir?"

"Cody. William F. Cody," Cody said.

"Cody, Will . . . ," the ticket agent looked up in surprise. "You—you mean you really are Buffalo Bill?"

"Guilty," Cody said.

"Oh, Mr. Cody, I'm so sorry," the ticket agent said. "I didn't mean anything by it, I was just shooting off my mouth. I, uh, I'm sorry."

"Think nothing of it, friend," Cody said.

Falcon was still chuckling as he stepped up to the table.

"Yes, sir," the nervous ticket agent said. "Your name?"

"McCallister. Falcon MacCallister."

"What? Are you *the* Falcon MacCallister?"

"I don't know," Falcon replied. "I may be, since I am the only Falcon MacCallister I know."

"I've read about you," the ticket agent said. "I—well, just a minute, let me show you."

The ticket agent reached down into a case that was on the ground by his table and pulled out a book. The title of the book was *Falcon MacCallister and the Mountain Marauders*.

"This is a real good book," he said.

"I'm glad you enjoyed it," Ingraham said. "Would you like me to autograph it for you?"

"Don't tell me you are . . ."

"Prentiss Ingraham," Ingraham said, answering the ticket agent before his question was completed. "And you have chosen well. This is one of my personal favorites."

The ticket agent shook his head. "My wife isn't going to believe this," he said.

Half an hour later, Falcon, Cody, and Ingraham were aboard when the captain stepped to the front rail of the wheelhouse.

"Draw in the gangplank," he shouted, and two deckhands responded by pulling in the ramp by which all had boarded.

"Cast off all lines!"

With that accomplished, the pilot called for full-reverse engine, and the stern paddle pulled the boat away from the bank to the middle of the narrow, shallow river; then it turned, nose downriver. The paddlewheel stopped, then started spinning in the opposite direction as the boat started its journey down the Tongue River.

An hour later, Falcon was standing at the stern, watching the paddlewheel spin through the water, leaving a frothing wake behind them. The river was not very wide and was quite shallow, so the boat was equipped with spars. They had not gone very far when the captain ordered the first use of the spars.

"Stand clear of the line, sir," a boatman said as he approached the spar on the starboard side of the boat, the side on which Falcon was standing. "When the line gets taut, if it breaks, it could hurt you bad."

"Thanks, I'll stay out of the way," Falcon replied.

"Stand by the spars!" the captain yelled through his megaphone from the Texas deck.

The boatman who had spoken to Falcon grabbed hold of the spar.

"Spars in the water!" the captain called through his megaphone.

The riverman stuck the end of the spar down into the water, then wrapped the line around a capstan. "Aye, Cap'n, spar in the water!" he called back.

The deckhand who was handling the spar on the other side of the boat repeated the call.

"Commence sparring!"

The boatman pulled a lever and the capstan, powered by steam, began putting pressure on the spar, while the same thing was being done to the spar on the port side.

Sparring lifted the bow of the *Queen of the West* as if it were on crutches, up and off the sandbar. With the bow raised, the paddlewheel got more purchase in the water and moved the boat forward. Because it was a particularly long sandbar, the action had to be repeated, in a procedure that Falcon knew was called grass-hoppering, or walking, the boat. The procedure had to be repeated several times until, finally, the boat was clear of the sand bar and the captain was able to proceed downriver at a rapid clip.

As the boat continued down the river, Falcon examined the banks sliding by. He saw a lot of deer coming down to the river to drink, amazingly unafraid of the huge fire bellowing, and the thundering monster that was moving down the river. He also saw elk, bighorn, and even a couple of bears coming down to get a drink.

Once he saw three Indians on horseback, high on

an overlook as they watched the riverboat pass by on its downriver transit. Shortly after they crossed from Montana territory into Wyoming territory, they saw a young white boy and girl standing on rock jutting out into the river. They were waving and Falcon waved back. Behind them stood a very small log cabin, and in a field alongside the cabin, a man Falcon presumed to be their father was plowing a field.

"Falcon," Cody called, and Falcon turned away from the railing to see what his friend wanted.

"We are getting a card game together in the salon. Come join us."

"I'll be glad to," Falcon replied.

The salon was the social center of the *Queen of the West.* Here the passengers could have a drink, take their meals, play cards, or simply engage in conversation. There were many more men on board than there were women, and the women passengers tended to gather in one corner to talk among themselves.

The game Falcon joined had six players: Falcon, Cody, Ingraham, and three others, all gold hunters. Reynolds, one of the card players, was a veteran of prospecting in the Big Horn Basin, and during the course of the game he was telling the others some of the places they could look for gold.

"Of course, I tell this, but with a warning," he said.

"A warning about what?" one of the gold hunters asked. "Bear? I know there are bear there. I plan to keep away from them."

"I ain't talkin' about bears," Reynolds said. "Though you'd be smart to keep a lookout for 'em. I'm talkin' about Injuns."

"Indians?" Cody said. "But the Crow live there. They are friendly."

"Yeah, I reckon they are supposed to be," Reynolds said. "But we've been havin' a little trouble with them. They've kilt a few prospectors, and here just recent, why they kilt a whole family, husband, wife, and their little child."

"Are you talking about the Kennedy family? That was Mean to His Horses, wasn't it?"

"No, sir, ain't talkin' about them. This was the Barlow family, and they lived right there along the Stinking Water River. And the closest Injuns to 'em is Crow."

"How do you know it was Indians who did it?" Falcon asked.

"How do I know? 'Cause they cut 'em up somethin' awful. And they scalped 'em too. Now I've heard of white men killing people for to rob them and such. But I ain't never heard of no white men scalping other whites. Most especial if it be a woman and a child."

"Has the army been called out?" one of the other card players asked.

"Nah," Reynolds said. "The people are takin' care of it their ownselves. Mr. Bellefontaine organized a posse, found some Injuns off the reservation, and kilt a couple of them. Then they left a note, lettin' the Injuns know the two was kilt 'cause they didn't stay where they belong. And it told 'em there'd be more killin' if the Injuns got off their reservation again."

"Bellefontaine did that?" Cody asked. "What right did he have to do something like that? Why didn't he take it to the army?"

"I don't know why he didn't take it to the army," Reynolds replied. "But seein' as he purt' nigh owns the entire town, I reckon that's about all the right he needs."

* * *

That evening, as the boat moved slowly, but majestically down the river, Falcon, Cody, and Ingraham stood out on the deck, enjoying the cool evening breeze, and looking at the wake of paddlewheel-churned water, breaking white and gleaming in the moonlight.

Cody lit his pipe, and for a moment the flare of his match cast a golden glow on the faces of the three men. He sucked on the pipe a few times until the tobacco caught, then he exhaled, the puff of smoke caught by the night air and drifting back over the churning paddlewheel where it was broken up.

"I don't mind telling you that I have been giving a lot of thought to what Reynolds was talking about at our poker game this afternoon," Cody said.

"Do you believe him?" Ingraham asked.

"I don't have any reason not to believe him," Cody replied.

"What do you know about this man, Bellefontaine?" Falcon asked.

"Well, I know that we are going to be competitors," Cody replied. "We'll be building Cody very close to where DeMaris Springs is, and when the railroad extends this far, why Cody and DeMaris Springs will just naturally be in competition for it."

"Is he the kind of man who would send out a posse on his own?" Falcon asked.

Cody paused for a moment before he answered. "Look, I don't want you to get me wrong here. I mean, I have already told you that Bellefontaine and I will both be competing for the railroad, so I don't want you to think that colors my assessment of the man. But to answer your question? Yes, he is exactly the kind of man who would send out a posse on his own, and not just for Indians. Reynolds was correct when he said that Bellefontaine owns the town. And he was also correct when he said that is all the right Bellefontaine thinks that he needs."

"I may need to meet this man," Falcon said.

"Oh, don't worry about that. You will meet him," Cody replied.

CHAPTER ELEVEN

Bismarck

As Ebersole had suspected, Billy Taylor had overheard the conversation that told him that Falcon Mac-Callister and Buffalo Bill were going to the Standing Rock Agency to talk to Sitting Bull.

"Talk to Sitting Bull? What the hell do they want to talk to that Redskin for?" Ebersole asked.

"I don't know," Taylor replied. "I never heard the why of it, just the doin' of it."

"Then we need to get there," Ebersole said.

"How we goin' to do that?" Dewey asked. "We didn't get no money at all from the train holdup."

"We was holdin' up the wrong thing," Ebersole said. "What we need to do is hold us up a bank."

"A bank? Are you serious?"

"Yeah, I'm serious," Ebersole said. "Banks have more money, and they don't move."

"Have you took a good look at the bank here?" Hawkins asked. "It's damn near like a fort."

"We ain't goin' to hold up the bank here," Ebersole said. "We're goin' to hold up the bank in Tyson."

"Tyson? Where the hell is that? I ain't never even heard of it."

"It's a little town 'bout thirty miles south of the railroad track."

Ebersole and the others rode into Tyson just after dark. The town consisted of a single street lined on both sides by squat, unpainted small houses. High above the little town stars winked brightly, while over a distant mesa the waxing moon hung like a large, silver wheel.

"What do you say we get a drink?" Ebersole suggested.

Tying off their horses, the five men went into the only building in town that was showing any light. There were two small windows and a door that was open onto the night. There was no sign suggesting that it was a saloon, but because of the light and the sound and the smell of whiskey and beer, they knew what it was.

There were only two tables in the saloon, and the bar. Four men were sitting at one of the tables, playing a game of cards. Nobody was at the other table, nor was anyone at the bar except for the bartender. Everyone looked up as the five men came in, because they more than doubled the number of customers in the place.

The barkeep slid down the bar toward them.

"What can I get you gents?"

"Whiskey," Ebersole said. "Leave the bottle."

"What kind?"

"The cheapest. We want to get drunk, not give a party."

The bartender took a bottle from beneath the counter. There was no label on the bottle and the color was dingy and cloudy. He put five glasses alongside the bottle, then pulled the cork for them.

"There it is," he said.

Ebersole poured himself a glass, then took a swallow. He immediately had a coughing fit, and almost gagged. He spit it out and frowned at his glass.

"Damn!" he said. "This tastes like horse piss."

"We just put in a little for flavor," the bartender said with a smile.

"What?" Ebersole shouted angrily.

"Take it easy, friend, I was just foolin' with you. You said you wanted the cheapest whiskey, and that's what you got. There ain't no horse piss in it. That's pure stuff. I don't even use a rusty nail for color and flavor."

Taylor took a smaller swallow. He grimaced, but he got it down. Dewey had no problem with it at all.

"How the hell can you drink that?" Ebersole asked.

"It's all in the way you drink it," Dewey explained. "This here whiskey can't be drunk down real fast. You got to sort of sip it."

Ebersole tried again, and this time he, too, managed to keep it down.

"You boys just passin' through?" the bartender asked.

"Ain't none of your business what we're doin'," Ebersole said. "Only thing you got to do is serve us whiskey when we ask."

"I was just tryin' to be friendly," the bartender replied.

Ebersole took in the other four men with him, with a gesture of his hand. "I got all the friends I need," he said.

"I see that you do," the bartender said, somewhat chagrined by the surly response.

After a few more drinks—they were limited by the amount of money they had—Ebersole and the others left the saloon. Without being too obvious, they checked out the bank, then rode on out of town to find a place to camp out for the night.

It was nearly noon of the next day when the five men rode back into town. Even though it was mid-day, the town was quiet, and festering under the sun. A few people were sitting or standing in the shade of the porch overhangs. A game of checkers was being played by two old men, and half a dozen onlookers were following the game intently. One or two looked up as Ebersole and the others rode by, their horses' hooves clumping hollowly on the hard-packed earth of the street.

A shopkeeper came through the front door of his shop and began sweeping vigorously with a straw broom. The broom raised a lot of dust and pushed a sleeping dog off the porch, but even before the man went back inside, the dog had reclaimed its position in the shade, curled comfortably around itself, and was asleep again.

Peters and Taylor stayed outside the bank, holding the reins of the horses, as Ebersole, Hawkins, and Dewey went inside. There were no customers in the bank; just one teller. He looked up at them with a smile as they came in, then, realizing that he didn't know any of them, instinctively knew that this wasn't going to be good.

"You know what we are here for, don't you, Mister?" Ebersole asked.

The bank teller nodded.

"Let's have all the money you've got."

"We don't have much," the teller said. "This is a very small town and a very small bank."

"How much do you have?"

"One thousand, seven hundred and twenty-six dollars," the teller said.

Ebersole smiled. "Well ain't that just fine, now, because that's just exactly how much money we wanted," he said.

As the bank teller was handing the money over to Ebersole, two men came into the bank.

"I told Joe, 'son, you've just learned a lesson. Never kick a horse apple on a hot day,'" one of them was saying.

The other man laughed, then both of them stopped, realizing what they had walked in on.

"What the hell is going on here?" the first man asked.

"I believe they're robbin' the bank," the second said.

"You ain't gettin' my money!" the first man said, going for his gun.

Dewey, Taylor, and Hawkins turned their pistols on the two men and began shooting. Both of the customers went down before they could even clear leather.

"You shot Mr. Simmons!" the bank teller shouted.

"And we're goin' to shoot you if you don't hurry up," Ebersole said with a growl.

With his hands shaking so that he could barely control them, the teller dropped the rest of the money into the sack Ebersole was holding.

"That's it," he said. "That's all the money we've got."

Peters was holding the horses for them out front when the robbers left the bank.

"What happened? What was the shootin'?"

"Don't worry about it, let's just get out of here," Ebersole said.

As they started down the street at a full gallop, the bank teller came out the front door.

"Bank holdup!" he shouted. He pointed at the galloping riders. "They kilt Mr. Abbott and Mr. Nash!"

A storekeeper ran out onto the front porch of his store and fired a shotgun at them, but missed. Ebersole returned fire and also missed, but his bullet crashed through a window and killed a young girl who was inside the store.

They made it out of town without any further incident, and because the town was too small for a marshal, there was no posse formed to pursue them. Also, because the town was not serviced by telegraph wires, they knew that they would be able to be well in the clear before any news of the robbery got out.

At Fort Yates they learned that Falcon MacCallister and Buffalo Bill Cody had gone on to Miles City, Montana Territory. Now, with enough money to buy train tickets, they put their horses on a special stock car, and went on to Miles City.

"And who did you say you was?" the sergeant at the gate of Fort Keogh asked when Ebersole and the four men with him showed up.

"The name is Brown," Ebersole lied. "Jim Brown. And we have a message for Falcon MacCallister. It's real important we get it to him."

"Mr. MacCallister and the party with him have already left," the gate sergeant said. "They took the *Queen of the West* south on the Tongue River. I expect they're near 'bout to Sheridan by now."

"Sheridan? Where is that?"

"That's a settlement in the north part of Wyoming.

Fact is, it is damn near the only settlement in north Wyoming."

"How do we get there?" Ebersole asked.

"Same way MacCallister got there, I reckon," the sergeant said. "You are goin' to have to take a boat."

"Yes, sir, we have two boats plying the river," the agent at the Montana and Wyoming Steamboat Navigation Company said. "They are fast, light-draft boats, especially built for operating on the Tongue River."

"You got 'ny idea when the next boat will go?"

"We got two boats makin' the run, takes two weeks to make the run so they're leavin' about a week apart. The *Queen of the West* is headin' south now, and I reckon tomorrow or the next day it will meet up with the *North Mist* that'll be comin' back."

"So when can we get on that *North Mist* goin' south?" Ebersole asked.

"I expect it'll be here around Monday, so it'll probably leave on Tuesday," the agent said.

"What about our horses? Can it take our horses?"

The agent shook his head. "Afraid not. It'll take your saddles and tack, but not the horses."

"What good will our saddles be without horses?" Ebersole asked.

"You can board your horses here for twenty-five cents a day. Or, you can sell 'em to the army back at the fort."

"The army will buy horses?"

"Oh, yes sir, as long as they are sound. The army always needs horses. They pay top dollar for them, too."

"I don't want to sell my horse," Dewey said.

"You got two choices, Dewey," Ebersole said. "You

can sell your horse and come with us, or you can keep your horse and stay here."

"We brought our horses here on the train," Dewey said. "How come we can't take 'em with us on the boat?"

"Because there are no facilities for horses on the boat," the ticket agent said.

"What will it be, Dewey?" Hawkins asked.

"I'll sell my horse," Dewey agreed.

Renegade camp of Mean to His Horses

"You are Crow," Mean to His Horses said, the expression in his voice showing his utter contempt for anyone of the Crow nation. "You were with Custer in the fight at Greasy Grass."

"We weren't with Custer. We were too young," Running Elk said.

"And now we want to join our brothers, the Cheyenne, to fight against the white man," White Bull said.

"Why do you turn now against your masters?" Mean to His Horses asked.

"They are not my masters," White Bull said emphatically.

"Nor are they mine," Running Elk said. "They have killed our people, for no reason."

"And now your blood runs hot and you want to kill them," Mean to His Horses responded. It wasn't a question, it was a statement.

"Yes," White Bull said.

"Why should I trust the Crow?"

"Have you not talked with the spirits?" Running Elk asked. "Have they not told you that we are all brothers? Have they not told you that the white man will be driven away, and the land that they took will be ours?"

Mean to His Horses stared at the two young Crow Indians before him for a long moment, then he nodded.

"You may stay," he said.

"Eiiiee yah, yah, yah!" White Bull shouted in excitement.

Although Mean to His Horses had accepted Running Elk and White Bull into his camp, when he went out on his first raid after their arrival, he ordered them to stay behind.

White Bull and Running Elk watched the raiding party ride off, angry that they had not been included.

"Why should we be left behind?" White Bull asked.

"Perhaps we must earn his trust," Running Elk said.

"Or perhaps we should prove ourselves to him."

"How can we prove ourselves if we are not allowed to go with him?"

"I will find a way. You will see."

CHAPTER TWELVE

Sheridan, Wyoming Territory

The Occidental Hotel was on North Main. A fine log structure, the hotel was built by Charles Buell. It advertised itself as the finest hostelry establishment between Chicago and San Francisco, and the boast was not without some justification. The lobby of the hotel was well appointed with overstuffed sofas and chairs, a dark blue carpet, and several brass spittoons. A chandelier and a few strategically placed lanterns provided some light, but not brightness.

There were several people in the lobby, but they were gathered in separate conversational groups speaking quietly, so that there was relative quiet. The desk clerk was sitting in a chair behind the sign-in desk, reading a copy of the *Sheridan Bulletin*. He was wearing a brown three-piece suit with a white shirt, detachable collar, and bow tie. Except for a small line of hair above each ear, he was bald. He looked up as Falcon, Cody, and Ingraham came into the hotel.

"Buffalo Bill Cody," the desk clerk said, setting his paper aside as the three men walked up to the desk.

"I heard that you had taken passage on the *Queen of the West.* How wonderful to see you again."

"Hello, Paul," Cody said. "May I introduce my two friends? This is Falcon MacCallister."

"Yes, indeed, I have heard much about you, sir. And all of it flattering," Paul said.

"And this gentleman is a writer who we can't seem to get rid of. His name is Prentiss Ingraham."

"Prentiss Ingraham? *The* Prentiss Ingraham?"

"You have heard of me?"

"Indeed I have, sir. And I have read every one of your books. In fact, I have one here that I would ask you to autograph for me, if you would be so kind."

"Why, I would be delighted to autograph your book for you," Ingraham said, beaming in delight over the unexpected recognition.

The clerk reached under the check-in counter and pulled out a copy of *Buffalo Bill's Spy Trailer—The Stranger in Camp* and handed it to Ingraham.

"Oh, you've chosen well," Ingraham said as he autographed the book. "This is one of my personal favorites."

That was the same thing he had said to the boat ticket agent about *Falcon MacCallister and the Mountain Marauders,* and as Ingraham signed the book with a great flourish, Falcon and Cody looked at each other and chuckled.

"Mr. Cody, I saw in the newspaper that you are going to be holding auditions for your show. Up in Cinnabar, I believe?"

"Indeed I am," Cody replied. "How about it, Paul? Do you want to try out for the show?"

Paul laughed. "Not unless you have a place in your show for hotel clerks," he said. He turned toward a board filled with keys hanging from hooks, took three of them down and handed one to each of them. "These rooms are on the second floor near the front," he said. "All three are together, two of them are adjoining rooms, and the third one is immediately across the hall."

"Thanks," Falcon and Cody said. Ingraham finished signing the book and then handed back to the clerk.

"Thank you, sir," the clerk said with a broad smile. "I will treasure this."

Like the lobby, the hotel room was nicely furnished. More spacious than most hotel rooms, this one had a bed, a settee, a chest of drawers, a chifforobe, and a dry sink. A porcelain pitcher and bowl sat on the dry sink.

After settling their luggage into the room, Falcon, Cody, and Ingraham decided to take a turn around the town to see what it was like.

"The reason I wanted to look over the town is because I expect that Cody will be much like this one," Cody said. "After all, Mr. Beck founded and built this town, and he is the principal architect for Cody, which is to be built some fifty miles west of here."

The town was well laid out, not only with a very fine hotel, but with many other conveniences a town would need: a mercantile, a leather goods store, a feed and seed store, a hardware store, a butcher shop, a livery, a gun shop, and, of course, a saloon. In this case the saloon was called the North Star Saloon, and it was a rather substantial building. Unlike many of the others, it was painted a gleaming white.

Buffalo Bill Cody had been to the town of Sheridan many times over the last few years, and he knew several of the people who were, at the moment, patronizing the saloon. They all greeted him effusively, and Cody returned the greetings with equal enthusiasm, introducing Falcon and Ingraham to them. Nearly all had heard of Falcon and Prentiss Ingraham, much to the delight of Ingraham, who enjoyed sharing stories of both his books and adventures.

As Falcon and the others listened with interest to Ingraham's tall tales, the sound of a slap could be heard all through the saloon.

"Ouch! Don't do that!" a woman called out, the pain and fear evident in the tone of her voice.

"Don't tell me what to do, whore!" a man's gruff voice replied. "I done bought you four drinks and you say you I can't lie in your bed?"

"I'm a bar girl, I'm not a prostitute," the woman replied.

"She's right, Slayton," the bar tender said. "Lucy is not a soiled dove. None of the girls here are. If you want that kind of woman, you need to go down the street to the cribs."

"Don't tell me where to go, and don't tell me she ain't no whore," Slayton said. He drew his hand back and turned toward Lucy. "You're goin' to lie with me, or I'm going to beat you to a pulp," he said with a menacing growl.

"Mister, back away from the lady," Falcon ordered, loudly.

"Say what?" Slayton replied. Slayton was nearly as big a man as Falcon. He didn't have a beard, but neither was he clean-shaven. He had what looked like a five-day stubble. The most noticeable thing about him was his teeth. Irregular and yellow, one front tooth was broken and the one next to it was missing.

"I said back away from the lady. Now," Falcon said.

Slayton turned toward Falcon and pointed at him. "Mister, you are buttin' in where you got no call. Now my advice to you is to sit down and mind your own business."

"Mister, you might want to rethink," Falcon said.

"Really? And what is it I need to rethink?"

"Your entire attitude."

Don't you be worryin' none about my attitude," Slayton said. "If there is anyone in here that's needin' to rethink, it's you for buttin' in where you got no business. You bein' a stranger in town, you may not know that I ain't the kind of man you want to mess with." He had been pointing at Falcon, but now he started to drop his arm.

"Huh, uh. Don't drop your arm, don't make a move," Falcon said.

"What?"

"You heard me," Falcon said. "Don't make a move. If you so much as twitch, I'll kill you."

"Mister, you don't even have a gun in your hand. Do you think you can run a bluff on me? Nobody runs a bluff on me."

"Friend," Buffalo Bill said. "I've known Falcon Mac-Callister for some time now, and I don't believe I have ever seen him run a bluff."

"I don't believe that is Falcon MacCallister," Slayton said. He started to drop his arm, but no sooner did he twitch than he found himself staring at the black hole of the business end of Falcon's pistol.

"I told you not to move," Falcon said.

"No! Wait!" Slayton shouted. He put both arms up. "Don't shoot, Mister, don't shoot!"

For the moment the loudest sound to be heard was the steady tick-tock of the regulator clock which hung just above the fireplace mantle. The other customers in the saloon were viewing the unfolding scene as intently as anyone who had ever watched a Buffalo Bill Wild West Exhibition. And in a way, they were spectators of a show, but in this case the scene being played out before them was much more intense than anything Buffalo Bill had ever produced. This was a drama of life or death.

Unable to control the sudden twitch that started in his left eye, Slayton looked around the saloon to see if he could count on anyone for help.

"Are you people going to just let him get away with this?" Slayton called out. "He's a stranger! I'm one of you!"

"You ain't never been one of us, Slayton," a cowboy over at the bar said. The cowboy was standing with his back against the bar, leaning back with his elbows resting on the bar. "You ain't done nothin' but run roughshod over the rest of us ever since you got here. As far as I'm concerned, he can shoot you right now and I'd say good riddance."

Slayton looked back at Falcon, realizing now that not only was he on his own, but he had come up against someone who was far his superior.

"Please, Mister," Slayton said with a whimper. "What are you going to do?"

"Yes, Falcon, what are you going to do?" Cody asked.

"What do you think, Buffalo Bill? Do you think

I should just shoot him and be done with it?" Falcon asked.

"My God," Slayton said, his bottom lip quivering now. "Falcon MacCallister and Buffalo Bill?"

"I'll tell you what," Ingraham said. "Falcon, suppose you put your pistol back in your holster. I'll count to three, then both of you can draw. A duel to the death like that would make much better story than if I wrote that you merely shot him. You would like that better, wouldn't you, Slayton? I mean if Falcon MacCallister put his gun away and actually gave you a chance to draw against him? It wouldn't be much of a chance, I admit—but it would be a chance. Better than him just shooting you, here and now."

"Yes," Slayton said.

Falcon put his pistol back in his holster.

"I mean no!" Slayton shouted, quickly, holding both his arms out in front of him, palms facing outward. "I mean no I don't want to draw against you at all. I ain't goin' for my gun! Do you see? I ain't goin' for my gun!"

The young woman was tending to her bleeding lip, and she looked up at Slayton. One of her eyes was black and nearly swollen shut. "If it was left up to me, I would tell you to shoot him," she said.

"No," Slayton said. He began shaking uncontrollably, and he wet his pants. "Please, don't kill me," he begged. "I swear, I'll never touch the girl again. Please, don't kill me."

Lucy turned to the others in the saloon. "Did you all hear the promise Mr. Slayton just made?"

"We heard it, Miss Lucy," one of the other patrons asked.

"Will you see to it that he keeps his promise?"

"Oh, he'll keep his promise, all right," the cowboy who was leaning back against the bar said. "'Cause if he don't keep it, me an' some of the boys will find him, and we'll string him up ourselves."

"Go home, Mr. Slayton," Lucy finally said in a cold voice. "And don't come back here until you know how to behave around a lady."

"Behave around a lady?" Slayton said in a contemptuous tone. "What do you mean around a lady?"

The next sound was the deadly double-click of a pistol sear engaging the hammer and rotating a shell under the firing pin. Once again, Falcon was holding his pistol pointed at Slayton.

"Are you going to try and say that you don't see any ladies around here?" Falcon asked.

"What? No, no, I see a lady," Slayton stammered. He looked around at the other bar girls. "I see a lot of ladies around here!" Still holding his hands out in front of him, as if warding Falcon off, he turned to leave.

"Wait a minute," Falcon called.

Slayton stopped.

"Before you leave, shuck out of that gun belt. The pistol stays here," Falcon said.

"Who the hell says that it stays here?" Slayton asked, in one last attempt at bravado.

"I say it," Falcon replied as calmly as if he were giving the time.

Slayton paused for a moment longer, then, with shaking hands, unbuckled his gun belt. He let it drop to the floor.

"Now you can go," Falcon said.

"When do I get it back?" Slayton asked.

"Whenever the lady says you can have it back," Falcon said.

"Are you crazy? I ain't leavin' my gun with no whore!"

"I will give it back to you, Mr. Slayton, when you have learned to behave as a gentleman," Lucy said.

As soon as Slayton stepped outside, there was a collective sigh of relief, then everyone started talking at the same time.

"Did you see that?"

"I ain't never seen nothin' like it in my whole life."

"Never thought I would see anyone back down Ethan Slayton," one of the patrons said.

"Well, it wasn't just anyone," another said. "It was Falcon MacCallister.

Falcon reached down to pick up the gun and belt that Slayton had shed. Carrying it over to the bar, he handed it to the bartender.

"It might be a good idea to empty the bullets before you hand the pistol back to him," Falcon suggested. "Someone with a temper like he has is liable to start shooting the moment he gets his hands back on it."

"Don't you worry none about that, Mr. MacCallister," the bartender said. "I'll have this gun empty before you can say Jack Sprat."

"Johnny," Lucy said.

"Yes, Miss Lucy?"

"Would you please pour these three gentleman a drink, on me?" she asked, referring to Falcon, Cody, and Ingraham.

"Yes, ma'am, I'd be glad to," Johnny said, reaching for the house's finest bourbon. "But you are only goin' to pay for half of it. I'm payin' the other half my ownself."

* * *

Preston Ingraham's notes from his book in progress:

After assuring the gallant General Nelson Miles that he did not believe the great Sioux Chief, Sitting Bull, was behind or planning any nefarious activity, Buffalo Bill Cody, Falcon MacCallister, and your humble scribe left the Standing Rock Indian Reservation to continue their sojourn through the West, proceeding from the above location by way of train to Miles City. There, the two Western heroes were feted by the commandant of the nearby army post, Fort Keogh, named for the gallant officer who died with Custer. Colonel Whitehead, the fort's commandant, allowed the ladies of the post to produce a military ball in their honor. Although the ball was held in the bare hall of a Suttler's Store, the ladies of the fort succeeded with their clever and colorful decorations to convert the stark building into as inviting a ball room as in the finest Eastern salons. And, as I am travelling with Cody and MacCallister, I was also privileged to attend the ball, and enjoyed dancing with the lovely ladies of the post.

Leaving Miles City, we traveled by riverboat on the Tongue River, with Sheridan as the destination.

Shortly after arriving in Sheridan, a small town in Wyoming Territory, a brutish fellow imagined himself offended by a young woman of the bar, and he struck her several times. Falcon MacCallister, upon seeing the altercation, interceded.

"Here, sir, do not strike that woman again."

His words rang with authority, and not one

*person in the room was there, who did not realize
that a challenge was being issued.*

*The brigand, a most disreputable fellow of the
lowest type, was a known bully by the name of Ethan
Slayton, a person whose disrepute was known by all.*

*"Mister, what I do to this woman ain't none of
your business," Slayton replied in a voice dripping
with arrogance and venom.*

*"You err, sir, for I have made it my business," the
valiant Falcon MacCallister said. "For one who
attacks a defenseless woman, attacks all that is good
and noble."*

*Pointing his finger at Falcon, Slayton issued a
challenge that would have made the blood run cold
in most men. "Mister, you have butted in where you
have no business. My advice to you is to back away
or be prepared to face the ire of Ethan Slayton."*

*It is to be supposed that brute was of the opinion
that mere mention of the name Ethan Slayton would
be sufficient to make most men withdraw meekly. But
Mr. Slayton made a serious miscalculation, for
Falcon MacCallister is not a man who is easily
frightened. His reply, intoned in a voice that was
dripping with danger, brought instant silence to all
in the saloon.*

*"Friend, if you so much as twitch, I will kill you,"
Falcon MacCallister said, his words cold and piercing.*

*"I will not be buffaloed, by you or any man,"
Slayton said, and to prove his point, moved his hand
in the direction of his pistol, but ere his hand reached
his holster, a Colt .44, as if by magic, appeared in the
hand of Falcon MacCallister. Slayton gasped in
surprise and fear.*

"You should feel no shame sir, for having been

bested by this man," Buffalo Bill Cody said from aside. "For this is Falcon MacCallister, and his gunmanship is superior to all in the West. Were you to test him any further, he would have put a ball in your heart."

Realizing that he was beaten, the disagreeable Slayton made no further attempt to extract his weapon from his holster. Begging for his life, he was allowed to leave the saloon, but only after offering his apology to the young woman whom he had assaulted, and surrendering his pistol.

CHAPTER THIRTEEN

Fort Keogh

For the most part there was harmony between the white troopers of the Sixth Cavalry and the black troopers of the Ninth Cavalry primarily because there was in effect a self-imposed segregation. The black troops stayed with their own, as did the white troops.

There were some points of interaction though, and at one of these points, the post quartermaster, there was discord between Sergeant Major Moses Coletrain of the Ninth Cavalry and Sergeant Lucas Depro of the Sixth Cavalry. Both were supply sergeants for their respective units, and though their ranks were equal, Sergeant Depro assumed more power than he actually had, using as his authority the fact that he was white.

The two men shared the same office in the supply room, each having a desk. Depro was already at his desk when Sergeant Major Coletrain came in.

"My, you are here early today, Sergeant," Coletrain said.

Depro, who was making entries in a ledger, nodded. "I had some extra work to do, so I came in early. I know that isn't anything you people would ever consider. From what I've observed, you people never do one thing beyond what is absolutely necessary. You are the worst soldiers I've ever seen."

Sergeant Major Coletrain did not respond to Depro's baiting. He knew that, even though there were more black troopers in the fort than white, the white soldiers had ten times more delinquency reports, and twenty times more incidents of absent without leave and desertion.

"I see they haven't shipped in the blankets yet," Coletrain said as he picked up a paper from his desk. "I hope they get them here before winter."

"They probably shipped them all to Arizona where they don't need them," Depro said.

In this, at least, the two sergeants were united, for the blanket shipment would benefit every soldier on the entire post whether black or white. Coletrain chuckled at Depro's comment as he walked back to the arms room.

Depro looked up from his desk at Coletrain as he opened the arms room. Putting his pen down, he waited for the expected reaction.

"Hey!" Coletrain said. "What happened?"

"What happened to what?"

"The weapons," Depro said. "The carbines, rifles, and pistols we were shipping to Jefferson Barracks. I had them right here, all boxed up, ready to go."

"I took care of that for you," Depro said.

Coletrain came back from the arms room, and standing right across Depro's desk, challenged him.

"What do you mean you took care of it, Sergeant Depro? Those arms belonged to the Ninth Cavalry. I was in charge of shipping them back."

"They belong to the army, not to the Ninth Cavalry," Depro said. "And we're in the same army. At least, that's what you're always tellin' me, ain't it? That we belong to the same army?"

"Yes, but that don't give you the right to interfere with my work. Shipping those weapons out was my job. I'm responsible for them, now they're gone, and I don't have any documentation for them."

"Relax," Depro said. "I knew you wouldn't be able to handle it, so I handled it for you. I had them sent by freight wagon to the railhead at Rawlins. I've got a hand receipt from the shipping officer of the wagon freight, and a Bill of Lading from Union Pacific that says they are on their way to Jefferson Barracks."

"Where are they?"

"I told you, they are on their way to Jefferson Barracks."

"No, I mean where are the documents you were talking about, the hand receipt and the bill of lading? Where are they? If I'm responsible for the arms shipment, I need some proof that the job was done."

"Are you questioning me?" Depro said angrily.

"Yes, I'm questioning you. I told you, I'm responsible for them. And I remain responsible for them, no matter who arranged to have them shipped. That's why I want the hand receipt and the bill of lading."

"You might have been responsible for it, but I'm the one who done the actual shipping," Depro said. "So if anything comes up, I'll be the one in trouble, not you. That's why I intend to keep the paperwork my ownself."

Coletrain stared at Depro for a moment longer. He knew that by rights he should have the paperwork, since the weapons had been on the property books of the Ninth Cavalry. But he knew, too, that if the question went to Major Benteen, Benteen, for all that he was commander of the Ninth, would back up the white NCO over Coletrain.

"All right, Sergeant, as long as we have proof that the weapons were shipped, I guess it doesn't really matter who has it."

At lunchtime Coletrain left the supply room and headed for the mess hall that served the Ninth. It was as big and as well kept as the white mess hall and the food, consisting mostly of salt beef or pork and vegetables raised by the soldiers, served along with coffee and cornbread, was about the same as the food served the white soldiers. The mess halls were across the quadrangle from each other, the sign on one reading: Colored, the sign on the other reading: White.

He saw Major Benteen going into the officers' mess. Many of the officers had their wives on post with them, but Benteen's wife and son were back in St. Louis. Because he had been with Custer and the Seventh Cavalry in their ill-fated fight with the Sioux, Benteen had been somewhat of a celebrity when he first arrived. Coletrain started toward him.

"Major Benteen?" he called.

Benteen stopped and turned toward him, the expression on his face showing his displeasure at being addressed.

"What is it, Coletrain? What do you want?" Benteen asked.

"It's about the weapons, Major. The ones we are supposed to be sending back to Jefferson Barracks?"

"What about them?"

"They are gone, sir. Sergeant Depro says that he sent them."

"Well, then, it isn't your worry, is it?"

"No, sir," Coletrain said. "I suppose not, sir. I just thought I ought to tell you."

"You told me. Anything else?" Benteen asked.

"No, sir, nothing else," Coletrain said, snapping a sharp salute.

Later that same day, Sergeant Lucas Depro stepped up to Captain Gilmore's desk and saluted. "You wanted to see me, Cap'n?"

"Yes, Sergeant. I'm told by Major Benteen that you took charge of an arms shipment that, by rights, was the responsibility of the Ninth Cavalry."

"Yes, sir."

"Why did you do that?"

"Cap'n, you know how them coloreds are. You can't depend on 'em for nothin'. I figured I was doin' the right thing by shippin' 'em like I done."

"How many were there?"

"Forty Winchesters, fifty-five Springfields and thirty-five Colt revolvers it was, all shipped back to Jefferson Barracks, Missouri."

Captain Gilmore whistled. "That's a lot of weapons. Did they get away all right?"

"Yes, sir, I got the bill of lading on file back in the arms room."

"I don't know as I like you taking on that responsibility. You work for me, and, as Major Benteen pointed out, that now makes me liable for them in case something happens to them."

"Ain't nothin' goin' to happen to 'em, Cap'n. Like as not, they are at Jefferson Barracks by now."

"Whatever you do, Sergeant Depro, you make certain that you keep up with that bill of lading. We certainly don't want to wind up having to pay for it ourselves, do we, Sergeant?"

"No, sir, we sure don't. But don't worry, Cap'n, I'll keep up with the bill of lading," Depro said.

After leaving Captain Gilmore's office, Sergeant Depro walked across the parade ground to an abandoned stable at the far end of the post property. The stable had been built ten years earlier as a place to hold captured Indian horses until they could be shipped off to factories in the East to be made into glue. That policy was dropped three years ago and the stable had been abandoned. Now, it was literally falling down.

Nobody ever came around it any more, not only because it was so far away from the main area of the fort, but also because of the stench. Unlike the stables of cavalry horses, which were kept clean by constant mucking of the stalls, these stalls had never been mucked, even when the stable had been in use.

After looking around to make certain that he wasn't being observed, Depro stepped into the building, taking shallow breaths in order not to be overcome by the odor. Going to the stall that was most distant from the opening, he brushed away some of the hay, then pulled back a tarpaulin. There were eight boxes beneath the tarpaulin. Lettering on two of the boxes identified the contents as: *Carbines, repeating, Cal .30-.30 Sixth U.S. Cavalry.* Three boxes read: *Rifles, breach-loading, Cal .51. Sixth U.S. Cavalry.* Lettering on the remaining three boxes read: *Pistols, revolver, Cal .45 Sixth U.S. Cavalry.*

"Yes, sir, Cap'n Gilmore," Depro said with a little chuckle under his breath. "I'll keep up with the bill of lading for you."

Leaving the stable, Depro saw two soldiers of the Sixth behind the building. At first he was frightened that they might have looked inside and seen the weapons. Then he saw that they had a bottle of whiskey, and were hiding behind the building because they were drinking on duty.

"All right you two!" he shouted angrily. "I've caught you! Drinking on duty ought to get you both a week in the stockade!"

He marched the two sullen soldiers to the provost marshal, where he said that he had seen the men sneak away and followed, only to find them drinking. Ordinarily, he would have done nothing about it, but this would give him a reason for being around the abandoned stable, just in case someone happened to see him over there.

Advertisement in the *Sheridan Bulletin*:

SHERIDAN AND YELLOWSTONE

STAGE AND FAST FREIGHT COMPANY

*The Sheridan and Yellowstone Stage Line leaves
Sheridan for DeMaris Springs every other day,
making the trip in two days, carrying U.S. Mails and
Wells, Fargo & Co's Express.
Passengers will spend the night in comfort at
Greybull Camp, on the Greybull River. Fare is $34.
Obtain tickets at the depot of the
Sheridan and Yellowstone Stage Line.*

*Full particulars will be given at the Sheridan Office
and all other offices on the line.*

                                        C.F. Cline, Agent

Falcon, Cody, and Ingraham stood outside the
Sheridan and Yellowstone Stage and Fast Freight Company as the coach was brought around. Six well-
matched fresh horses stood in harness, as if anxious to
get underway. The driver of the coach set the brake
and remained on the seat, reins in hand as the shotgun
guard used the step and front wheel to climb down.

"Folks, if you'll bring your luggage around to the
boot I'll put it away for you, all nice and tidy."

In addition to Falcon, Cody, and Ingraham, there
was an attractive young woman with two small children
who would be taking the trip as well. Smiling at her,
Falcon took her luggage and handed it to the shotgun
guard who put it in the back of the boot.

"There you go, ma'am," the shotgun guard said.
"Your bag is all safe and steady."

"Thank you," the woman said.

Buffalo Bill Cody held the door open to the coach,
then helped the lady aboard. Once she was aboard, he
picked up the children one at a time and handed them
up to her.

It took only a few moments more before all were
aboard.

"You folks all ready down there?" the driver called.

"We're ready, driver. Take it away," Cody called up
to him.

The driver swung his whip, making a loud crack
over the head of the team, and they lurched forward.
The coach left the town of Sheridan at a rapid trot, and
held the trot until they were almost a mile out of town,

at which time he slowed the team down to a brisk walk of about eight miles per hour.

The passengers introduced themselves. The woman was Mrs. Juanita Kirby; her two children were Gary, who was six, and Abby, who was four.

"Wait until you see where we are going to build my town," Cody said. "It is the most beautiful area you have ever seen. It is very near Yellowstone Park."

"I've been to Yellowstone," Falcon said. "That is certainly a beautiful area."

"Beautiful yes, but strange too," Cody said. "It is filled with boiling lakes and steam gushing from the ground, sometimes erupting into huge geysers that stream hundreds of feet into the air. And there is land that you cannot walk on without fear of falling through it into the very bowels of the earth. No, the land where my town will be built is nothing like that."

"How close will it be to the place where we are going?" Ingraham asked. "What is the town called? DeMaris Springs?"

"Yes, DeMaris Springs. Cody will be very close to where DeMaris Springs is now, and there is no doubt in my mind but that Cody will so overtake DeMaris Springs in development and desirability, that DeMaris Springs will cease to exist."

"Oh, I'm afraid Mr. Bellefontaine may have something to say about that," Mrs. Kirby said.

"I'm sure he will," Cody said.

"Do you know Mr. Bellefontaine?" Falcon asked.

"Yes, my husband is a mining engineer and he works for Mr. Bellefontaine." She paused for a moment. "For now."

"For now?" Cody asked.

"Yes. My husband has been offered employment in

the lead mines back in Missouri. And with the recent Indian incidents, he has decided to accept the offer. And, though I shouldn't be telling tales out of school, Mr. Bellefontaine is not the most—pleasant of men."

"Mama, you don't go to school," Gary said.

"What?"

"You said you shouldn't be telling tales out of school. But you don't go to school."

Mrs. Kirby smiled at her son. "No, I don't, do I? How foolish of me."

Ten Sleep way station

The way station at Ten Sleep was in the shape of the letter T, with the cross of the T running east and west. The dining room was in the front, the west wing was a bunk room for the men passengers, and the east wing was a bunk room for female passengers. The driver, whose name was Bo, and the shotgun guard, named Hank, had quarters in the barn, but they ate at the table with the others. Hodge Deckert and his wife Ethel ran the way station. Hodge took care of the livestock and Ethel did the cooking. They lived in a room at the bottom of the "T."

"Mrs. Deckert," Cody said, rubbing his stomach as he pushed away from the table. "That's about the best thing I've tasted in a month of Sundays."

"Oh, but you haven't had your pie yet," Ethel said. "I made a couple of apple pies."

"Pie? Well, I can't imagine anyone wanting apple pie after a meal like this. You can just save the pie for the next stage to come through, I'm sure no one here wants any."

"I do," Gary said.

"You? You want some apple pie?" Cody teased.

"Yes, sir. I like apple pie."

"Oh, so because it is apple pie you want it. If it was cherry pie, or blueberry pie, you probably would not want any, would you?"

"No, I like cherry pie and blueberry pie too," Gary said.

"All right, Mrs. Deckert, I guess I'll have to have some pie too. I sure wouldn't want Gary to eat all of it by himself."

"Oh, I don't think I could eat all of it," Gary said, and the others laughed.

After the meal, Mrs. Kirby and her two children went into the room that was reserved for them and the stage crew went out to the barn, while Falcon, Cody, Ingraham, and Hodge Deckert sat out on the front porch, watching the play of light as the sun set behind the distant Absaroka Mountain range.

Cody, Ingraham, and Deckert smoked their pipes, Falcon rolled his own cigarette.

"Mr. Deckert, what have you heard about any Indian trouble?" Cody asked.

Deckert took a long puff of his pipe before he answered, as if thinking about the question.

"Well now, it's just real strange," he said. "The only Injuns we've got close to us are the Crow, and it's been more 'n twenty years since we had any trouble with them. High Hawk is the chief of the local tribe, and he has always been friendly to the whites. But over the last couple of months, there's been some incidents. A couple of prospectors was found scalped, then, I understand there was some Injun hunters kilt, then a white family was kilt, the husband, wife, and their boy. Scalped they was, all three of 'em. And that seemed to set off the whole town."

"Has the army been called in?" Falcon asked.

"Don't know as they have. What I think happened was Bellefontaine, you'll prob'ly meet him when you go into DeMaris Springs, or if you don't meet him, you will sure hear about him. He seems to be the cock-of-the-walk there. Anyway, what I was sayin' is, Belle-fontaine put together a posse, I think, and they kilt a couple of Injuns, and left a note on one of 'em. I don't know as anything has happened since then."

"What about Mean to His Horses?" Cody asked. "Have you heard of him?"

"Oh, yes, I've heard of him. And from what I've heard of that red devil, it ain't only his horses he's mean to."

Suddenly the loud cry of a child interrupted their conversation, and then they heard Mrs. Kirby call out.

"Gary!"

The crying continued and, curious, the four men went back inside, just as a distraught Mrs. Kirby came from their room.

"Oh," she said. "Gary was jumping on the bed and he fell. I'm not sure, but I think he may have broken his arm."

"Ingraham, you're a doctor," Cody said. "Why don't you take a look?"

"I was in medical school, but I didn't finish," Ingra-ham said. "But I will take a look.

All went into Mrs. Kirby's room, where they saw young Gary sitting on the floor, crying and holding his arm. It was immediately obvious that a bone was broken, because of the protrusion just above the wrist of his left arm.

"Let me take a look at it, Gary," Ingraham said. He sat down on the floor beside Gary and looked at the arm, then nodded. "It's broken."

"Can you do anything about it?" Falcon asked.

"I think so. I can put it back and splint it. You wouldn't have any laudanum, would you, Mr. Deckert?"

"No, I wouldn't have anything like that," Deckert said.

"All right, we'll just have to do it without it. I need a couple of flat boards about this long," he said, holding his hands apart equal to the length of Gary's forearm. "And enough strips of cloth to bind them."

"I can get the boards easy," Deckert said. "I repaired a door on a coach last week, I've got some of that wood left over."

"How thick is it?"

"Oh, it isn't thick at all, not more'n an eighth of an inch."

"That will be perfect."

"I have some cloth," Ethel Deckert said. "I got it to make some new curtains, but this would be a better use for it."

Within a few moments, Ingraham had everything he needed, and he lay it down beside Gary. No longer crying out loud, Gary was still sniffing as he tried to hold it back.

Ingraham took his arm. "Now, son, I'm going to set the bone back in place. But, when I set the bone it's going to hurt you again."

"How bad will it hurt?" Gary asked.

"I won't lie to you. It's going to hurt pretty bad, but it won't hurt as bad as it did when you first broke it."

"Do you have to set it?" Gary asked.

"Yes, I have to do that so that your arm will grow back just as good as it was. If I don't set it, you could wind up not ever able to use that arm again."

"All right," Gary said.

"Cody, have the splints ready," Ingraham said. "Mrs. Deckert, when I get the splints in place, you start wrapping the cloth around it."

Cody nodded and picked up the splints, then held them apart so Ingraham could get to them easily.

"Are you ready, Gary?"

"Yes, sir," Gary answered in a frightened voice.

Ingraham moved the arm and pressed the bone down until he knew it had reconnected. Gary winced, and cried out, but he did not cry again.

Quickly, Ingraham put on the splint, then held it in place as Mrs. Deckert began the wrap. Within a moment the splint and bandage were in place.

"Son, I saw soldiers in the war who weren't as brave as you were when they were doing that," Falcon said.

"Really?" Gary replied, forcing a smile now through his pain and tears.

"Really. You are one brave young man," Falcon said.

Gary looked up at his mother. "Did you hear what he said, Mama?"

"I heard. And you are a brave little boy," Mrs. Kirby said.

"No, Mama, I'm a brave young man," Gary said. "He called me a young man."

Mrs. Kirby kissed her son on the forehead. "And you are a young man," she said. "A brave young man."

"You are the bravest person I know," Abby said. "I won't ever be afraid anymore if I am with you."

Mrs. Deckert had a hearty breakfast ready for them the next morning, biscuits, country ham, gravy, fried potatoes, and eggs. The pain had subsided in Gary's arm, and he now showed it proudly to Bo and Hank.

"Mr. MacCallister said I was as brave as a soldier," Gary said.

"I don't doubt it," Bo said. "And I reckon you'll be showin' that broke arm to all your little friends when you get back home too, won't you?"

"I want him to show it to my friends as well," Abby said.

Bo finished his coffee, then stood up. "Folks, we'll have the coach around front in about fifteen minutes. So if you got 'ny last minute things to do, you'd best be gettin' 'em done."

Chapter Fourteen

.

Mean to His Horses and ten warriors had wandered far south from the Cheyenne reservation, and were waiting at a ford on the Big Horn river. They had no particular target in mind, though they knew that any wagon or coach that traveled the road between Sheridan and Yellowstone Park would have to cross the river here, and when they did so, they would be vulnerable to attack.

They heard the coach before they saw it, the sound of a popping whip, the whistles and calls of the driver, and the drumming hooves of six trotting horses.

"Make yourselves ready," Mean to His Horses said.

Only Mean to His Horses and one other of his band had firearms. The rest of the warriors had bows and arrows only. But Mean to His Horses believed that would be enough to overcome the stagecoach, which normally had only one armed guard. Then he would be able to take the guns the stage passengers had.

* * *

The six passengers inside the coach were relatively quiet, just enjoying the scenery or lost in their own thoughts. Even though Gary's arm was in a sling he was holding it, and it was obvious that every bump made it hurt because he winced in pain, though he did not cry out.

Cody looked him, then smiled. "Gary, did you know that Mr. Ingraham writes stories?" Cody asked Gary and Abby.

"What kind of stories?" Gary asked.

"Oh, all kinds of stories," Cody answered. "Ingraham, why don't you entertain us with a story? One that the children will like."

"Well, what kind of stories do you like?" Ingraham asked.

"I like stories about princesses," Abby said.

"And sailing ships," Gary added. "Have you ever been on a big sailing ship?"

"Indeed I have," Ingraham said.

"And have you ever seen a real princess?" Abby asked.

"Yes, I've seen a real princess. And it so happens that I can tell a story about a princess and a sailing ship."

"Oh, good," Abby said.

"Once upon a time, in a land far, far away," Ingraham began, and within moments he had both children spellbound as they lost themselves in his story.

The serenity of the interior of the stagecoach was broken by a whizzing sound, followed by a loud "thock." An arrow had embedded itself in the stagecoach, less than an inch away from the window opening where Falcon was sitting. Looking through the window, Falcon saw several mounted Indians galloping toward the coach. Even as he saw them, he also saw several arrows in flight, streaming in the same direction. At least three more hit the stagecoach with the same "thocking" sound as the first.

"Indians," Falcon said, though he didn't have to tell them. By now everyone in the coach was aware of what was happening.

Falcon opened the door of the stage, which had increased its speed as the driver whipped the team into a gallop.

"Where are you going?" Cody asked.

"On top," Falcon said. "I'll be in better position to shoot from up there, and it will also draw the Indians' fire away from the inside of the coach."

"Good idea, I'll join you," Cody said. "Ingraham, you stay with Mrs. Kirby and the children."

"I'll do that," Ingraham shouted back, his pistol already in his hand.

The two men climbed up to the top of the stagecoach, one on either side.

"Good to see you boys comin' up here!" Hank yelled.

"Bo, keep the team running as fast as you can!" Falcon shouted.

"If we go any faster we're going to start flying!" Bo replied as he popped the whip over the galloping team.

Falcon and Cody lay on their stomach on the coach, then began shooting. With their first shots, two Indians fell. The shotgun guard got one, and as one of the Indians galloped up alongside the stage, Igraham shot him. Then Falcon got another one.

* * *

Mean to His Horses saw five of his warriors fall in the first few minutes of their attack, including the only other Indian who was carrying a rifle. That was half of his band, so he called a halt to the chase.

"Why do we stop?" one of the warriors asked.

"They have many guns, we have one," Mean to His Horses said. "We will fight another day."

"It would be better if we had guns."

"We will get guns," Mean to His Horses said.

"They're gone!" Falcon said to the driver. "Hold it up!"

"Whoa!" the driver said, hauling back on the reins as he also put his foot on the brake.

The stagecoach came to a halt, and as it set there, the dust kicked up by the rapid pace caught up with them and began billowing around the coach. The horses twitched and tossed their heads and whickered in discomfort at having had to stop so quickly without cooling off.

"Hank," the driver said. "Keep an eye open in case them heathens decide to come back. After a run like this, I'd better check out the harness."

"All right, Bo," Hank replied. Holding his rifle at the ready, he searched the road behind them.

Falcon and Cody climbed down from the top of the stagecoach. It wasn't until then that Falcon noticed an arrow sticking out of the top of the coach, less than an inch from where he had been lying.

On the ground, Falcon opened the door to the coach and looked inside. Mrs. Kirby was holding both her children close to her. Ingraham, with a wide grin on his face, was still holding a smoking pistol.

"Are you folks all right in here?" Falcon asked.

"Yes, we are fine," Mrs. Kirby said, "thanks to you three gentlemen."

"And the shotgun guard," Falcon added.

"I have taken the trip to Sheridan many times," Mrs. Kirby said. "I have never known the Indians to be so bold. I have no idea what might have provoked them to such a thing."

When they rolled in to DeMaris Springs two hours later, several people noticed that there were arrows sticking out of the side of the coach. And because they had noticed it, they began running alongside, keeping pace with the coach until it pulled into the depot.

"What happened?" one of the townspeople called up to the driver.

"What happened? We was attacked by injuns, that's what happened," the driver said. "But we run them heathens off."

"And we kilt five of 'em while we was runnin' 'em off," the shotgun guard said.

"You kilt five of 'em, did you, Hank?"

"No, far as I know, I only got one," Hank said. "Buffalo Bill, Falcon MacCallister, and Mr. Ingraham got the others."

"Buffalo Bill is here?"

"Yep, he's in the coach."

"Are you sure it was Indians, and not just some bandits dressed like Indians?" someone asked.

"Oh, they was Injuns all right. There ain't no doubt about that," the driver said.

When Cody and Falcon stepped out of the stage, Cody was recognized immediately.

"It's Buffalo Bill!"

"Buffalo Bill, what are you doing here?" another asked.

"I'm here to show my friends where my new town is to be built," Cody said.

"Does Bellefontaine know about that?"

"More to the point, will he approve of it?"

"I have not discussed this with Mr. Bellefontaine," Cody said. "And to be honest, I don't care whether he approves of it or not. My business dealings are with Thornton Beck, not with Pierre Fontaine."

Five minutes later, Davis and Regret were in Bellefontaine's office, smiling broadly.

"Did you hear about the stagecoach from Sheridan gettin' attacked?" Regret asked.

"I heard. Are you boys responsible for that?"

"No, sir. This attack was for real," Davis said. "What we've been doin' is workin'. We've been stirrin' folks up and the Indian war has started."

"It's good that it has started," Bellefontaine said. "Now we need to keep it going."

"We're working on that," Davis said. "I've got a line on some guns that we're goin' to sell to the Injuns."

"The army will have to come in here then," Regret said.

"And once the army comes in, the whole valley will be cleared out, Injuns, prospectors, homesteaders, the lot of them," Davis said.

Bellefontaine smiled and took down a bottle of good blended whiskey. He poured three glasses, then handed one to each of the other two men. He held his glass up.

"Gentlemen, to our success," he said.

"To our success," Davis repeated.

* * *

Later that morning there was a town meeting held in the community center to discuss the growing Indian problem. The meeting was chaired by Mayor Joe Cravens, but Pierre Bellefontaine had a seat at the head table. Falcon, Cody, and Ingraham were sitting in the front row, as were Bo and Hank.

Mayor Cravens called the meeting to order.

"Now, friends, I reckon you know why we have called this meeting. The truth is, this Indian problem is beginning to get out of hand. First off, we had some prospectors kilt, and it was plain that it was Indians that done it. Then we had a rancher, Frank Barlow and his whole family, good people they were, get kilt by Indians too. And all of 'em was scalped, includin' even the woman and the boy.

"Mr. Bellefontaine has somethin' he wants to say to us now. Mr. Bellefontaine?"

Bellefontaine was a tall, slender man with silver hair and light blue eyes. He was exceptionally well dressed, and looked like the wealthy entrepreneur he was.

"As most of you know, after the incident where the Barlow family was slaughtered by the heathens, I authorized a posse to go after the Indians. Some of you may think that, as a private citizen, I had no right to do this. But I have several employees who are required to work all up and down the valley between here and the Crow camp. I have their safety in mind. I also have the safety in mind of all the independent prospectors, homesteaders, ranchers, and farmers who are trying to live peacefully out there. To that end, I am proposing to pay one hundred dollars to any prospector who will abandon the valley, and five hundred dollars to any rancher or farmer now living out there who will give up his land."

"Where are we goin' to get that kind of money to pay those people to do that?" one of the citizens of the town asked.

Bellefontaine shook his head and held up his hand. "Don't get me wrong, friends. I'm not asking the town to come up with that money. I will personally come up with the money to pay people to leave."

"That's real decent of you, Mr. Bellefontaine, but I know for a fact that there are some ranchers and farmers out there who won't think that's enough. Fact is, I don't think you could pay some of 'em to come out."

"Whether they stay or come out, the trouble has started. If any of you have contact with any of these people, please let them know that the offer is there."

"Why don't we call in the army?" one of the men in the audience asked.

"Funny that you should bring that up," Bellefontaine said. "For I am indeed calling in the army, and I am going to ask them to relocate the Crow. They have shown by their actions that they are not peaceful. And today, they were so bold as to attack a stagecoach. It's one thing to get all the settlers out of the valley, but the way I see it, that's not even enough. With the Crow on the warpath, not even our town is safe."

"It wasn't Crow that attacked the stagecoach," Falcon said, speaking up from the audience.

Falcon's remark elicited several responses from the audience, but it was Bellefontaine who had the floor and his voice is the one that got through.

"I beg your pardon?" Bellefontaine replied. "And who are you?"

"The name is MacCallister. Falcon MacCallister."

"Falcon MacCallister!" someone in the audience said, and his name spread throughout the hall where the meeting was being held.

"I've heard of MacCallister."

"He's nigh as famous as Buffalo Bill his ownself."

"Well, Mr. MacCallister, your name seems to have evoked some response from the citizens of DeMaris Springs. I apologize for my ignorance, but I must confess that I have never heard of you."

"No reason why you should have heard of me," Falcon replied.

"Tell me, why do you say that it was not the Crow who attacked the stage coach?"

"I was on the stagecoach, I saw them. They were not Crow, they were Cheyenne."

"They were Cheyenne, you say," Bellefontaine said. "And tell me, Mr. MacCallister, am I to believe that you are so knowledgeable about such things that you can tell the difference between one heathen and another?"

"I brought one of the arrows that were sticking out of the stage," Falcon said. Reaching under the chair he held it up, then pointed to the markings just before the feathers. "This crooked black and yellow line here, on the arrow shaft, is the mark of the Crooked Lance Warrior Society. That's Cheyenne."

"He's right!" someone else called out loudly. "I've seen the mark of the Crooked Lance Warrior Society myself. If that's what's on that arrow, then the Injuns that attacked the stage was Cheyenne, not Crow."

"It was Crow that attacked the Barlow family though!" someone else yelled and for the next few minutes there was so much shouting going on that no one could hear what anyone was saying. Picking up his gavel, Mayor Cravens began banging on the table.

"Order!" he shouted. "Order! Folks, we can't conduct this town meeting unless we have order!"

Mayor Cravens continued to bang his gavel until, finally, order was restored.

"Now," he said. "Perhaps we can get on with the meeting. Mr. Bellefontaine, you may continue."

Bellefontaine waited a moment before he resumed.

"Perhaps, Mr. MacCallister, you are correct. In fact, I am willing to accept that you probably are correct, as you seem to know about such things. But, even if they are Cheyenne, that just broadens the picture and makes our own position here more untenable. You see, that attack happened well east of DeMaris Springs, whereas the prospectors and the tragedy that befell the Barlow family happened west of us.

"It may well be that there has been an alliance made between the Crow and the Cheyenne, and if that is the case, we are caught in the middle."

"The Crow and the Cheyenne are enemies," Cody said. "I don't live out here anymore, but even I know that."

"You say they are enemies and they may have been so in the past," Bellefontaine said. "But perhaps you have not heard of this new movement that has begun among the Indians out here. It is called Spirit Talking, which I am led to believe is a new kind of religion. I am also told that this heathen religion seems to have reached out beyond tribal lines, and is infecting all the Indians."

Buffalo Bill held up his hand. "May I speak, Mr. Mayor?"

"Yes, of course, Mr. Cody," Mayor Cravens said.

"Falcon MacCallister and I are well aware of the Spirit Talking movement. Indeed, that is why we are out here. I was summoned to a meeting with General Miles at his headquarters in Chicago. There, he asked me to meet personally with Sitting Bull in order to ascertain, one, whether Sitting Bull was behind this movement and, two, whether this movement represented the potential outbreak of a new Indian war.

"I am pleased to report that Sitting Bull has nothing to do with it. And I think the answer to the Indian question is a simple one. So long as philanthropists are allowed to weep over the Indians, while politicians plunder them, while the Indian Agency fails on their promise of decent treatment, there will be trouble.

"What we should do is make them feel that we will deal with them honestly and fairly, and that they will be held accountable for their crimes as individuals, and not be held accountable as an entire tribe. When we can do that, I believe that the Indian difficulties will be at an end."

Cody's remarks met with a mixed response. There were those who applauded, and called out, "here, here." However, there were others who renewed their demand for the army to be called in to "settle accounts once and for all."

After the town meeting Bellefontaine invited Falcon, Cody, and Ingraham to his office. The conference room in his office was as large as the meeting hall had been, and a big window on the west side of his office afforded a magnificent view of the snow-peaked Absaroka Mountains. There were comfortable chairs and sofas everywhere, buffalo-skin rugs on the floor, and elk heads and antlers on the walls.

"I hope you enjoy the wine," he said as one of his employees began pouring. "It is a fine wine that I import from France." He passed goblets around to all of them, then they each took a swallow.

"I'll bet none of you have ever tasted anything this good, have you?" he said.

"It is quite a good wine," Cody agreed. "But I prefer Beaujolais from the vineyards in the Pierres Dorées region. I had quite a good conversation with the vintner when I was there."

"Yes, Beaujolais is quite good as well," Bellefontaine said, somewhat deflated.

Falcon smiled at Bellefontaine's reaction.

"Are you really planning on calling in the army?" Falcon asked.

"Yes. I cannot be expected to continue to supply posses to take care of the Indians when, by rights, that should be the job of the army."

"I agree you have no business sending out posses," Falcon said. "But if these are isolated incidents, don't you think calling in the army would make it even worse?"

"What would you propose?" Bellefontaine asked.

"I would say we follow Mr. Cody's suggestion, that we call a meeting with the Crow and tell them that we do not hold the entire tribe responsible for these atrocities, but only those who actually committed them. It is my belief that the Indians would turn the guilty parties over to us."

"And what makes you believe that?"

"The Crow have been friendly with the white man

for some time now. It simply does not make sense that they would suddenly start making war."

"That's because you don't know anything about the Spirit Talking movement," Bellefontaine said. "Ever since they started on that, the Indians have gone crazy. Crazy, I tell you."

"Have there been any incidents here in town?" Cody asked.

"No, nothing here in town. But I understand the town that you wish to build will be even closer to the Crow Reservation."

"A little closer, yes."

"If you are asking my advice, Cody, I would say, don't build it."

Cody took a swallow of his wine before he answered.

"I'm not asking for your advice," he said.

Prentiss Ingraham's notes from his book in progress:

The area where Buffalo Bill intends to build his town is in the Absaroka Range, a mountain segment of the northern Rocky Mountains, in northwestern Wyoming Territory. This magnificent vista extends in a northwest-southeast direction. It is a large plateau with spectacular features and many very high mountains. The Yellowstone valley is formed by the Stinking Water River, which, despite its name, is a quite beautiful and refreshing stream of water.

There is already a town situated here, called DeMaris Springs, named after the natural hot springs herein located. The town is small and mean-spirited, inhabited by a poor class of citizens who, for the most part, are dependent upon one man, Pierre

Bellefontaine, for their livelihood. As a result of this unholy alliance, Bellefontaine treats the townspeople more as subjects than citizens.

Buffalo Bill Cody has expressed his belief that upon the emergence of his town, to be called Cody, that DeMaris Springs will dry up. Those citizens who currently reside in DeMaris Springs would then be well served to move to Cody, where they will be able to establish a more independent life and enjoy that promise offered by the Declaration of Independence to freely engage in the pursuit of happiness.

CHAPTER FIFTEEN

Rattlesnake Mountain, Wyoming Territory

"Are you sure he can be trusted?" Regret asked.

"Yeah," Davis said. "The deal was, he was to show up alone. That means there's two of us and only one of him. If anyone is worried, it should be him."

"But what if he ain't alone?"

"He's got to come that way," Davis said, pointing toward a wide, open plain. "If there is anyone with him within a mile, we'll see 'em."

"Yeah, I guess you are right," Regret agreed.

The two men were waiting for their meeting in an area known as Colter's Hell. They were here to carry out the next part of their plan to maintain the momentum of the growing Indian problem. But it was also a plan that entailed a great deal of risk, such as the risk they were taking today in meeting with Mean to His Horses. If the plan failed, it could cost them their lives.

"Are you sure Depro will come up with the guns?" Regret asked.

"You heard him same as I did," Davis said. "Last time we talked to him, he said he already had the guns."

"Do you believe him?"

"Yeah, I believe him. Don't you?"

"I guess. The only thing is, if we promise Mean to His Horses that we are going to furnish him guns and we don't, it's goin' to make him pretty mad."

"Yeah, well, if we don't get the guns, we'll just stay away from him."

"How long we been waitin' here?" Regret asked.

"I don't know. An hour, maybe two," Davis replied.

"Maybe he ain't goin' to come."

"Oh, he'll come all right," Davis said.

"What makes you so sure he'll come?"

"Because he wants those weapons."

"Which we ain't got with us, I remind you," Regret said.

"We don't want the weapons with us when we first meet. Else he might just up and take 'em."

"How's he goin' to do that? You said he was comin' alone."

"He is supposed to, and I believe he will. But, just in case he don't come alone, our best bet is not to have the weapons with us."

"Hey, look out there. Ain't that him?" Davis asked, pointing.

Looking in the direction Davis had pointed out, Regret saw a lone rider coming toward them. Even though he was some distance away, they knew it was an Indian, and as he drew closer they saw his face, painted red on one side and white on the other, so they knew it was Mean to His Horses.

"Let's go meet him," Regret said.

"Wait until he gets a little closer," Davis replied.

The two men watched the Indian as he rode across the last three hundred yards, then when he was within one hundred yards of them, they rode out from the tree line where they had been waiting and started toward him. First Davis, and then Regret held up their right hands as they approached him. Mean to His Horses held his right hand up as well.

"Hello, Chief, it is good of you to come," Regret said.

"You have guns to sell?" the Indian asked.

"Yes."

"How many guns you have?"

"Many guns, and I can get many more."

"I will buy."

"With gold," Davis said. "I'm only going to deal in gold."

"In gold."

"Then we have a deal."

"Where are the guns?"

"I will deliver them to you. I did not bring them with me until I knew we would have a deal. Where is the gold?"

"You will have gold when I have guns," Mean to His Horses said.

Davis chuckled. "Why, Mean to His Horses, you mean you don't trust the white man?"

"You will get gold when I get guns," Mean to His Horses repeated.

"All right, I'll go along with that."

"Why?" Mean to His Horses asked.

"Why what?"

"You are white, I am Indian. If you sell guns, I will make war on white man. Why do you sell?"

"I think the white man has done the Injun wrong," Davis said. "I will sell the guns to you because I want to see justice done."

"I think you lie," Mean to His Horses said.

"What?"

"I think you sell guns because you want the gold I will give you, and you do not care if I make war on the whites."

Davis laughed. "You are a pretty smart Injun," he said. "You are right. I want the gold."

Mean to His Horses nodded, then he looked toward the tree line near where Davis and Regret had waited for him. He held his hand in the air and four mounted Indians emerged from the woods, riding toward them.

"What the hell?" Davis said. "Where did they come from?"

Sheridan

Angus Ebersole, Clay Hawkins, Ike Peters, Jim Dewey, and Billy Taylor were in the Fireman's Exchange Saloon, having just arrived in Sheridan on board the *North Mist* riverboat. Relatively flush, having the money they took from the bank plus the money they got from selling their horses to the army, they were sitting around a table drinking, planning their next move, when they heard the name of Falcon MacCallister.

"Ha!" one of the others in the saloon said, laughing as he told the story. "I wish ole' Pelham had been here with his camera so he coulda' took a picture of Slayton when MacCallister stood him down."

"Yeah, we could hang it up on the wall here so's Slayton would see it ever' time he come in," another said.

"Maybe there ain't no picture, but don't forget the writer feller that was with them," one of the others said. "And I'd sure like to read what he wrote about this. I seen him writin' somethin' no sooner than Slayton went out of here with his tail tucked up between his legs, like as if he was a beat dog or something."

"Yeah, I've heard tell that the biggest reason Mac-Callister and Buffalo Bill are famous in the first place is because that writer feller made them famous. Can't think of his name, though."

"His name is Ingraham," Lucy said. "Prentiss Ingraham. And he is a real good writer, because I have read some of his books."

"Ha! I wonder if Slayton will turn up in any of his books," the bartender asked.

"Excuse me, gents," Ebersole said, interjecting himself into the conversation. "This here MacCallister feller you are talking about. Would that be Falcon MacCallister?"

"It would indeed," one of the talkers replied. "Do you know him?"

"Yes, as a matter of fact, I do. He is an old friend of mine," Ebersole said. "But who is this gentleman, Slayton, you are talking about?"

"Slayton ain't no gentleman, Mister, and that is for sure and certain. He ain't nothin' but a bully. You see Lucy's eye there? How it's black? Slayton done that to her."

"But he got his come uppance," Lucy said. "Slayton thinks he is pretty good with a gun, only, as it turns out, he wasn't good enough to go against MacCallister."

"MacCallister kill him, did he?"

"Kill him? Nah, he didn't kill him, and that's what makes it so good," the bartender said. "MacCallister just stood him down, made Slayton shuck out of his gun belt and leave it here."

"His gun is still here," one of the others said, laughing. "It's there behind the bar. Show it to him, Jake."

Jake, the bartender, held the gun up.

"Here it is, Ken," Jake said. "Only thing is, Slayton ain't got the gall to come back in for it."

"My, my, I wish I had been here to see that," Ebersole said. "Don't you boys think that would have been a good show to see MacCallister stand down Slayton?" he asked the others at the table with him.

At first, Dewey and the others didn't know what Ebersole was getting at. They certainly would not have enjoyed seeing MacCallister in a heroic role. But seeing the expression in Hagan's face, they knew to go along with him, and so they enthusiastically agreed that they wish they had been here.

"It wasn't just a show," Lucy said. "Mr. MacCallister came to my aid when Slayton began hitting me."

"That's true," Ken said. "MacCallister wasn't just showin' off or nothin' like that. Slayton deserved what happened to him."

"Where is he now?" Ebersole asked.

"Who?" Ken replied. "Slayton? Like as not, he's still down at the livery. He works there. Don't reckon we'll see him back here very soon."

"No. I mean Falcon MacCallister. Like I said, he's an old friend of mine and I'd like to look him up. Is he still in town?"

"No, he ain't here no more," Ken said. "He left. Him, and Buffalo Bill and that writer." He turned to his friends. "Say, that was really somethin' in itself, wasn't it? I mean Falcon MacCallister and Buffalo Bill, both here at the same time."

"They didn't stay here long, though," one of the others said.

"They couldn't stay too long. Buffalo Bill is havin' that big audition up in Cinnabar," Jake said.

"What kind of audition? What are you talkin' about?" Ebersole asked.

"Why, you know about Buffalo Bill, don't you? He has a Wild West Show," Jake said.

"Yes," Ken said. "I ain't never seen it, 'cause mostly he plays it back East, like in New York, and Philadelphia, and St. Louis and the like."

"In London and Paris and Vienna too," Lucy added.

"Anyhow," Ken continued, his show has bronco bustin', and stagecoach drivin', all sorts of things like that, and it has done made him one of the richest men in the country."

"And the cowboys that works for him makes good money too," Jake said. "That's why there will be so many showin' up in Cinnabar to try and get signed on to his show."

"Where is Cinnabar?" Ebersole asked.

"It's just north of Yellowstone Park. Why? You plannin' on tryin' out for the show?"

"Who knows?" Ebersole said. "I might be interested. When is this audition bein' held?"

"It's a week from now," Jake said. "It was printed up by the newspaper. Lucy, show him the newspaper article about the audition."

Lucy walked down to the end of the bar, then brought a copy of the *Sheridan Bulletin* over to show to Ebersole.

Cowboys! Cowboys! Cowboys!

Come one, come all! If you can ride, or shoot, or rope, come to Cinnabar on the Seventh instant to audition for the BUFFALO BILL CODY WILD WEST EXHIBITION.

> Cowboys who are selected will become members of the show. Honest wages will be paid, and you will travel to St. Louis, Chicago, New York, London, and Paris. Buffalo Bill will be present to judge and make the selections.

"And you say that MacCallister went to Cinnabar with Buffalo Bill?" Ebersole asked after he finished reading the article.

"Yeah, only they didn't go right there," Jake said. "They took a stage coach from here to DeMaris Springs. Buffalo Bill, MacCallister, and that writer fella that's travelin' with 'em."

"Ingraham," Lucy said. "The writer is named Prentiss Ingraham."

"Yeah, Ingraham. Anyhow, the word I heard is that Buffalo Bill is going to build himself a town there. Well not right where DeMaris Springs is, but real close," Jake said.

"And like as not, it'll be the end of DeMaris Springs," Ken said.

"That's pro'bly right. And get this. He's goin' to name it after himself."

"Yeah, well, if I had as much money as Buffalo Bill Cody, I'd like as not build me a town too. And I'd name it after myself too. I'd call it Hickenlooper," one of the other saloon patrons said.

The others in the saloon laughed.

"Ha. Hickenlooper. Now that would be a name, wouldn't it? Folks, welcome to Hickenlooper," Ken said.

Finishing their drinks, Ebersole and the others left the saloon and walked down Central Street to the livery stable.

A man came out of the stable to meet them. He was a big man, with stubble on his chin, and irregular, yellowed, broken and missing teeth.

"Yeah, what do you want?" he asked.

"Do you have horses for sale?"

"Horses for sale? Yeah, we got horses."

"Good. We'll need five," Ebersole said.

"Five? I don't know as I can sell you five, that would purt' nigh clean us out. You'll have to wait till Mr. Giles comes back."

"Is your name Slayton?" Ebersole asked.

"Yeah, how did you know that?"

"I've heard you are pretty good with a gun, Slayton."

"I ain't bad," Slayton said.

"I've also heard that you don't care much for a man named Falcon MacCallister."

The smile turned to a frown. "Are you trying to be funny, Mister? 'Cause I don't like it when folks try to fun me."

"No," Ebersole said. "I'm not trying to be funny at all. In fact, I will tell you why we want these horses. We are on MacCallister's trail, and we plan to kill him."

Slayton's scowl turned to an expression of surprise and curiosity. "You plan to kill him?" he asked.

"We do," Ebersole answered. "MacCallister and Buffalo Bill Cody."

"And that writer son of a bitch who is traveling with them," Hawkins added.

"Why?" Slayton asked. "Why are you going to kill him?"

"Does it make any difference why? As I understand it, you may have a bone to pick him as well. I would think you would welcome the idea that we're goin' to kill him."

Slayton drummed his fingers on the top rail of a stall and was silent for a long moment.

"Any of you fellas got an extry gun?"

"Why do you ask?" Ebersole asked.

"'Cause my gun and holster is still in the saloon, and I ain't goin' back in there to get it and be made a fool of."

"There's a gunshop here," Dewey said. "I seen it when we got off the boat."

"I ain't goin' to go buy one, either, for the same reason. But I'll make you a deal."

"What kind of deal?" Ebersole wanted to know.

"If one of you fellers will go buy a gun for me, I'll give you these five horses for free."

"What? How are you going to do that?" Hawkins asked.

"'Cause Giles has gone down to Laramie and by the time he gets back, we and his horses be long gone."

"We?" Ebersole asked.

"Yeah," Slayton said. "That's part of the deal. I'm goin' with you."

Fort Keogh

Lieutenant Colonel Whitehead glanced up at Benteen when Benteen came into his office.

"You wanted to see me, Colonel?" Benteen asked.

"Yes, thank you. Fred, we have a request that has been approved by General Colby to send troops to the Big Horn Basin in Wyoming Territory. I'm going to ask you to respond to the request with elements of the Ninth Cavalry. And I will leave it to you to decide what the troop makeup would be."

"What, exactly, is the problem?" Benteen asked.

"The request came from a man named Joe Cravens, who is the mayor of DeMaris Springs."

"DeMaris Springs? You mean where the hot springs are? I thought that was a geographical location, I had no idea there was a town there."

"It isn't on any map that we have, and I'm not certain that it has ever actually been incorporated as a town. However, there are, as I understand, in excess of three hundred people living there, most of them employed in one way or another by Pierre Bellefontaine."

"So then the man calling the shots will be this man, Bellefontaine, not Mayor Cravens," Benteen said.

"That would be my guess," Whitehead agreed.

"How will Bellefontaine feel about my colored troops?"

"What is there to feel?" Whitehead asked. "Bellefontaine wants soldiers there to protect him; your soldiers will be doing that. If he doesn't like it, tell him to protect himself."

Benteen chuckled. "Good idea. Who are the Indians I'll be dealing with? Brule? Sans Arc? Cheyenne?"

"Crow."

"Crow?" Benteen said. "Are you serious?"

"The Crow have a reservation just east of Yellowstone Park on the Meeteetsee River," Whitehead said. "And the complaint is that they have been killing the prospectors and raiding homesteaders."

"But the Crow have long been our allies," Benteen said. "Curly, White Man Runs Him, Half Yellow Face, White Swan, Bloody Knife, they were all with us at Little Big Horn. They were Crow. What would make the Crow go on the warpath against the white man now?"

"Fred, you know Indians better than I do. In fact,

I would say that right now, you are probably the most experienced officer in the army as far as Indian fighting is concerned. You know better than anyone how they get caught up in their cults and rituals. General Colby thinks it is this Spirit Talking that has them all riled up."

"He may be right," Benteen said. "I'll get my men ready."

"How many companies will you be taking?"

"I think two will be enough," Benteen said. "I can't believe that the entire Crow nation is involved. If it is related to the Spirit Talking, it is more than likely going to be just handful of trouble makers."

After his meeting with Lieutenant Colonel Whitehead, Benteen walked across the parade grounds to the supply room. When he stepped inside he saw Sergeant Major Moses Coletrain taking an inventory.

"Sergeant Major Coletrain," Benteen said.

Coletrain came to attention. "Yes, sir?"

"How are you doing with the inventory?"

"I'm doing very well, sir, thank you. I'm just about concluded."

"Are we missing anything?"

"Not exactly, sir."

"Not exactly? What does that mean?"

"The major might remember that we were ordered to turn in some rifles, carbines, and pistols," Coletrain said. "I had them all packed, ready to go out, but Sergeant Depro shipped them instead. So far, I still haven't gotten a receipt from Jefferson Barracks saying they arrived, and until I do, I can't close my property book on them."

"I do remember that," Benteen said. "Not to worry, Sergeant. If something has happened to the weapons, I will see to it that it will be Depro's fault, not yours." Benteen looked around the supply room. "Where is Sergeant Depro, anyway?"

"He took a one-week furlough," Coletrain said.

"One week? As I understand it, he is from Ohio. He can't get to Ohio and back in one week. Where did he go?"

"He didn't tell me, sir."

"Well, he isn't my problem," Benteen said. "The reason I came over, Sergeant, is because we have been ordered to the field. I am going to take two troops of the Ninth. What I want you to do is get our equipment together for the march."

"Yes, sir. Any idea how long you will be gone, sir?"

"I have no idea, how long we will be gone," Benteen said. "We are going up into the Big Horn Basin. And it isn't just an expedition. There is a very strong possibility that we may expect some fighting," Benteen said. "So I will want 100 rounds of carbine ammunition and 24 rounds of pistol ammunition per man."

"Yes, sir, I'll get right on it," Coletrain replied.

"Oh, and Sergeant, since we will have only two companies going, I am going to leave Sergeant Major Wilder here at the post. That means I will need an acting Sergeant Major. I would like you to fill that position."

"Yes, sir!" Coletrain replied proudly.

CHAPTER SIXTEEN

Jim Mountain, Wyoming Territory

Lee Regret and Sam Davis rode down to the river at the base of the mountain and dismounted. Leading their horses down to the water, they stood holding the reins as the horses began to drink.

"I don't see him anywhere about," Regret said.

"He'll be here," Davis said. "You know Sergeant Depro as well as I do. You know that when he tells you he's goin' to do somethin' that he does it."

"Yeah, well, only if he's goin' to get somethin' out of it for his ownself," Regret said.

"Well, he is goin' to get somethin'," Davis insisted. "He's goin' to get his cut of the money."

"If there is any money," Regret replied. "You ever seen any Indians with money?"

"You were there when we talked to Mean to His Horses. You heard me tell him that we wanted to be paid in gold. He agreed, and that's what we'll be dealin' in."

As the two men stood there talking and watching their animals take water, they heard a low whistle from just beyond the tree line on the opposite side of the river.

"What was that?" Regret asked.

"Sounded like a bird," Davis replied.

"Didn't sound like no bird I ever heard."

Davis returned the whistle and a moment later a man wearing an army uniform with the stripes of a sergeant walked through the tree line.

"Howdy, troopers," he called from the other side of the river.

"We ain't troopers no more," Regret said. "We done been out of the army for nigh onto a year."

"Hell, Regret, you wasn't no soldier when you was in the army," the sergeant said. "You wasn't bad though, Davis."

"Thank you, Sergeant," Davis said.

"What the hell you suckin' up to him, for?" Regret asked. "He can't make me muck out stables, and he can't give you no stripes. Me 'n you both is out of the army and there ain't nothin' he can do to hurt us or help us. Ain't that right, Sergeant Depro?"

"That all depends," Depro replied.

"Depends on what?"

"On whether or not you want the weapons I got."

"You got 'em, Sarge?" Davis asked, now, suddenly animated.

"Come over here with me, and I'll let you take a look."

Regret and Davis waded through the water, then followed Sergeant Depro to the other side of a large rock outcropping. There sat an old weather-beaten wagon, its markings so dim that it was barely identifiable as a one-time army wagon.

"Here they are," Sergeant Depro said, jerking the canvas cover away to reveal eight closed boxes.

Davis pried off the lid from the first box. He picked up one of the rifles and tossed it over to Regret, then picked up another for himself. It was a lever-action rifle, and he pumped the lever as he examined the action. "How many do you have here?" he asked.

"Forty Winchester repeaters, .44-.40, fifty-five Springfield .51 caliber breach-loading rifles, and thirty-five Colt revolvers, .45 caliber," Sergeant Depro answered. "Or, put another way, enough weapons to start a small war."

"Funny you should say that," Regret replied. "For that is exactly what we have in mind."

"Have you got a buyer?"

"Yeah, we have a buyer," Davis said. "Mean to His Horses."

"Mean to His Horses?" Depro replied. "Wait a minute. Are you tellin' me I stole these guns to sell to Injuns? And not just any Injun, you're going to sell them to Mean to His Horses? You can't be serious."

"Yeah, we are serious. Why wouldn't we be serious?" Davis asked.

Depro shook his head. "I don't know, Mean to His Horses is one bad son of a bitch. I just can't believe you sold weapons to him."

"Who did you think we would sell them to?" Regret asked. "Some squaw, somewhere?"

"No, I guess not. But I'm sure you remember the skirmish we had with Mean to His Horses a couple of years ago. He had fifty braves who went off the reservation, and we ran into them at Crazy Woman Creek. That was the fight where Miller, Tucker, and Jimmy Clark was all three killed."

"Yeah, I remember that," Davis said.

"They captured Jimmy Clark, and tortured him that night. We all heard him screaming for two or three hours before he died," Depro said. "You remember that too, do you?"

"Yes, of course I remember. Something like that ain't all that easy to forget," Regret said. "So what is your point?"

"My point is, is that really the kind of Injun you want to sell these guns to?"

"I don't care who we sell the guns to, as long as we get paid," Davis said. "And seein' as how you done stole the guns, looks to me like you don't have no choice but to go along with it your ownself. 'Cause when you think about it, you are in this for the money, same as we are."

"Yeah, you're right," Depro agreed. "It don't really make me no never mind what happens to the guns as long as I get paid for 'em. What price do you think we can get for them?"

"We've already set the price at ten dollars apiece so, with what we've got here, I figure that comes to about thirteen hundred dollars," Davis said.

"How much will that be for each of us?" Regret asked.

"Four hundred and thirty-three dollars each, with one dollar left over," Davis said. He looked at Depro. "Which is damn near a year's salary for you."

"Here's another way we can make some money," Depro said. "I've already got me about ten thousand rounds, all divided up according to caliber. If we don't give the Injuns bullets when we sell 'em the guns, why, we could charge them for the bullets too, oh, say maybe a nickel a round and that would be another five hundred dollars."

"Sounds good to me," Davis said. "But how did you come by the bullets?"

"When we were told to ship them guns back to Jefferson Barracks, what they also done was ask for the ammunition too," Depro explained. He smiled. "But I hid all the bullets away same as I hid the guns. That means I've got all the ammunition we will need."

"I tell you what," Davis said. "What do you say we just let the Indians play with the guns without bullets for a while? I'm sure they can come up with some on their own, but probably not more 'n a handful. And all that's goin' to do is make 'em hungry for more."

"Ha! They might get so hungry for them bullets that we could fetch a dime apiece for 'em," Regret said.

"I wouldn't be surprised," Davis said.

DeMaris Springs

As it so happened, Buffalo Bill Cody had several horses being kept for him at the livery at DeMaris Springs, so the day after their meeting with Bellefontaine, Cody, Falcon, and Ingraham walked down to the DeMaris Corral.

"I keep horses here so that I have them handy when I come out," Cody said. "It helps that the DeMaris Corral is one of the few business establishments in town that Bellefontaine doesn't own."

When they stepped into the livery barn, they saw two men putting a wheel on a buckboard.

"Karl, are you sure you know what you are doing?" Cody called out.

A big man, whose rolled-up sleeves displayed well-developed biceps, turned toward the three men.

"More better than you know, I think," Karl replied.

Grabbing a rag to wipe his hands, the big man advanced toward the three, then a wide smile spread across his face. "Cody, in town I heard you were," he said as he stuck out his hand.

"It is I heard you were in town, you dumb Dutchman, not in town I heard you were," Cody said.

That there was no animosity between the two men was indicated by the mutual smiles, and a hearty handshake.

"Gentleman, this thickheaded Dutchman is Karl Maas. And you aren't likely to find a better man anywhere. Karl, this is Falcon MacCallister and Prentiss Ingraham."

"Falcon MacCallister, *ja*, of you I have heard," Karl said as he shook first Falcon's hand, then Ingraham's.

"When are you going to sell this place and come join my Wild West Exhibition? I would put you in charge of all my stock and rolling equipment. I was in Germany two months ago. Why, just think, if you had been working for me then, you could have gone back."

"And why to the place I left, would I want to go back?"

Cody chuckled. "A good enough question, I suppose. Listen, how about picking out three of my best horses and having them saddled for us?"

"You are going to look at the site where the town you will build?" Karl asked.

"Yes. Then we are going to ride through Yellowstone, and go on to Cinnabar. I'm going to try out some new cowboys for my show there."

"Al," Maas called to one of his employees, "three of Herr Cody's best horses, you saddle."

"Yes, sir, Mr. Maas," Al replied.

"You weren't at the meeting this morning when we talked about the Indian problem," Cody said.

"There is no Indian problem," Maas said, shaking his head. "I think it is something Bellefontaine wants."

"Why would he want that?" Falcon asked.

"I think he wants all the basin for himself so he can build his mine. If there is Indian problem, then all prospectors and homesteaders will not be able to stay. And the Indians too, will not be able to stay because the army will come in and move them."

"Is there that much gold in this valley?" Falcon asked.

"I think there is no gold," Maass said, "but there is much coal. Bellefontaine wants to mine the coal to sell to the railroad. That will make him much money, I think."

"Damn," Cody said, snapping his fingers. "You know, Karl, you may not be as thickheaded as people think. Bellefontaine is making everyone think he is looking for gold, but that is just a ruse. He has been after coal all along."

"*Ja*, that is what I think," Maas said.

Al returned with three saddled horses.

"Ah, thank you, Al," Cody said, giving him a generous tip. He turned to Falcon and Ingraham. "Gentlemen, all three are excellent riding horses, with strength and endurance. You may choose your mount."

Half an hour later the three men were at the exact site where Cody planned to build his town.

"One problem in this area is the lack of potable water, which is why I am building on the river," Cody said. "This is the Stinking Water River." Dismounting, he walked down to the river. "But as you can see," he said, as he dipped his canteen cup into it, then took a drink. "The water is as sweet as a good wine."

He held the cup out toward Falcon and Falcon took a drink as well. "It is good water," Falcon agreed.

"Why do they call it Stinking Water River?" Ingraham asked.

"It has nothing to do with the water at all. There are several fumaroles about," Cody said, "and they give off an odor, rather like rotten eggs. Once we get my town established, I intend to get the name changed to the Shoshone River."

"I must confess that the scenery here is **be**autiful," Ingraham said. "But this a very remote and isolated location. It will be very hard for people to get here."

"There is already a railroad to Cinnabar just on the other side of Yellowstone Park," Cody said. "And the Burlington railroad is planning to build a railroad from Billings to Denver. I am trying to convince them to bring the track through Cody."

"Knowing your power of persuasion, Cody, I would bet that you get the job done," Falcon offered.

"And that will completely destroy the town of De-Maris Springs," Ingraham said.

"Unfortunately, yes," Cody said.

Ingraham laughed. "Unfortunately my foot. That is your intention."

"I must confess that it is unlikely this area could support two towns in such close proximity," Cody replied. "So if one town is to succeed, I would hope it would be my town."

"Nobody can fault you on that," Ingraham said.

"Cody, did you say we are going through Yellowstone before we get to Cinnabar?" Falcon asked.

"Yes."

"But there is no east entrance to Yellowstone. The mountains are too high."

"There is a pass," Cody said. "It is called Sylvan Pass. I am proposing that they make an entrance using that pass. That would add to the attraction of my town when I get it built."

"Sylvan Pass. I don't think I have heard of it."

"It's very high," Cody said. "But I am convinced that, with a series of switchbacks, a road could be constructed that would take visitors from my town into the park. And I intend to prove it."

"By taking us through it," Falcon said.

"Yes. Are you game?"

"I'm not the one you need to ask," Falcon said. "The question is, are the horses up to it?"

"There's only one way to find out," Cody replied.

From Cody's town site, they had a day's ride through Big Horn Basin to the Yellowstone Park. Their ride took them close to, but not through, the Crow Indian village.

"I have known High Hawk for a long time," Cody said. "We are friends of long standing, and I cannot believe we are in any danger. Nevertheless, it would probably be wise to keep an eye open."

The three men were alert for the entire ride, but they did not see one other person, Indian or white. They camped that night, just east of the park.

The next morning they entered Yellowstone by way of Sylvan Pass. Without a road, they had to follow the natural terrain of the mountain, finding enough ground for their horses to get footing as they made a series of switchbacks to enable them to gain altitude. The climb was long and arduous, and soon they were so high that they were actually looking down on the snow-capped peaks of adjacent mountains. In fact, though it was the middle of June, there were several areas where they actually passed through snow that came up to the horses' knees.

Several times they had to dismount and lead the horses until, at last, they were at the top of the pass. There they stopped to give themselves and their horses a chance to catch their breath. That was made even harder due to the thinner air at this elevation.

"How high are we?" Ingraham asked, panting heavily as they stood at the top of the pass, as he looked around at the vista their position afforded.

"I'm not sure exactly how high we are," Cody said. "But if this were nighttime and we were hungry, why we could just reach up and get a piece of cheese from the moon."

Falcon and Ingraham laughed.

"Actually, the pass is somewhere between eight and nine thousand feet high," Cody said.

Yellowstone had been established as a national park in 1872. Both Falcon and Cody had been to Yellowstone prior to its establishment as a park, and Cody had been many times since it became a national park. But Ingraham had never been, and he took in the park with the awe of someone who was transfixed by the wonders that he beheld.

Falcon and Cody pointed out Yellowstone Lake, which Cody declared was the most beautiful lake in the entire country. Coming down from the pass, they saw travertine terraces, geysers, mud volcanoes, giant hot springs, and the Upper and Lower Falls in what Cody called the Grand Canyon of the Yellowstone Park.

At midday Falcon shot a goose. Ingraham started gathering wood and Cody called out to him.

"What are you doing?"

"I'm gathering wood for a fire so we can cook the goose," Ingraham replied.

"No need for that."

"What are you planning for us to do? Eat the goose raw?"

"No need for that either," Cody said. "Let me show you."

After cleaning the goose, Cody tied a long piece of rawhide around the goose's feet, then lowered it into one of the boiling cauldrons of the natural hot springs.

"Because of the pressure, the water is much hotter than normal boiling temperature," Cody said. "So the goose will cook much faster."

In less than ten minutes, Cody pulled the goose from the hot water, then lay it on a fallen tree trunk. Cutting it open showed that the goose was thoroughly cooked, through and through.

"I wonder if the Indians used to cook their food this way?" Ingraham said and he pulled some meat away from the breast and ate it.

"No," Falcon said. "Because of all the hot springs, geysers, mud pots, and sink holes, the Indians considered this area to be filled with bad medicine."

"You have to be careful where you walk here," Cody added. "There are places where the ground looks quite secure, but if you step on it you will find that it is only a very thin crust, and you can fall through to a boiling cauldron like this one."

"Thanks a lot," Ingraham said. "Now you'll have me scared to death to take a step."

"Do like me," Falcon said. "Walk behind Cody. If he falls in, we'll know not to step there."

Ingraham laughed. "Good plan," he said.

"I'll say this," Ingraham said. "The wonders of this park will never cease to amaze me."

"Here is another amazing wonder," Cody said. "Once, many years ago, before this became a park, I came here to hunt bighorn sheep. I saw one, took a perfect aim at him and fired, but missed. Not only did I miss, the bighorn sheep paid no attention to me.

"I moved closer and fired again, missed again, though I don't know how that could possibly have been so. And what was even more amazing is the fact that the bighorn paid no attention whatever, not even reacting to the sound of the gunshot. I rushed toward the sheep to see what was wrong and I ran smack dab into a solid glass wall."

"A glass wall?" Ingraham said.

"Yes, sir, well, it wasn't exactly a glass wall. It was more like a glass mountain. Because, believe it or not, that glass mountain was acting just like a telescope. As it turns out, even though that bighorn sheep looked like he was no more than a hundred yards away, he was actually ten miles off."

Falcon and Ingraham laughed out loud.

"Of course, that mountain isn't here anymore. No sir, the government found out about it and they sent folks in here to chop it down and make it into field glasses and telescopes for the army and navy," Cody added.

"Cody, you have missed your calling," Ingraham said. "With a tall tale like that, you are the one who should be writing."

After dinner they continued their sojourn through the park, riding by sheer-sided cliffs that rose a thousand or more feet straight up and enjoying the colors, from canary, to orange, to bronze. During their ride through the park they saw buffalo, elk, deer, and grizzly. One grizzly bear made a few feints toward them and all three men drew their rifles, but the bear, with a few grunts and a toss of his head, turned and ambled away from them.

Within the boundaries of the Yellowstone Park rise the headwaters of the greatest river system in the United States. The Gallatin, Madison, Gardiner, Jefferson and Yellowstone join the Missouri River, which joins the Mississippi to empty into the Gulf of Mexico. The Snake has its head here as well, and it flows to the Pacific, while the headwaters of the Colorado lead to the Gulf of California.

It took them all day to see the sights, and they camped outside one more night, reaching the Mammoth Spring Hotel mid-morning of the next day. This was a large building, over 300 feet long, with a broad porch that ran the entire length of the hotel. There were a number of people lounging on the porch, including several tourists from Europe, a couple of army officers in uniform, and a very pretty black-haired, dark-eyed girl who was selling photographs of the park. From the porch there was a particularly fine view of mountains covered with pines, with their tips above the tree line, covered year-round with snow.

The most noticeable feature was a mountain, no more than one hundred yards away from the hotel. At first glance it looked like ice, but was actually a sedimentary formation from the hot springs which formed a succession of steps, terraces and plateaus of irregular height and width. From various terraces emerged trickles of hot water which then passed down over the plateaus in thin, pulsing waves.

When the three men went into the hotel they were greeted by Rufus Hatch, the owner of the hotel.

"Buffalo Bill Cody," he said. "What a pleasure to see you. How goes your town? Have you built it yet?"

"I am still working on it," Cody replied. He turned to Falcon. "You know that the only reason he is interested in my town is because he thinks it will mean more business for his hotel."

"But of course it will," Hatch said. "Did you come down from Cinnabar?"

"No, we came from DeMaris Springs."

"DeMaris Springs? Are you trying to tell me you came from the east?" Hatch asked.

"I'm not trying to tell you, Rufus, I am telling you. We came in from the east."

"But no, that is impossible."

"We are proof that it is possible."

"Ah, yes, but you came by horse, and foot, did you not? I suppose one could enter the park that way. But that would not be a practical way to enter for tourists."

"It would be practical if we built a road," Cody said.

"Are you saying that you think a road could be built that would enter the park from the east?"

"I believe so," Cody said. "In fact, I will personally hire surveyors to mark out the route for a road."

"You are indeed a friend," Hatch said. "That would be of immense benefit to the park."

"I see that you are doing a very good business, despite the lack of a road from the east," Cody said.

"Yes, well, the trains come from Livingston to Cinnabar now, and of course we have stagecoaches that maintain a steady run from the Cinnabar depot to here," Hatch said. "Oh, by the way, as you will see in the

lounge, I have put up posters about the audition you
will be holding in Cinnabar for your show. I predict
you will get cowboys from all over Wyoming, Montana,
and Utah."

Prentiss Ingraham's notes from his book in progress:

*The hotel at Mammoth Hot Springs is one of the
most remarkable hotels I have ever seen. It is built
upon a plateau of the vast formations of sulfur and
magnesia, deposited by the Hot Springs. A level area
of many acres surrounds the hotel, with mountains
and forest on every side except far below, where the
Gardiner River rushes through a beautiful valley
toward its juncture with the Yellowstone.*

*The hotel is built of wood, except for the chimneys
which are of brick. The rooms and corridors are
generous in their dimension and surprisingly so in
this remote area, illuminated by Mr. Edison's electric
lights. The hotel attracts hunters, settlers, and
cowboys as they congregate in the great halls, wearing
sombrero hats, high leather boots and leggings,
revolvers and cartridge belts.*

*The residents of Yellowstone expressed a great deal
of surprise that we gained entrance to the park from
the east, marveling at the fact that we were able to
negotiate a pass which rises to nearly nine thousand
feet in elevation.*

*Leaving the hotel and the park, we journeyed by
horseback some ten miles, gradually descending in
altitude by way of a dusty but well-travelled road to
Cinnabar. Here, announcements had been duly posted*

to attract applicants for the coveted position of being a performer in Buffalo Bill's Wild West Exhibition. This is no small thing as Buffalo Bill is a man of great honesty and integrity who believes in giving the audiences for his show an authentic look at America's great West as it really is.

CHAPTER SEVENTEEN

Cinnabar, Montana Territory

Perhaps the greatest promoter of Yellowstone Park was the Northern Pacific Railroad.

NORTHERN PACIFIC R.R.

*Wonderland Route
to the "Land of Geysers"*

Yellowstone Park

With colorful brochures and national newspaper advertising, the Northern Pacific brought several hundred visitors per year, discharging them at Livingston, where the Yellowstone tourists would take another train to the depot in Cinnabar. Cinnabar was a town that had grown up specifically to service Yellowstone, and on any given day during the summer season there were many more tourists in town than there were residents. Today Cinnabar was even more crowded than usual, for a large number of cowboys had gathered to audition for a position with the Buffalo Bill Cody Wild West Exhibition, and an even larger crowd had gathered to watch the performance.

Although there were several stagecoaches that maintained a route between the Mammoth Springs Hotel and Cinnabar, Falcon, Cody, and Ingraham rode the ten miles, covering the distance in just under an hour.

Cody had given Sherman Canfield the authority to make all the arrangements for him. It was an established relationship, since Canfield had long worked with Cody and had even traveled to Europe with the exhibition. Canfield met them when they arrived in Cinnabar.

"Of course I know who Falcon MacCallister is," Canfield said when he was introduced. "And Ingraham, it is good to see you again. Are you writing any new books?"

"My boy, I am always writing new books," he said. He smiled. "But this time, I am actually living the book as I write it."

"Living the book as you write it? Whatever do you mean?"

"He is following Falcon and me, taking notes on every little detail. We can't seem to get rid of him," Cody said.

"You love it, Cody, you know you do," Ingraham said, laughing.

"Mr. Cody, if you'll come down here to the end of the street, you'll see where I've got us set up," Canfield said. "I had some bleachers built especially for the occasion and I expect we'll have three hundred or more who will show up to watch the auditions."

"You aren't charging them, are you?" Cody asked.

"No. Do you think I should have charged them?"

"No, we charge the Easterners, but these people out here are my people, so let anyone in who wants to come. I want it to be more like a party."

"Well now a lot of them will be tourists, just gettin' off the train to take the stage into the park," Canfield said. "So they'll be Easterners."

"All the better," Cody said. "We will whet their appetite so that when they go back East, they will be anxious to see the entire performance. It will just sell more tickets to the exhibition. What about the cowboys? Have many shown up?"

"Ha! I'll say they have. They've come from three or four states. Quite a few of them have been here for a week or more. The saloon has been doing a heck of a business ever since word of this got out."

"Good, that should give us a large enough field to find some really good riders."

Canfield led the three men down to the end of the street to show them what he had done to prepare for the event. A large arena had been marked off by use of ropes and poles, and, facing the arena were recently built bleachers. On the opposite side of the bleachers, stock pens had been built. In one set of pens were cattle to be used for roping, another pen held horses selected for their ability to throw their riders.

Several cowboys were already practicing for the event.

"Hey!" one of them shouted. "There's Buffalo Bill!"

Upon being recognized, Cody was quickly surrounded by visitors who were here to see the show as well as many of the cowboys themselves.

Falcon and Ingraham stepped aside as Buffalo Bill Cody's fans swarmed around him.

"How in the world is he able to put up with all that?" Falcon asked Ingraham.

Ingraham chuckled, and shook his head. "You don't understand, do you, Falcon? Cody lives for that."

"Better him than me," Falcon said.

"It's all a matter of business," Canfield said. "The more people that recognize his name, the more people will come to one of the exhibitions. It's a matter of promotion, and Mr. Cody is better at this than anyone I have ever known."

They heard the sound of a train whistle.

"Here comes another train load," Ingraham said. "By the time we get around to doing the show, I'll bet the bleachers won't be big enough to hold everyone."

Livingston, Montana Territory, was a stop on the Northern Pacific transcontinental line. From there, Northern Pacific built a special track down to Cinnabar, which was located at the edge of Yellowstone Park. The trip was fifty-five miles long, and was covered in just under three hours. That was the train that Falcon and Ingraham heard arriving. What they could not know was that this train carried six passengers who were dedicated to one purpose, and that was to kill Falcon MacCallister, Buffalo Bill Cody, and Prentiss Ingraham.

Angus Ebersole, Clay Hawkins, Ike Peters, Jim Dewey, Billy Taylor, and their newest recruit, Ethan Slayton, stepped down from the very train Falcon and Ingraham heard arriving. Once out of the train, they waited on the depot platform as their horses were off-loaded from the special stock car. Then they led them over to the cart on which baggage was being loaded.

"When our saddles come out, no need to put them on the cart," Ebersole said to the station agent. "We'll take them right here."

"Are you boys here for the tryouts?" the station agent asked.

"Yeah, we thought we might give it a try," Ebersole said.

"Well there's a good bunch of cowboys here to try out," the station agent said. "I know a bunch of 'em myself. So it sure ought to be a good show."

"That's what we was figurin'," Ebersole said. "Is there any place here to keep our horses?"

"Not really. I mean, bein' as we're so small, we don't have no livery here as such. But we do have a barn where they keep the horses for the stagecoaches that take the tourists on down into the park. It's run by a fella named Dempsey. If you tell 'im that Deekus sent you, that's my name, Deekus Smart, well, like as not he'll let you keep your horses there till you're ready for 'em."

It wasn't hard to find the stagecoach depot. It was right across the street from the railroad depot, and it had two coaches standing out front, the teams already in harness, ready to take tourists down into the park.

Leading their now-saddled horses across the street, Ebersole inquired of one of the drivers as to where to find Dempsey.

"That's him over there," the driver said, pointing to a heavyset man who was bald, but sported a bushy beard and equally bushy sideburns.

Ebersole and the others led their horses over to him.

"Would you be Mr. Dempsey?" Ebersole asked.

"I am. What can I do for you?" Dempsey replied.

"We just came in on the train, and Deekus Smart said that if we was to mention your name, you might put up our horses for us."

"He said that, did he?"

"Yes."

Dempsey cut off a chew of tobacco and stuck it in his mouth before he answered. "You know this ain't no livery, don't you? All the horses here are team horses for the stagecoaches."

"Yeah, I know."

"But, Deekus is right. From time to time I will put up a horse for someone."

"Good. We'd like you to keep these for us. Not sure how long we'll be here. Probably no more than today and tomorrow."

"All right. That'll be a dollar a day. Pay me for the first day now. If you stay any longer, come back and make the arrangements."

"A dollar a day?" Ebersole replied. "Damn, that's kind of steep, ain't it, Mister? Liveries don't normally charge more 'n a quarter a day. Some charges half a dollar a day, but I ain't never run across none that charges a dollar a day."

"Well, you don't have to pay it," Dempsey said. "You can always put your horses in a livery."

"I thought there weren't any liveries here," Ebersole said.

Dempsey spat out a quid.

"There ain't none here," he said. "They's one up at Livingston. 'Course, you ain't in Livingstone, are you?"

"All right, a dollar a day," Ebersole agreed, snarling the words to show his displeasure in the arrangement.

"In advance," Dempsey said.

"In advance," Ebersole agreed as all of them dug out a dollar for the payment.

"Where at is the tryout being held?" Hawkins asked.

"Don't you hear all the shoutin'? It's just down the street at the south end of town," Dempsey said. "They've put up bleachers there, you can't miss it. Hell, near 'bout the whole town is there, all you got to do is follow the noise."

Grumbling, the six men turned their horses over to Dempsey, then as he led them back into the stable, they walked down the street toward the crowd.

"Taylor, you and Slayton need to hang back a bit," Ebersole said. "They're sure to recognize you two. I don't think they'll recognize me or Peters or Dewey, or Hawkins, 'cause it was dark the only time he seen us, and we wasn't right up against the train."

Renegade camp of Mean to His Horses

Running Elk and White Bull had been with Mean to His Horses for at least three weeks. In that time, Mean to His Horses had led his warriors out for several raids, but he had not taken Running Elk or White Bull with him. In addition, there were at least twelve others who had joined Mean to His Horses's group who had also not been allowed to go on raids.

Running Elk was willing to wait until they were invited, but White Bull had other ideas.

"We will make our own raid," White Bull said. "We will show Mean to His Horses that we are warriors with courage and honor."

"Do you think that is wise?" Running Elk asked.

"Yes. It will be like it was when we were young and

hunted together," White Bull said. "And when I killed the bear. Do you remember?"

"I remember when you killed the bear."

Running Elk recalled the incident White Bull was talking about. They were young, no more than fourteen summers. It was the last year before Running Elk was selected to go back East to the white man's school.

Running Elk had shot an antelope, and it ran into some trees. He went into the trees after it, and saw where it had fallen. It was still alive, and Running Elk knelt beside it to cut its throat. That was when he heard White Bull calling out to him.

"Running Elk! There is a bear!"

Looking up, Running Elk saw a bear coming toward him. It wasn't a grizzly, it was a black bear, but it was frightening enough. Running Elk had put down his bow when he went after the antelope, so all he had was his knife. Frightened, he knew it would do no good to run, so he stood up and turned toward the bear to face it, with his knife in his hand.

That was when he heard the whizzing sound of an arrow pass only inches from him. The bear had stood up, and the arrow buried itself in the bear's heart, killing him instantly. White Bull had saved Running Elk's life. Even in the difficult days after Running Elk had returned from the school, when the relationship between them had cooled, when they became rivals for the hand of Quiet Stream, Running Elk was aware that he owed his life to White Bull. And it was because of that that their relationship had never gone from being rivals to being enemies.

"Hear me!" White Bull called to the others. "Mean

to His Horses thinks that we are not ready to go with him, but I say we can show him we are ready. I am going now to claim coups against the white man! If you are brave of heart, you will go with me."

"I will go," Jumping Wolf said.

"And I will go," Standing Bear said.

Within moments, everyone had declared their intention to go but Running Elk."

"Running Elk, will you not go with me?" White Bull asked.

Running Elk smiled, and put his hand on White Bull's shoulder. "I will go with you," he said.

Cinnabar

"Hang on there, Tommy! Hang on! You can do it!" someone shouted as the six men walked around the edge of the bleachers. The bleachers were overfilled with spectators and scores were standing on each side of the bleachers, right up to the rope that marked off the riding arena. In the arena a cowboy was trying to stay in the saddle of a bucking horse.

He wasn't able to, and a groan went up from the crowd.

"There they are," Slayton said, pointing to a table that was set up in front of the bleachers.

"You sure that's them?" Ebersole asked.

"The three on the left are," Slayton said. "That's MacCallister and Cody. I don't know the name of the man on the right, but he was with MacCallister and Cody back in Sheridan."

"Slayton is right," Taylor said. "That's MacCallister, Cody, and the other man is a writer named Prentiss

Ingraham. I met all three of 'em while they was takin'
me to jail."

"What do we do now?" Dewey asked. "We can't shoot
them in front of all these people."

"We'll just wait and watch," Ebersole said. "We'll get
our chance."

The tryouts continued for another three hours,
until it began to get too dark. Because this was an im-
promptu arena, there were no lights, neither electric
nor gas, that could provide enough illumination for it
to continue.

Cody got up from the table, stepped out into the
arena and, holding a megaphone in front of his
mouth, made an announcement to the crowd and the
participants.

"Ladies and gents, and all the cowboys who took
part today, this ends the performance."

The crowd applauded.

"I want to thank all of you for coming." He turned
the megaphone toward the group of cowboys who had
participated in the auditions. "Now, if you cowboys will
just wait around for a bit, we'll be calling some of you
up for interviews."

Prentiss Ingraham's notes from his book in progress:

> *The bucking contest was held on the arena in
> front of a specially built grandstand at noon. It
> began just as the last stage rolled out of Cinnabar
> taking tourists to the park, but several tourists
> remained behind for the show and were part of a
> crowd of approximately five hundred spectators.
> Those who were present bore witness to one of the*

*greatest exhibitions of bronco busting this writer has
ever witnessed. In order to give the audition the
greatest show of honesty, Buffalo Bill chose Falcon
MacCallister and this writer as judges of the contest.*

*It was a magnificent exhibition of horses that had
never been ridden trying to throw cowboys who had
never been thrown. The horses leaped and spun,
reared on first their back legs then their front legs,
doing all in their power to get the objectionable weight
off their backs. Oft times they were successful, and
more than one cowboy suffered the ignominy of
finding himself facedown in the dirt as the noble steed
pranced around the ring in victory. But, just as
often, the cowboys succeeded and it was the horse who
found himself humiliated before the large crowd there
gathered. Along in mid-afternoon a funny incident
occurred. A young man, barely out of his teens,
applied for permission to compete. Much younger
than the other participants, he also stood out for his
dress and appearance. He was wearing cowboy boots
and spurs, but no chaps, sombrero or the customary
vest. He asked to ride in the tryouts.*

*Stares, sneers and sniggers were openly directed in
his direction but Buffalo Bill Cody said that the boy
would be permitted to ride. Some of the cowboys, who
were not themselves applicants, selected the wildest of
all the horses from the remuda. A cowboy then held
the wild horse while the young stranger removed his
old and very worn saddle from his own horse, and
transferred it to the wild horse that had been selected
for him.*

*Those in the crowd, consisting mostly of tourists
from the East, were totally unaware of what they were
about to see. They had already seen wonderful*

*exhibition of riding and roping, but they had no idea
that this young man was about to mount the wildest
horse of all. I could tell by the expression in the faces
of some of the cowboys who did know, that they were
now having second thoughts and some, I think,
would have gone out to stop the rider and thus
prevent any injury.*

*With an expression that was set and determined,
the young man climbed aboard.*

*With that the fun was on. With his head to the
ground and back arched like an angry cat's, the wild
cayuse bucked and pitched and sunfished; jumped
straight up and came down twisting and then shook
himself in an effort to get rid of the man on his back,
but it was all for naught.*

*Unable to unseat his rider, the horse broke into a
run down the road. The horse galloped at breakneck
speed, going so far down the road that he
disappeared.*

*"Now we have done it," some of the cowboys said,
and expressions of remorse circulated through the
cowboys as they appeared truly remorseful over the
trick they had pulled on the young rider.*

*Then a great cheer spread through the crowd as the
young man was seen returning, this time riding on a
horse that was trotting and well under control. As the
young man returned to the arena, he leaped down
from the horse on one side, then back on to the horse
and leaped down from the other side, and then back
on again, all to the appreciative roars of the crowd.*

*Finally he rode up to the stand where Falcon
MacCallister, Buffalo Bill, and I were sitting.
Swinging down from the horse he removed his hat
and made a sweeping bow.*

"Sirs, I present you with a fine horse, tamed and eager to serve his master, but not broken, sir. Never broken. His spirit is as great as it has ever been."

"Young man," Buffalo Bill said. "I do not even need a response from the judges, for I make the judgment myself that this is one of the finest rides I have ever seen."

With that announcement, the cowboy who had practiced every spare moment for a year for the event, but who did not have enough money to purchase a cowboy outfit, got the job.

CHAPTER EIGHTEEN

"Look there. MacCallister is leaving," Slayton said. "And he's the son of a bitch I want the most."

"Dewey, you, Slayton, and Taylor follow him. Keep an eye on him and find out where he's going. When you find out, come back and tell us."

"How about we just kill him?" Slayton asked.

"No, don't do anything yet. We're going to do this right, so we have to plan everything all out," Ebersole replied.

"He's going," Taylor said.

"Come on," Slayton said. "I don't intend to let him get away."

After the audition and judging, Buffalo Bill began interviewing several of the participants to see who wanted to join his Wild West Exhibition, and who in fact he wanted to recruit. Prentiss Ingraham was part of the interviewing process, but Falcon had no particular interest in it, so he decided to take a walk through the small town of Cinnabar. He, Buffalo Bill, and Prentiss Ingraham had made arrangements to stay at the Cinnabar Hotel, which was the only hotel in town. The Cinnabar Hotel was run by George Canfield, who was Sherman Canfield's father, and he, like Sherman, was an old friend of Buffalo Bill's.

Nearly every cowboy in Cinnabar, those who had performed well and those who had performed poorly in the tryouts, now seemed bent on getting as drunk as they could. Falcon had no more desire to get drunk than he did to be a part of the interview process, and nothing seemed more unappealing to him than to be around a lot of men who were drinking heavily when he wasn't drinking at all, so he had no problem in avoiding the saloon.

Though he did not go into the saloon, it was nearly impossible to avoid it, as the laughter, shouts, hurrahs, and singing spilled out of the saloon to fill the streets of the little town.

"Hey! Hey! Hey!" a cowboy's loud voice carried over all the others. "Did you boys see me ride that sumbitch? I stayed in that saddle liken as if I was glued to it."

"Well, hell, Connie, that ole' cayuse didn't buck more 'n two or three times!" someone replied.

"Yeah, but on them times when he did buck, I stayed on," Connie insisted, and his reply was met by a lot of a laughter.

"Hey, anyone know the song 'Buffalo Gals'? What do you say we sing 'Buffalo Gals'?"

"The piano player ain't playin' that."

"That don't make no never mind. He can play what he wants and we'll sing what we want."

Discordant singing followed, joined by other singers, but not the piano player who continued with his own tune.

Heart Mountain, Wyoming Territory

At that moment, some one hundred miles away as the crow flies, Sam Davis, Lee Regret, and Sergeant Depro were waiting at Heart Mountain for their rendezvous with Mean to His Horses. The army wagon that Depro had used to transport the guns and ammunition up from Fort Keogh was pushed up into a ravine and covered with sage brush.

"Here they come," Davis said.

"They?" Depro said. "What do you mean, they? I thought we were dealing with just Mean to His Horses."

There's five of them, and each one of them is leading a pack horse," Davis said. "It makes sense when you think about it. There's no way Mean to His Horses could get all those guns back by his ownself."

"I reckon you are right," Depro said. "But I don't like it."

"Bet you'll like spending all that money though," Regret said.

"Yeah, I'll like that just fine," Depro agreed.

"You have guns?" Mean to His Horses asked as he and the other Indians rode up.

"You have gold?" Davis replied.

Mean to His Horses threw down two bags. Davis opened the bags and dumped the contents out on the ground. They were all twenty-dollar gold pieces.

"Good Lord," Regret said. "There must be two hundred of them."

"Give me guns," Mean to His Horses said.

"They are in the wagon," Davis said, pointing to the ravine where the wagon lay, covered with sage.

"You're going to need bullets for them guns, chief," Depro said. "And that's goin' to cost you extry."

"Already I give you more money than you ask," Mean to His Horses said. "I will take bullets too."

"Huh, uh. Not without payin' extry, you ain't," Depro said.

Mean to His Horses was already armed, and he raised his rifle and pointed it at Depro.

"Give me bullets," he said. "Or I will kill you and take the bullets."

"Back off, Depro," Davis shouted. "The chief is right. There is more money here than we asked for."

"All right, all right!" Depro said, holding up his hands. "Take the bullets. Davis is right. I reckon you have already paid for 'em."

All the Indians but Mean to His Horses had already gathered around the wagon and were jabbering excitedly among themselves as they broke open the boxes and began pulling out the guns. They started whooping and hollering and dancing around, holding the rifles over their heads.

"Boys, I think we would be smart to ease on out of here while they are busy with those guns," Davis suggested.

"What about the wagon?" Depro said. "We can't leave it here."

"Why not?"

"It's got army markings on it. Sixth Cavalry markings. If someone finds it here, they can trace it back to me. I ain't leavin' without that wagon."

"Depro, take it from me," Davis said. "If you don't leave without the wagon, you won't leave at all. I think them Injuns mean to kill us."

"Davis is right," Regret said. "We need to get out of here now."

"Yeah," Depro finally agreed. "Yeah, that's probably a pretty good idea."

The three men slipped off quietly, leading their horses until they were some distance away. Then, mounting, they rode off at a gallop.

One hour later, after the three divided the money, Depro started back to where he had left the wagon. It was his intention to burn it so that nobody would ever be able to recognize it and connect it to him. He had just gotten the fire started when two Indians came out of the brush and grabbed him.

Cinnabar

Falcon had not gone far when he realized that he was being followed; but who it was, and for what purpose, he didn't know. He altered his route, leaving the main street and choosing the new route, not only to see if he actually was being followed, but also because he saw ahead of him several open lots. One of the lots was filled with cut logs, preparatory to building a cabin. If he was being followed, this would be good place to confront them.

When Falcon reached the lot where the construction was pending, he stepped off the street and slipped in behind the logs. Pulling his gun, he looked back into the direction from which he had come.

By the light of a full moon and the ambient light of the nearest street lamp, he saw the men who were following him. He could see their forms, but not their faces, so he would have been unable to identify them even if he had known them.

There were three of them, all with drawn pistols. They had come off the main street and were now walking in the same direction Falcon had taken, pausing for a moment to look around. Evidently they had not seen him slip behind the logs and now they were wondering what happened to him.

From the center of the town could still be heard the raucous sounds of cowboys celebrating their selection or lamenting their failure. There were shouts, laughter, and loud conversations, even as the discordant singing continued to do battle with the tinkling of the only piano in town.

"What the hell?" Slayton asked. "Where did he go, Dewey?"

"I don't know, one minute he was right in front of us, the next minute he was gone," Dewey answered. "He just disappeared, like a haint or somethin'."

"MacCallister ain't no haint, I can tell you that," Taylor said. When you and the others left me behind back at the train robbery, I got a chance to see him up real close, remember?"

"Yeah, well, we didn't have no choice, we had to leave you," Dewey replied. "But we come to break you out of jail, so you really ain't got no complaint now, have you?"

"Keep your eyes open. He has to be down here, somewhere," Slayton said.

"Yeah, Slayton, we know he is here somewhere," Dewey said. "We all seen him come this way. The question is, where?"

"Wherever he is, I aim to find him, and I aim to kill the son of a bitch," Slayton said.

"Ebersole said don't kill him yet," Dewey said.

"I don't care what Ebersole said, I say we should kill him. Hell, I should have killed the bastard back in Sheridan when I had the chance."

"Haw," Taylor said. "From what I heard, you didn't have no chance with him back in Sheridan."

"That's 'cause he got the drop on me when I wasn't lookin'," Slayton said. "Well, I'm lookin' now, and I aim to kill 'im."

"I don't know," Taylor said. "Maybe we should go back and get Ebersole, Peters and Hawkins."

"No, I think Slayton is right," Dewey said. "Ebersole and the others is keepin' an eye on Buffalo Bill, and we may not get another chance this good. Besides, there's three of us and only one of MacCallister. Just how damn hard can it be for three people to kill one man?"

"From what I've heard of MacCallister, it ain't goin' to be easy, even with the three of us," Taylor said.

Because he had overheard the conversation, Falcon now knew who was after him. He recognized Taylor's voice and knew that he was the one they had captured after the aborted train robbery. And from Taylor's comment about being left behind, he knew that the other man must have been one of the train robbers who escaped. He recognized Slayton too, from the run in he had with him back in Sheridan. What he did not understand is why Slayton was with the train robbers.

Looking around, Falcon saw a fairly good-sized rock lying on the ground. He picked it up and tossed it toward a rock outcropping. As he hoped it would, it made a loud, chinking sound.

"He's over there, by them rocks!" he heard one of them yell out loud.

"Shoot him! Shoot the son of a bitch!"

All three men began shooting then. The night was illuminated with muzzle flashes as guns roared and bullets screamed as they ricocheted off into the darkness. There were flashes of orange light as the bullets sparked little fireballs when they hit the rocks.

Falcon was well positioned to pick out his targets. The three shooters were clearly visible in the moon's glow, backlit by the street lamp behind them, and illuminated by their own muzzle flashes. They made perfect targets, and Falcon picked one of them off with one shot.

"Damn! He's seen us!"

"Son of a bitch! He ain't by the rocks, he's over there! Kill him! Kill the son of a bitch before he kills us!" the other yelled.

Amazingly, the remaining two attackers made no attempt to find cover or to run away. Instead, they stood their ground and continued to shoot at him.

Falcon shot two more times, and the final two went down.

Then it was quiet, except for the barking of some nearby dogs and the ongoing singing and celebration from Cinnabar's lone saloon. A billowing cloud of gun smoke drifted up over the deadly battlefield and Falcon walked out among the fallen assailants, moving cautiously, his pistol at the ready.

He needn't have been so cautious. All three men were dead.

By now the insistent singing of the cowboys had won

over the piano player and the piano joined them as more began to sing, the words and celebratory music incongruent with the scene that had just played out in this open lot, could be heard all over the little town.

> *Buffalo Gals won't you come out tonight,*
> *Come out tonight, come out tonight?*
> *Buffalo Gals won't you come out tonight*
> *And dance by the light of the moon?*

CHAPTER NINETEEN

Leaving the empty lot, Falcon went to get George and Sherman Canfield, Bill Cody, and Prentiss Ingraham so he could bring them back to the scene of the shooting. George Sherman was carrying a lantern and he held it down low, enabling them to see the faces of the three men Falcon had shot.

"Do you know them, Falcon?"

"I can't say as I know them," Falcon said. "But I know the names of two of them." He pointed. "That one is Billy Taylor. Last time we saw him, he was in jail back in Bismarck."

"And this fella is named Slayton," Ingraham said. "Last time we saw him, he was in Sheridan."

"I wonder how Taylor got out of jail," Cody said.

"From what I overheard, this man is one of the ones who attempted to hold up the train," Falcon answered, pointing to Dewey's body. "And they broke Taylor out of jail."

"*They* broke him out?" Cody asked, emphasizing the word "they."

"Yes."

"That means the rest of them might be here."

"That's what I'm thinking," Falcon said.

"Seems strange that Slayton was with them though," Ingraham said. "I mean, how do you suppose that came about?"

"My guess is they were looking for us, and when they came through Sheridan they recruited Slayton," Falcon said.

"Yes, I can see that," Cody said. "It's for sure that Slayton had ill feelings toward you."

"What will we do with them?" Ingraham asked.

"We could strap them to a board, stand 'em up in front of the hotel with a sign asking if anyone knew who they were," Sherman suggested.

"Heavens no, Sherman," George said. "Most of the people who come through here are from back East. Something like this would scare them off for sure. If you ask me, the best thing to do would be to just let Marv Welch bury them. It won't be the first time he ever buried someone without knowing who they are."

Within an hour after the shooting, everyone in Cinnabar, at least those who were still awake, knew what had happened.

The bodies were not embalmed, so the idea was to get them buried as quickly as possible. Because of that, Marv Welch began preparations right away. Welch was not a real undertaker; he was a carpenter, and he had assumed the position of undertaker only because he was able to construct simple wooden coffins. And even though the bodies were not strapped to a board and stood up in front of the hotel as Sherman had suggested, that didn't mean that they were not objects of attention. Morbid curiosity caused two score and more people to come out of the night and wander through Marv Welch's carpentry shop to view the bodies. Marv, who had three coffins to build, paid no attention to his nighttime visitors.

Not only did Welch not embalm the bodies, he made no effort to clean them up in any way, so those who came to view them saw them just as they fell, bloodied from their bullet wounds and smudged with dirt from the ground where they fell.

It made a rather macabre scene: visitors strolling through the carpenter shop to view the bodies while the flickering kerosene lanterns cast disproportionately large and grotesque shadows against the wall, giving the illusion of otherworldly wraiths come to earth to welcome their new residents. All the while the visitors arrived and departed, Marv Welch continued to saw and hammer together the three traditionally shaped coffins, flared at the top to accommodate the shoulders and torso, then narrowed toward the bottom for the legs.

Three of the viewers who came through were Ebersole, Hawkins, and Peters.

"MacCallister kilt 'em," Hawkins said once they went back outside into the night. "He kilt all three of 'em."

"How did he do that?" Peters asked.

"He shot 'em," Hawkins said.

"I know that. What I mean is, how could one man kill all three of them like that? Taylor and Dewey weren't no slouches with a gun. And Slayton was supposed to be pretty good."

"Ahh. Slayton was probably pretty much of a loud mouth," Ebersole said. "I wouldn't have brought him at all, except for the horses."

"Still, MacCallister must be awful good to have kilt all three of them, though," Peters said.

"I'll tell you how he did it," Ebersole said. "He did it because the damn fools didn't listen to me. I told them just to keep an eye on 'em, until we could come up with a plan."

"Yeah, well, what plan can we come up with now?" Peters asked. "I mean if MacCallister kilt all three of 'em, and he's only one man, what are we goin' to do now? There's only three of us and when you count Cody and that writer, that makes three of them. I would like it a lot better iffen the odds was on our side."

"Just because someone has a reputation, that doesn't mean he is invincible," Ebersole said. "Look at Wild Bill Hickok. They say he was about the deadliest gunfighter of all of 'em, and how many men did it take to kill him? Just one."

"Yeah, just one, but from what I heard, the fella that kilt him snuck up on him while he was playin' cards and shot him in the back."

"Front, back, it don't matter. The point I'm making is, Hickok is still dead, ain't he?" Ebersole said.

"So, what you're sayin' is, wait until MacCallister is playin' cards then sneak up behind him?" Hawkins asked.

"No. What I'm sayin' is, wait until the son of a bitch goes to sleep, then sneak up on him," Ebersole said. "He's spending the night in the Cinnabar Hotel. All we got to do is find out which room it is."

"How are we going to do that?" Hawkins asked.

"I'm going to register at the hotel," Ebersole said. "When I sign the register book, I'll be able to see which room he's in."

* * *

After the bodies of the three men who had tried to kill him were removed, Falcon returned to the hotel. He was always somewhat ill at ease after killing someone, even if they had been trying to kill him. And though it wasn't something he had ever expressed in words, he knew that he never wanted to get over that sense of unease. If it ever got to the point to where killing another human being came as easy to him as stepping on a bug, he would know that he had lost his soul.

When he went to his room he walked over to look out the window. From here he had a good view of the main street. The street, scarred with wagon ruts and dotted with horse droppings, formed an X with the track. The railroad station was halfway down the street but the train had already gone back to Livingston. It would return in mid-morning the next day with another batch of Yellowstone visitors.

On the far side of the track he saw a scattering of buildings, fashioned from log and rip-sawed lumber. On this side of the track the buildings were all commercial so they were somewhat more substantial. Some had false fronts, and a few were even painted. Right across the street from the hotel was the livery stable. Below him and next door to the hotel was the saloon. Because it was nearly midnight, the saloon was much quieter, not because the cowboys were concerned about disturbing anyone's slumber, but because so many of them were now passed out drunk.

This would be the first night Falcon had spent in a bed in over a week, and he was rather looking forward to it. Walking over to his bed he hung his pistol belt on the headboard, loosed the revolver in its holster, then extinguished the lantern. He was asleep within a few minutes.

By two o'clock in the morning, all the celebration was over. The cowboys who had been serenading the town most of the night were now either passed out drunk or sound asleep, wherever they had been able to throw down their bedrolls.

As he had explained to the others, Ebersole was able to ascertain which room Falcon was in simply by looking at the register when he signed in. Now, Ebersole, Peters, and Hawkins were standing in the lobby of the hotel. It was dark except for one dimly glowing kerosene lantern that was attached to the wall just over the check-in desk. The hotel clerk was sound asleep, and the air was rent by his loud snoring.

Every room in the hotel was rented, as evidenced by the fact that only one key was hanging from each of the hooks which designated a room. Ebersole leaned over the desk, and quietly lifted the key from the hook for room number five.

"All right, you two, you need to be very quiet now," he whispered. He pulled his pistol from the holster and the others did the same; then, as quietly as possible, the sound of their steps softened by the carpet, they started up the stairs to the second floor.

If anyone had asked Falcon what awakened him from a sound sleep, he probably would not have been able to explain it. He knew only that, in the midst of a deep slumber, a sudden feeling of danger passed over him, a feeling so strong that even as he was awakening, he was slipping his pistol from its holster.

The full moon that had served him well in the empty lot earlier in the night was now in position to send a splash of silver in through the open window. It was that, and the fact that because he had been sleeping, his eyes were accustomed to the dark, that he could see the door.

Falcon did not stare directly at the door but looked slightly to the left of it. If asked, he could not tell anyone the scientific reason for it, he knew nothing about visual purple, or that the *fovea centralis* in the exact center of the retina stops functioning in darkness. Only the rods in the peripheral field of the retina function in darkness, which meant that in order to see in the night, one must use the peripheral field of vision.

He did not need to know the scientific or physiological reason for this, nor had anyone ever told him about it. It was a trick he had discovered on his own, many years ago. It had served him well many times, and it was serving him well now, because even as he heard the tumblers in the lock fall, he could see the doorknob turning, slightly.

With gun in hand, Falcon slid out of bed, then moved quickly across the room to stand in the far corner opposite of the bed. The door swung open.

"Now!" a voice shouted, and three pistols began firing through the doorway, the noise deafening, the muzzle flashes, like successive streaks of lightning, illuminating the room. The intruders fired several shots at the bed, then stopped.

"Can I help you boys with something?" Falcon asked.

"What? What the hell?" a voice called.

"He's over there!"

Actually, Falcon wasn't "over there," because as soon as he spoke, he dropped to his knees and crawled quickly back over to his bed.

Again the pistols fired through the door, this time into the corner where Falcon had been. And this time Falcon returned fire, using the flame patterns from the muzzle flashes as his target. When he stopped firing, all was silent, except for a quiet moaning.

Even before Falcon could light his own lantern, he saw a light moving down the hall way toward his room.

"Falcon! Falcon, are you all right?" he heard Bill Cody call.

"Yeah," Falcon called back. "I'm all right."

By now, other guests in the hotel were coming down the hall as well.

"Who are you?" Falcon recognized Ingraham's voice. "Who are you? Are you connected with the other three men who tried to kill Mr. MacCallister?"

"I told Ebersole it was a dumb idea," a pain-filled voice said. "When you run us off from the train robbery, we should have . . ." that was as far as he got.

"Oh," a woman said. "My goodness! Is it always like this out here? George, I want to go home. I want to go back to Baltimore."

"We just arrived today. We haven't even seen the park yet," George replied.

"I don't care. I had no idea the West was this wild. Why, we could have been killed in our beds."

"You were never in any danger, madam," Ingraham said.

"How do you know?"

"Because these men weren't after you."

"Who shot them?"

"I did, ma'am," Falcon said. By now he had pulled on a pair of trousers and was standing just inside the door of his room.

"Heavens! You shot all three of them?"

"Yes, ma'am."

"But, why?"

"It seemed to be the thing to do at the time," Falcon said.

CHAPTER TWENTY

Rocking B Ranch

Oliver Bowman owned the Rocking B Ranch. His nearest neighbor and close friend, Doyle Clayton, owned the Lazy C. They were small ranchers, but their ranches were productive, and this year, between them, they would be taking over five hundred cows to market. In order to market them, they were going to have to drive them north to the rail head at Livingston, Montana Territory.

To that end, Doyle Clayton and his wife had been invited over to the Bowmans for supper. They enjoyed a good meal, then the Claytons' six-year-old daughter Diane and the Bowmans' eight-year-old son Clyde went into another room to play while the adults remained at the table and talked over coffee.

"We can put our cowboys together," Bowman said, "and they should be able to handle the drive all right. But I'm thinking that perhaps you and I should go on ahead to scout the best route."

"There's only one route, Oliver, and that's to follow the Yellowstone River," Clayton said.

"That's what I'm thinking, but I would like to check it out. Also, we'll need to make reservations at the rail head up in Livingston."

"You are probably right. So, when do you want to go?"

"I was thinking first light, day after tomorrow," Bowman said.

"I'll be here."

"Oh, Doyle, Oliver, you two be very careful," Mrs. Clayton said. "I just don't like it that the Indians have gotten so bold of late."

"Everyone agrees that it's nothing more than a handful of renegades," Clayton said. "This is a big country, the odds of us running into any of them are pretty small."

"Especially since we won't have the cattle with us the first time. Indians only attack when they want something. With just the two of us, it's not likely we will have anything they want," Bowman added.

"Oliver, you have a Winchester, don't you?" Clayton asked.

"Yeah, I do."

"Tell you what, if it will make the ladies feel any better, we'll both take our Winchesters, in addition to our pistols," Clayton said.

"Good idea. I'll also bring along an extra box of bullets."

"Why is that supposed to make me feel better?" Mrs. Clayton said. "If you think you have to carry extra guns, that means you are worried too."

"No, dear. It just means we are being careful," Clayton said.

Cinnabar, the next day

There was a telephone in the Cinnabar Hotel, so on the morning after the shooting a call was put through to the sheriff and circuit judge in Livingston. They came down to Cinnabar on the morning train to hold a hearing into the shooting incidents in which Falcon had been involved.

There were eyewitnesses to the shooting in the hotel, so it was easy to establish that the gunman had attacked Falcon. And, though there were no eyewitnesses to the shooting in the empty lot, the sheriff and the judge listened to Falcon, Cody, and Ingraham tell about the train robbery and the incident with Slayton in Sheridan. In addition, a telegram from the city marshal in Bismarck told of Taylor being broken out of jail. Another telegram from the city marshal in Sheridan told of six horses being stolen, with Slayton as the principal suspect. By extrapolation, the judge declared the shootings to be justifiable, and no charges were brought against Falcon.

Later that same morning, Ingraham made another entry in his book.

Prentiss Ingraham's notes from his book in progress:

> *The reader may well remember the names of Ethan Slayton and Billy Taylor, desperadoes whom Falcon MacCallister had encountered upon previous occasions. The third name, Jim Dewey, may be new to the readers, but the brigand himself is not new, for he was one of those whose nefarious scheme to rob the Northern Pacific Railroad met with disaster at the*

*hands of the aforementioned Falcon MacCallister and
Buffalo Bill.*

*One can only wonder what motivates such men to
commit acts of such brazen wantonness as were
perpetrated by these three men when they made their
ill-advised attempt to murder Falcon. Encountering
MacCallister in an empty lot in Cinnabar on the very
night of celebrating the auditions for the Buffalo Bill
Cody Wild West Exhibition, Dewey, Slayton, and
Taylor discharged their pistols toward him repeatedly,
but with no effect. Falcon MacCallister fired but three
shots in reply, all balls finding their targets with
devastating results.*

*But the night of danger was not yet ended for the
brave and stalwart Falcon MacCallister, for even as
he lay in peaceful slumber in his hotel room, Angus
Ebersole, Clay Hawkins, and Ike Peters made plans
to ply their murderous intentions against him. Their
motivation, no doubt, was that they held Falcon
MacCallister responsible for the failure of their plot
and the justifiable killing of their friends.*

*Like the most loathsome of vermin who prowl
under cover of darkness, the three men acquired the key
to Falcon MacCallister's room, and brazenly attempted
to kill him in his sleep. Their attempt, as had been the
earlier attempt of their partners in crime, failed, and
with disastrous consequences for the perpetrators. Once
again, the gallant Mr. MacCallister avoided death.
Instead, he dispatched those who would have killed
him to the final adjudication of He whose final
judgment we all await.*

*This writer feels a particular sense of gratitude to
Mr. MacCallister, for no doubt had the brigands
succeeded, they would then have turned their*

murderous intentions toward Buffalo Bill Cody and your humble scribe, as we were also participants in their failed attempt to rob the train upon which we were passengers.

Falcon MacCallister's killing of the outlaws was warranted and he was totally exonerated by a legal hearing held by the sheriff and circuit judge.

Ingraham had just finished his notes when Cody knocked on his door. "You still asleep in there?" Cody called.

Ingraham got up from the table and jerked open the door. "Not at all," he said. "I was just making some notes."

"More entries in your great American novel?"

"I'll have you know, sir, that it is not a novel," Ingraham said. "It is a scholarly work of nonfiction."

"Is it now? Well, if you want to continue your scholarly work of nonfiction, you'd best get moving. Falcon is seeing to our horses. We are going back a different way."

"Not back through Yellowstone?"

"No. We're going through Dead Indian Pass, and will join the Yellowstone River back in Wyoming."

"Sounds interesting," Ingraham said.

With Bowman and Clayton

It took Bowman and Clayton half a day to reach the Yellowstone River from their respective ranches. The ride had not been difficult, and was even easier once they reached the river. Here, they had an abundant source of water, and because of the river, there was an abundant source of forage for the cattle.

They caught a couple of trout and cooked them over an open fire. That night they had roasted rabbit. They could have eaten elk; there were plenty to be taken, but as there were only two of them, they didn't want to waste the rest of the meat that they wouldn't be able to eat or store.

"I hope I'm not speaking too early," Clayton said as they bedded down for the night. "But seems to me like this drive is likely to be pretty easy."

"Yeah, I'm thinking the same thing," Bowman said. "But, just to be safe, let's extinguish the fire. No sense in leaving a beacon for anyone."

With the White Bull raiding party, the next day

White Bull gave the reins of his pony to Running Elk, and then climbed to the top of the hill. He knew the warrior's secret of lying down behind the crest of the hill so that he couldn't be seen against the skyline, so he lay on his stomach, then sneaked up to the top and peered over. There, on the valley floor below him, he saw two white men. It was obvious that the whites had no idea they were in danger. It would be easy to count coups against them. He smiled, then slithered back down the hill into the ravine where Running Elk and the others were waiting.

"Did you see them?" Running Elk asked.

"Yes," White Bull answered.

"How many are there?"

"There are two white men."

"Only two? But we are thirteen," Running Elk said. "Where is the honor in thirteen attacking two?"

"Where is the honor in the whites killing Many Buffalo and One Feather? Where is the honor in attacking White Deer and Quiet Stream and White Deer's children?" White Bull replied. "Have you forgotten how the blood ran hot in your veins?"

"No, I have not forgotten."

"We will claim coups on these white men, then we will show Mean to His Horses that the Crow can be as good warriors as the Cheyenne."

"When do you attack?" One of the others asked. He was Face in the Wind, a Shoshone. Standing Bear and Jumping Wolf were also present.

"Now," White Bull replied. He pointed down the ravine. "We will follow the ravine around the side of the hill. We will attack them before they suspect our presence."

Doyle Clayton and Oliver Bowman had gotten an early start this morning and were well into their trip when Clayton saw a substantial group of Indians coming toward them from the east.

"Look over there, Oliver," Clayton said. "What do you think that is all about?"

"I don't know, but there are too many of them to suit me. I think we should get out of here," Bowman answered.

The two ranchers urged their horses into a gallop, keeping it up for at least two miles until they came into the breaks of the Yellowstone River. There they dismounted, pulled their rifles from the saddle-sheaths, then slapped their horses to keep them running, hoping that would draw off the Indians. Finding a spot in the sand dunes next to the river, they hunkered down to wait for the Indians. The Indians poured over the bluffs, then crossed over the sand dunes so that the two ranchers were surrounded. Bowman and Clayton had cover from the front, but no cover behind except for the river.

One of the Indians tried to sneak up from the river, but Clayton shot him. For the rest of the day, the cattlemen and the Indians exchanged shots, though Clayton's response was measured to preserve ammunition. They warned each other not to waste a bullet until they had a good, clear target.

The two were well-positioned, and for the first hour or so they were able to hold the Indians off, killing no fewer than four of them. Finally, the Indians quit trying to advance on them, but stood off and fired arrows from over a hundred yards away, launching them high into the air so they would rain down on the other side of the dunes.

Clayton was hit in the arm, and again in the side. Bowman pulled both of the arrows out.

"Damn," Clayton said, grunting with pain. "Those things go in easier than they come out."

"I know, but we can't leave 'em in or they'll start festerin', and the next thing you know you'll have gangrene," Bowman said.

Bowman was bandaging Clayton's arm when one Indian came over the top of the dune to claim coups. Clayton was lying on the ground, and even though his left arm was being bandaged he was holding his pistol in his right hand. When the Indian appeared over the top of the dune, Clayton raised his pistol and shot him at point-blank range. After that, no other Indian tried to breach their defense.

That night Clayton developed a fever. "I'm going to die," he said.

"No you ain't."

"Yes, I am. I'm goin' to die, so here's what I want you to do. I want you to leave me here. It's nighttime so I think you can get away."

"I ain't leavin' you here by yourself."

"Leave, damnit!" Clayton said. "Don't you understand? You are our only chance. If you can get away, you can bring help back."

Bowman thought for a moment, then he nodded his head. "All right," he said. "I'll go. But I'll be back." Bowman handed his rifle and a handful of .44-.40 cartridges to Clayton.

"You take my rifle and bullets, I'll just keep my pistol."

"All right, if they come after me, I'll take out as many as I can before they get me," Clayton said.

Even though it was relatively cool, Bowman stripped down to his underwear, thinking that if he stayed in the river he would be less likely to encounter an Indian. But shortly after he left, he encountered a mounted Indian riding down the middle of the river. He moved over to stay as close to the bank as he could.

Bowman stayed in the river, continuing downstream until daybreak. Then, cold and barefooted, he started south across the rocks, cactus, and sage.

"I think they are both dead," Jumping Wolf said.

"I think they are not dead," White Bull replied.

"I am going to see. If they are dead, I will count first coups."

"I think we should wait until first light," Running Elk said.

"I think Running Elk is a coward, afraid to see if the white men are dead," Jumping Wolf said.

"I am not a coward, I am pragmatic," Running Elk said, saying the word "pragmatic" in English. It was a word he learned in the white man's school, and he thought it fit this situation perfectly.

"What is pragmatic?" Jumping Wolf asked. He had trouble pronouncing the word.

"It means I have good sense," Running Elk replied.

"I think it means you are a coward," Jumping Wolf said.

Running Elk stood and drew his knife. "I will show you who is a coward," he said.

Jumping Wolf held out his hand. "I do not want to fight you now. Now I will claim coups on the white men. When I return, I will fight you."

"You will not return," Running Elk said.

Clayton was trying to stay awake but he kept dozing off. Each time he would doze off he would dream, and in one of his dreams he was talking to Diane, his six-year-old daughter. She was showing him the new dress her mother had made for her doll.

"That is a very nice dress," Clayton said.

"It is the prettiest dress, so I put it on my favorite doll," Diane said.

"Yes, I think that is the one I would put it on too."

"You had better wake up now, Daddy, because there is an Indian coming."

Clayton opened his eyes just in time to see an Indian kneeling over him, with his war club raised.

"Ahhh!" Clayton shouted, and, raising his pistol, he

242 *William W. Johnstone*

shot the Indian in the head. The Indian fell across him, dead.

It was a struggle to get out from under the Indian's body, but he managed to do so, then he lay there, breathing hard, feeling his heart pounding in his chest.

He vowed not to go back to sleep.

With the White Bull raiding party

Jumping Wolf did not come back. Running Elk, White Bull, and the others had heard the shot in the middle of the night, and because Jumping Wolf had carried only a war club with him, they suspected that he had been seen.

White Bull had left their encampment with Running Elk and eleven others. But in the time they had been here, they knew for sure that four of their number had been killed, and now they believed that Jumping Wolf had been killed as well.

"Perhaps he claimed coups, then left," Face in the Wind suggested.

"Why would he do that? Would he not want to return and brag of his coups?" Standing Bear asked.

"Yes, and did he not challenge Running Elk to a fight?" Red Eagle asked.

"Perhaps he is afraid of Running Elk," Face in the Wind said.

"No," Running Elk said. "Jumping Wolf was a brave warrior. I do not think he feared me. But I think he is dead. I think the white men killed him."

CHAPTER TWENTY-ONE

When Falcon, Cody, and Ingraham left Cinnabar, they went across the top of the park, then cut south, crossing the Montana border back in to Wyoming Territory. From the lofty heights of Dead Indian pass it was as if they were on top of the world. They could see far down into the valley where the Yellowstone River snaked its way through, and they had a wonderful view of the surrounding mountains, range after range.

"You know, I write my Western novels about this land, but I've never really seen it," Ingraham said. "The scenery here is magnificent. I love the way the light and shadows play upon the mountains, and down in the valleys. We don't have anything like this down in Mississippi, I can tell you that for sure."

"Look at Falcon," Cody said. "He is as at home here as a mountain goat."

"Kind of hard to breathe up here though. I'm getting winded," Ingraham said.

"That's because you have those little Mississippi lungs," Cody said. "You see how big Falcon's chest is?

That's because it is all lung. He has no heart, no liver, nothing in there but one big lung."

Ingraham laughed. "Cody, after that tall tale about the mountain of telescopic glass you told the other day, and this wild tale, you have definitely missed your calling. You should give up show business and become a full-time writer," Ingraham said.

"The Life of Honorable William F. Cody, the famous hunter, scout, and guide known as Buffalo Bill, by William F. Cody," Cody said. "How does that sound?"

"Everyone in America will want to read it, of that I am sure," Ingraham said.

"Hmm, I just may give that a thought," Cody replied.

They continued their banter for several more minutes, then Falcon held up his hand.

"Hold it," he said.

"What do you see?"

"Look, down there. Alongside the river."

"Is it an Indian?" Ingraham asked.

"No, it's a white man."

"What are those clothes he's wearing?"

"Long johns," Falcon said. "He's wearing nothing but his underwear."

Falcon slapped his legs against the side of his horse, urging it into a lope, and the other two followed.

"I think I know that man," Cody said as they drew closer to the strange figure.

When they reached Oliver Bowman, they saw that Falcon was right. He was half-naked and barefoot. In addition, his eyes were bloodshot, and his swollen feet were leaving bloody footprints in the sand.

"Oliver? Is that you?" Cody asked.

"Hello, Buffalo Bill. Fancy meeting you here," Bowman said, just before he passed out.

By the time Bowman regained consciousness, Falcon had already started a fire and brewed some coffee. He gave Bowman a cup, and Bowman drank it down greedily, not caring that it was so hot that it burned his lips.

"You wouldn't have anything to eat, would you?" Bowman asked.

"Some elk jerky," Falcon said, offering him a piece.

Between deep swallows of coffee, Bowman wolfed down the jerky. "I'm mighty obliged to you," he said. "Sorry to be puttin' you folks out like this."

"Nonsense, you aren't putting us out," Ingraham said.

"It's nice of you to say so."

"Oliver, what are you doing out here like this?" Cody asked.

"You mean with purt' nigh no clothes on? I thought if I had to swim it would be easier if I didn't have my clothes." He looked at his hand. "I thought I had my pistol with me. Did you see a pistol?"

"You were unarmed when we saw you," Cody said.

"Oh, yeah, I reckon I was," Bowman said. "I left my pistol with Doyle Clayton. Or, was it my rifle? I don't remember now. All I remember are the Injuns."

"Indians?" Falcon asked.

Suddenly Bowman seemed to come out of his stupor.

"My God! Injuns!" he said. "We was attacked by Injuns yesterday, me and Doyle was! He's still up there, if he's alive. He's been shot, I know that."

"Where is he?" Cody asked.

"I don't know for sure, he's upriver, that's all I know. Maybe ten or twenty miles or so."

"We'll find him," Falcon said.

"Ingraham, Mr. Bowman doesn't live too far from here," Cody said. "How about you take him home?"

"I thought I might come with you two," Ingraham said.

"And just leave Mr. Bowman here?"

"Oh, yeah, I guess you are right."

Bowman began shivering then, from the cold.

"Here, Mr. Bowman," Ingraham said, taking a blanket from his saddle roll. "Wrap yourself in this, then climb on to the horse behind me. How far is it to your place?"

"Ten, maybe twelve miles," Bowman answered through chattering teeth.

"Climb up behind me, keep the blanket wrapped around you, and hold on," Ingraham said. "I'll get you safely home."

"I think we should return," Running Elk said. "Already we have lost nearly half our number."

"You may return if you wish," White Bull said. "But I will stay until I have claimed coups."

"They are but two men," Running Elk said. "Where is the honor in killing but two men? Especially as they have already killed so many of us."

"That is all the more reason we should kill them," White Bull said. "There is honor in killing enemy. It matters not how many there may be."

Although Running Elk was opposed to it, he knew that he could not abandon White Bull without violating a lifelong friendship, and he could not leave the fight without losing face, so he stayed. But now it had been two days, and the white men were well armed and well dug-in alongside the river, so, despite their many efforts, they had been unable to defeat them.

Jumping Bear and the others grew frustrated and a few suggested that perhaps White Bull was not the leader for them. White Bull challenged any other to take his place if they could, but none accepted the challenge. Running Elk felt honor-bound to defend White Bull's position, so he let the others know that he would continue to follow White Bull. But he knew that if the fight went on for one more night and day that the other Indians would leave, and if that happened, White Bull, and by extension he as well, would be disgraced and dishonored.

White Bull began shooting toward sand dunes where the white men were. Running Elk and the others joined in the shooting.

As Falcon and Cody approached the spot in the river where Bowman told them Clayton would be, they heard shooting from ahead. The Indians, as Bowman had explained, were located on the east side of the Yellowstone, so Falcon and Cody crossed over to the west side as they continued their approach.

In this they were lucky, for there was a long, high ridge that ran along the west side of the river, shielding their approach. They rode as close as they could get, then they dismounted, and securing their horses, continued on foot. When they heard one of the bullets whizzing just overhead, they knew that they must be even with Clayton, so they crawled up to the top of the ridgeline and looked across the river.

There they saw Clayton. They saw too that he was badly wounded, and was moving with great difficulty in order to return fire. He was no longer aiming his shots, but merely shooting to let the Indians know that he was still alive.

"Clayton!" Falcon called.

Clayton looked around, as if not certain he had heard his name called.

"Clayton!" Falcon called again. "We are over here, across the river."

"Thank God you have come!" Clayton said. He tried to get up.

"No! Stay there! We will come to you!" Falcon shouted.

Clayton got back down as instructed, and Falcon and Cody climbed over the ridge, then ran across the river to join him. The river was deeper than they thought, coming all the way up to their armpits, so it slowed them considerably, but they made it across without incident.

"Bill Cody, what are you doing here?" Clayton said. "I thought you were in New York."

"I was," Cody answered. "But Mr. Bowman told me you were in trouble, so I asked my friend here to come along, and here we are."

"From New York?"

"Sure, why not?" Cody said, laughing, and trying to make Clayton feel better.

"Well, wherever you came from, I'm damn glad to see you," Clayton said. "These Injuns have been givin' me hell."

"Looks to me like you gave that one hell," Falcon said, pointing to a dead Indian who was lying over to one side.

"Yeah, he sneaked in last night," Clayton said. "I

guess he figured I was asleep and he could bash my head in."

"There are a couple more out there," Cody said. "I'd say you have put up a pretty good defense."

"Yeah, well, between Bowman and me, I'm purt' sure we've kilt at least four or five of 'em. Oh, that reminds me, Bowman! He's out there somewhere."

"Bowman is safe," Falcon said. "He is the one who found us."

"Good for him," Clayton said. He looked at Falcon. "I don't reckon I know you. Who are you?"

"The name is MacCallister. Falcon MacCallister."

"Damn! I've heard of you," Clayton said. Despite his wounds, he was able to muster a chuckle. "I reckon if I can't get the United States Cavalry out here to rescue me, gettin' Buffalo Bill Cody and Falcon MacCallister would be the next best thing. Maybe even better."

"Let's see what we've got here," Falcon said, easing up to the top of the dune where Clayton had taken shelter. Looking out across an open area, he saw a line of Indians, and he counted eight.

"I see eight," Falcon said. "How many are there?"

"I expect that's about all that's left," Clayton said. He wriggled up the dune so he could peer over it with Falcon, then he pointed. Do you see that fella there? The one wearing the buffalo horns?"

"I see him."

"I don't know his name, but he seems to be the leader of them. But now, here's the funny thing. He and one of the others are dressed like Crow. This here fella is Shoshone." He pointed to the Indian who had tried to sneak up on him last night. "And I know that some of 'em are Cheyenne. What are the Crow and Shoshone doin' fightin' with Cheyenne? And agin' us?

I thought we was friendly with the Crow and the Shoshone."

"It is a curious thing," Falcon said. He cocked his rifle and aimed it at the Indian who was wearing the buffalo horns.

"You can't hit him from here," Clayton said. "And that Injun knows it. He's been struttin' back and forth out there all day, just rubbin' it in that he's out of range."

Falcon's answer was to squeeze the trigger of his rifle. The rifle boomed and the recoil kicked his shoulder back. The Indian stiffened, then one arm went up as he fell from his horse. The rest of the Indians, seeing their leader fall, turned and galloped back into the trees.

"Damn!" Clayton said in admiration. "That was one hell of a shot."

"Let's get you home," Falcon said.

When the other Indians fled, Running Elk waited. He watched as the white men left, seeing that one of the horses was carrying two men. He was sure there had only been two men when the battle started. Someone else must have joined them during the night. That meant that there had never been more than three men against them. Three white men against thirteen Indians, yet the white men had prevailed. This was not a good sign.

When Running Elk was certain the three white men were well gone, he went out to check on White Bull. As he expected, White Bull was dead. Running Bull constructed a travois, then put White Bull's body on it. He was taking his childhood friend and recent rival home.

* * *

Running Elk traveled for the rest of the day, then camped out that night. It seemed strange, lying on the ground sleeping beside White Bull's body. Once, when they were children, they watched as an old man of the tribe was dressed in his finest clothes, then elevated onto a burial platform.

"Where do you think he is now?" Running Elk asked.

"He is in the great beyond, where hunting is always good and there is always feasting," White Bull had replied.

Running Elk had always found the Happy Hunting Ground to be a comforting thought for those who died. But, when he went to the white man's school, he was told there was no such thing as a Happy Hunting Ground. He was told that only if one followed the white man's Jesus, could one be saved, though he never quite understood what it meant to be saved.

When Running Elk rode into the Crow Village the next day many came to see who was being pulled behind him on the travois. White Bull's mother saw him, and began weeping, as did his sister and even Quiet Stream.

"Were you with Mean to His Horses?" High Hawk asked.

"No," Running Elk replied. "Mean to His Horses would not take us with him. So White Bull led a raiding party, and was killed."

When he saw White Bull's mother put her hand on White Bull's face, he wanted to comfort her.

"White Bull died very bravely," he said.

Brown Cow Woman shook her head as she continued to weep. "I do not care that he died bravely," she said. "I did not want him to go. I feared when he left that this would happen."

"Are you going back to join Mean to His Horses?" Quiet Stream asked. "Did you come back, only to return White Bull's body?"

"I am not going back," Running Elk said. "I was wrong to leave. I will stay here, with my people, in peace."

William W. Johnstone

said, "I did not want him to go. I feared when he left
pen.

ing back to join Mesin to His Horses."

CHAPTER TWENTY-TWO

Major Frederic Benteen held up his arm to signal
a halt. "Battalion!" he called.

"Troop!" the troop commanders sang out, issuing
their supplementary commands.

"Halt!"

The battalion, riding in columns of twos, came
to a halt.

"Dismount! Trumpeter, sound Officers' Call and
First Sergeant's call."

The trumpeter blew the calls, first for officers, then
for the first sergeants.

Benteen and two troops of the Ninth Cavalry had
come up from Fort Keogh, reaching the Greybull River
without seeing any hostile Indians. The guideon-bearer
planted the unit colors and stood by them to keep the
wind from blowing them down. Benteen filled his pipe
and had just lit it when Captain Pope and Lieutenant
Bond, acting Sergeant Major Coletrain, and the two
first sergeants responded to the bugle call.

"I think we will bivouac here for the night," Benteen

said. Troop commanders, get your sentries posted. First sergeants, see that the horses are cared for."

"Yes, sir," all responded.

"Return to your companies. Sergeant Major, you remain," Benteen said.

Benteen watched as the troop commanders and first sergeants returned to their units. He puffed on his pipe for a long moment before speaking and Coletrain stood by in silence.

Not until the men started unsaddling their horses and getting out their shelter-halves did he speak.

"Sergeant Major, I understand you were at Willow Springs."

"Yes, sir, I was," Coletrain replied.

"Tell me about it."

"Not much to tell, Major," Coletrain said. "There were thirty of us. We were well mounted and armed, but Sergeant Winston and I were the only two veterans. I was a corporal then. The rest were all raw recruits, and we were taking them to Fort Shaw for training. We had just stopped for lunch when we were attacked by sixty to seventy Lakota.

"With the opening shots, ten of the recruits threw down their weapons and ran." Coletrain was silent for a moment. "It was such a damn fool thing for them to do. The Indians had sport with them, running them down easily, then clubbing them or running them through with lances.

"The rest of the men stayed, whether because they knew it was the right thing to do, or because they saw what happened to the ones who ran, I don't know. But they stayed, and we formed a circle. Some of the men, despite being raw recruits, were pretty good shots, and we held the Indians off for the rest of the day, though we had three more killed and another eight wounded.

"Come night time, we pulled out, but we ran into the Indians at least three more times during the night. We exchanged fire with them every time. Sergeant Winston was killed during one of the nighttime fights. Finally, we reached Fort Shaw just before dawn, bringing our wounded with us. But in all, we lost fourteen killed."

"What were the Indian casualties?" Benteen asked.

"Yes, sir, I knew that's where you were going with this. The next day a reconnaissance in force retraced our route, they brought back all of our dead, all them had been scalped and mutilated, but they did not find any Indian bodies. So the official report says that there were no Indian casualties at all."

"Is that true?"

"No, sir, it isn't true," Coletrain said. I personally saw nine Indians killed, and that was just on my side of the defensive circle. Winston told me he saw as many himself, though some of them might have been the same ones I saw. But without any proof, the official report remained—no Indians killed."

"No Indians killed," Benteen repeated.

"That was the report, yes sir."

"You may wonder why I asked you about this," Benteen said. "I asked you about it because many of the officers and men of the Sixth Cavalry have taken great delight in telling me that story. They use it to point out that nearly half of your platoon ran at first contact, and that the rest of the men did nothing more but hold on until they could run away come nightfall. All that, and not one Indian killed. It is proof, they say, that colored soldiers can't be depended on in a fight. I wanted to hear it from your own lips."

"Major, as God is my witness, I have told you the truth. I can only guess at how many Indians were killed, but I know there were at least fifteen or more."

"Which is nearly as many men as you lost," Benteen said.

"Yes, sir. But considerably less than Custer lost."

Benteen blinked a couple of times, then nodded. "You are right about that, Sergeant Major," he said. "You are right about that. And, if it is any consolation to you, I believe you."

"Thank you, Major."

"What is the mood of the troopers?" Benteen asked.

"It's very good, Major. Many have been in battle before, and the ones who have not been in battle are looking forward to it. And, Major, if you don't mind my saying so, they feel good because you are our commanding officer. Even the rawest recruit knows that there is no one in the army with more experience than you."

"That may be true, Sergeant Major. But not all my experiences have been positive ones," Benteen said.

DeMaris Springs

When Major Benteen brought the Ninth Cavalry through town, the townspeople turned out to welcome them.

The volunteer firehouse band played stirring marches and the soldiers rode in close formation. As they passed the mayor's office, Benteen ordered eyes right, and the guideon-bearers dipped their colors as the soldiers in every file except the extreme right file turned their eyes right in salute.

"Damn," Regret said. "Did you see them soldiers? They're all colored."

"All the better," Bellefontaine said.

"Why all the better?"

"Because they won't have enough sense to figure out that we're the ones that started all the trouble."

"Yeah," Regret said. He smiled. "Yeah, that's right, ain't it?"

"The mayor is holding another meeting tonight, and he's invited the officers."

"Colored? Comin' to a town meetin'?" Davis asked. "How's the rest of the town goin' to take that?"

"The officers are white."

"Oh. Well then, I reckon that will be all right."

The Rocking B Ranch

Clayton was lying in bed now with fresh bandages on the wound on his side, and wrapped around his arm. His daughter Diane was sitting on the bed beside him. Mrs. Clayton, Falcon, Cody, and Ingraham were in the bedroom as well.

"I can't thank you enough for bringing my husband home safely," Mrs. Clayton said.

"He had a lot to do with it himself," Falcon said. "Don't forget, he held the Indians off for twenty-four hours."

"And he was all alone," Cody added.

"I wasn't quite alone," Clayton said. "I had Diane with me."

"I wasn't with you, Daddy," Diane said.

Clayton had already told his wife about the dream in

which Diane warned him of the Indian, so she smiled and reached over to put her arm around her daughter.

"He means you were with him in spirit, dear," she said.

"And I owe thanks to Oliver Bowman as well," Clayton said. "I know now, what an ordeal he went through to find help. But what I can't understand is why the Indians have suddenly gone bad. We have lived here for ten years without the slightest bit of trouble. In fact, we have had Indian guests in our home."

"I've dealt with Indians for most of my life," Cody said. "And the most important thing I have learned is that they are always unpredictable."

"They're having a town meeting tonight in DeMaris Springs," Ingraham said. "Do you plan to go?"

"Yes," Falcon said. "I think we need to."

"I heard that they have brought in the cavalry," Mrs. Clayton said. "I'm glad. I hate it that it has come to this, but since it has, I feel safer knowing that the cavalry has been called in."

"When you men go to that meeting in town, give them my excuses for not being there," Clayton said.

Cody chuckled. "I'm sure they will understand."

The Crow village on the Meeteetsee

"Why have the whites turned on us?" Grey Dog asked.

"Did we not fight at their side against the Sioux?" Black Hand asked.

"Now we know, they are our enemy."

"Soldiers have come," Running Elk told High Hawk.

"Where are the soldiers?"

"They are very near to here," Running Elk said. "They are camped along the river the whites call Stinking Water."

"I think that is good," High Hawk said.

"Why do you think it is good?"

"I think the soldiers will see that we are not the ones doing these terrible things. And I think they will stop the whites from attacking us."

DeMaris Springs

Again, the citizens of the town gathered in the town center for a meeting called by Mayor Joe Cravens. As before, Pierre Bellefontaine was seated at the head table with the mayor, but joining them tonight was Major Benteen. Falcon, Cody, and Prentiss Ingraham were, once more, in the front row. And though Clayton had been unable to attend due to his wounds, Oliver Bowman, still showing the effects of his ordeal, was present.

"Ladies and gentlemen," Mayor Cravens said. "We are met again to discuss the Indian problem. In a few minutes, I'm going to call on Mr. Oliver Bowman to give us a firsthand report of his experience with the Indians, but first I want to introduce Major Benteen and his gallant officers. Would you gentlemen stand, please?"

Benteen and his officers stood to acknowledge the applause.

"Major Benteen and his soldiers are camped out on Stinking Water River, some west of here. I know that will make you feel better to realize that they are between us and the Crow village."

"If all the officers are here, who is in charge of the

soldiers right now?" Don Bailey asked. Bailey worked for Bellefontaine as a freight-wagon driver.

"Sergeant Major Coletrain is in charge at the moment," Benteen answered.

"I understand all your soldiers are colored. Is this fella Coletrain a colored man as well?"

"He is."

"Well, what if the Injuns decide to attack tonight, while you and all your officers are here? Do you think it is safe to leave a colored man in charge?"

"Sergeant Major Coletrain would be quite capable of mounting a defense if it became necessary," Benteen said.

"What I want to know is when are you going to go out to that village and clean it out?" one of the men in the audience shouted.

"And just what village would that be?" Benteen asked.

"Hell, you know what village. I'm talkin' about that nest of crows that's between here and Yellowstone."

"I don't believe that the Crow are our enemy," Benteen said.

"What do you mean they ain't our enemy? Didn't they kill the Barlow family? Ever' last one of 'em?"

"Indians may have killed the Barlow family . . ." Benteen started, but he was interrupted in mid-sentence.

"What do you mean may have kilt 'em? If you had seen 'em strapped to boards in front of the hardware store, you wouldn't of said may have. They was all butchered up, exactly the way Injuns do it."

"Even if it was Indians who killed them, there is no proof that it was Crow. And even if it was Crow Indians, chances are that it was no more than one or two renegades. I just do not believe that the Crow are our enemy."

"Then who is? Sioux?"

"More than likely it is Mean to His Horses and a few renegades, mostly Cheyenne, though I am willing to admit that he may have attracted Indians from some of the other bands as well."

"So, what do you plan to do about it?" Bellefontaine asked.

"Our first duty is to provide safety for the town of DeMaris Springs," Benteen said.

"The best way you can do that is to go after the Injuns and take care of them," one of the others said.

"I agree," Benteen said. "It is my intention to establish a very aggressive pattern of scouting. If we find armed Indians wandering around off the reservations, we will deal with them."

"You're making a mistake," Bellefontaine said. "The first thing you should do is attack the Crow Indian village near Yellowstone. Run them completely out of here, back up into Montana somewhere. Then, with that taken care of, you can start your scouting."

"Thank you, Mr. Bellefontaine," Benteen replied. "But I am in command, and I will conduct the military operation as I see fit."

DeMaris Springs bivouac

After the meeting broke up, Benteen invited Falcon, Cody, and Ingraham to the bivouac area of his two companies. There they had lunch together, and Benteen discussed his plans with them.

"I intend to send out a couple of scouts in strength," Benteen said. "I shall want one element to go down to the Graybull River, then follow it up to the Big Horn River. The other group will follow the Stinking Water River up to the Big Horn. Colonel Cody, if you would, I would like you to act as guide for the men who will take the Graybull scout. Colonel MacCallister, if you are agreeable to it, I would like you to act as guide for the group that will take the Stinking Water River scout. Proceed to the Big Horn, then go south until you effect a rendezvous with Colonel Cody, who will be coming north. If for some reason you do not effect the rendezvous then that will probably mean that the other detail is engaged, in which case I want you to continue on until you do make contact."

"All right," Falcon agreed.

"Colonel, MacCallister, I will send Sergeant Major Coletrain with you. Colonel Cody, Lieutenant Bond will be with you."

"Very good," Cody said.

"I will flip a coin to see which of you I will accompany," Ingraham said.

"I'm not sure having a civilian along is such a good idea," Benteen said. "I don't want any of my men to be distracted by having to look out for you."

"Major, I will speak for Mr. Ingraham," Cody said. "He has been in battle all over the world. He is more likely to be looking out for the soldiers than to have one of them looking out for him."

"Very well, if you say so," Benteen said.

Ingraham flipped the coin, then looked at Cody and smiled. "I'm going with you," he said.

"Aren't I the lucky one?" Cody replied, but his smile ameliorated the response.

"Trumpeter?" Benteen called.

"Yes, sir?"

"Would you please get Lieutenant Bond and the Sergeant Major and ask them to come to my tent?"

"Yes, sir."

As the trumpeter left to perform his mission, Benteen turned back to the others. "I see no reason for delay," he said. As soon as Bond and Coletrain arrive, I will instruct them to put together their scout. I think twenty men each will be sufficient. If you encounter an Indian force larger than that, don't engage, but keep an eye on them. Send one courier back here and another to the other scout platoon. That way we can strike them with maximum force."

CHAPTER TWENTY-THREE

After the meeting, Bellefontaine asked Sam Davis
and Lee Regret to come to his office.

"This isn't working out the way it was supposed to,"
Bellefontaine said. "If the soldiers don't drive the
Crow out of their village, we haven't accomplished
anything."

"Seemed to me like none of the folks in town was all
that happy about the way things is turnin' out either,"
Regret said.

"No, they weren't very happy about it, were they?"
Bellefontaine said. He drummed his fingers on his
desk for a moment. "Davis, those men who were with
you when you attacked the Indians a couple of weeks
ago. Do you think you could get them to go with you to
attack the village?"

Davis held out his hand. "Whoa now, Mr. Bellefontaine, there was only six of us done that. That ain't
near enough to attack a whole village."

"You wouldn't need too many, if you attacked in the
middle of the night, when they were all asleep."

"Even then, we would need more than six."

"What about twenty? Would that be enough if you attacked the village in the middle of the night, when nobody was expecting it?"

Davis nodded. "Twenty might do it," he said. "But I'm not sure I can come up with twenty men."

"If I paid them one hundred dollars apiece?" Bellefontaine said. "And two hundred dollars to each of you?"

Davis smiled broadly, and nodded. "Yeah," he said. "For a hundred dollars apiece, I can get twenty men for sure."

Confluence of the Stinking Water and South Fork Rivers

Falcon and Coletrain's platoon had come twenty miles up the Stinking Water River when they reached South Fork. Here, the water widened considerably to accommodate the two streams, and the men dismounted with the intention of having their lunch. The horses were watered, then ground-tethered in the grass so they could feed as well.

Just as they were settling down to their meal, someone shouted "Indians!" There were no more than half a dozen Indians, but their yelling, whooping and firing guns frightened the cavalry horses, causing them to pull away from their ground tethers and run away. Sergeant Major Coletrain and the others fired at the Indians, and the Indians retreated.

The soldiers stood there, holding smoking weapons in their hands, watching as the Indians rode away.

"What'll we do now, Sarge? All our horses is gone," one of the soldiers said.

"We're goin' to go get 'em," Coletrain replied.

Within fifteen minutes, half the horses were retrieved, and the men were about to get mounted to go after the remaining horses when the Indians returned. This time there were at least two hundred of them, against Falcon, Coletrain, and no more than twenty soldiers. The cavalrymen had no choice but to retreat onto an island in the middle of the river. There they formed a defensive circle, the soldiers lying belly-down on the ground while Falcon and Coletrain were on their knees inside the circle.

Within the first five minutes all of the recovered horses were killed, along with one of the soldiers. Sergeant Major Coletrain had been hit twice, once in the right thigh and once in the left leg.

Mean to His Horses, who was easily identified by the red and white painted face, led his Indians in a second charge toward the cavalry. The Indians fired volley after volley, but the soldiers returned fire and, because they were in the prone position and the Indians were exposed, the soldiers got the better of it. When Mean to His Horses pulled his Indians back he left almost fifty of them behind, dead in the water or along the banks of the river.

"They're gone!" one of the soldiers said.

"Not for long," Coletrain replied, his voice strained with pain.

"How bad is it?" Falcon asked. "Your wounds, I mean."

"I can't rightly tell," Coletrain said. "I guess you are going to have to take a look and let me know."

Falcon used his knife to cut open Coletrain's trousers so he could look at the wounds.

"Well, the one on your thigh isn't that bad," Falcon said. "Looks like it just caught the edge of it, left a crease, but there's no bullet."

"The other one?"

"It didn't hit a bone, and it didn't sever an artery that would cause you to lose a lot of blood, but the bullet is still inside, so it is going to need to come out."

"Think you can get it out?"

"I can try, but it's going to be hard with just a knife," Falcon said.

"I got me some tweezers," one of the other soldiers said.

"Tweezers? Yes, let me have those."

The soldier reached into his knapsack and pulled them out. Falcon was pleased to see that there were at least six inches long.

"Good, I can use this. Get fire going, boil some water, and drop this in the water."

"Colonel, you ain't plannin' on boilin' that, then stickin' it in Sarge while it's still hot, are you?"

"Yes. I've read that if you boil the instruments a doctor uses it helps keep the wound from festering," Falcon said.

"I don't know, I ain't never heard of such a thing," the soldier said. "I know I wouldn't want it stuck down in me if it was boilin' hot."

"Bates, do what the colonel says," Coletrain said.

"All right, Sarge, you the one he's goin' to use it on, not me."

Half an hour later, Falcon held up the bullet to show it. Then, tossing it aside, he found the cleanest piece of cloth he could find, and bound up Coletrain's wounds.

He had no sooner finished with Coletrain than the

Indians attacked again, and again the casualties among the Indians were very high. The cavalry suffered casualties as well, and because their numbers were so small, each loss was multiplied in its effect. Three more soldiers were killed and one more wounded.

Somewhat later the Indians made another charge, but were again repulsed, though not without cost, as two more soldiers were killed and two more wounded. After that, it turned into a waiting game. Now, there were only fifteen soldiers left alive, four of whom were wounded. The nature of the wounds ranged from slight to serious.

Mean to His Horses changed his tactics. Realizing that he had the soldiers trapped on the island, he decided he could wait them out, so he put his men on both sides of the island to deny the soldiers any opportunity to escape.

"Sergeant, they's Injuns all around us," one of the troopers said. "We are trapped here!"

"Look out there, Schuler," Coletrain said, pointing to the river and the riverbank. The river and the bank were strewn with bodies. "What do you see?"

"I see Injuns," Schuler said.

"Dead Injuns," Coletrain said. "We've killed nearly a hundred of them now."

"Yeah," Schuler said. He smiled. "Yeah, we have, ain't we?"

"Ol' Mean to His Horses has already decided that he can't run us off this island, so he plans to try and wait us out. Only, he can't do that, either."

"How come he can't?"

"We have plenty of ammunition, we have water, and we have fifteen days of rations. And if we had to, we can cut up one of the dead horses and cook it. But we aren't goin' to have to wait here fifteen days, because by then Lieutenant Bond will connect with us."

"Yeah," Schuler said. "Yeah, that's right, ain't it?"

Coletrain came back over to Falcon, then sat down, painfully, beside him.

"How is Jackson?" Coletrain asked, inquiring about the most seriously wounded of the soldiers.

Falcon shook his head. "I don't think he's going to make it," he said.

"Jackson is a good soldier," Coletrain said.

"Sergeant, from what I have observed, they are all good soldiers," Falcon replied.

"Thank you, Colonel," Coletrain said. "Comin' from you, that means a lot."

That night, two of the men volunteered to try and sneak through the Indians to go for help, but they were seen by the Indians and had to return to the island.

Near the Crow village on the Meeteetsee

Bellefontaine personally led the group he called the Wyoming Citizens Militia to the Crow village on the Meeteetsee River. It was two o'clock in the morning as the men rode across the Meeteetsee River, the hooves of their horses churning up the water and sending up a froth of bubbles as they did. As Bellefontaine had said, no one in the village expected anything.

High Hawk, perhaps to show the loyalty of the Crow, was flying an American flag over his tipi.

"Look at that," Regret said. "That Injun bastard is flyin' an American flag. Where do you reckon he got that?"

"More than likely he stole it from some soldiers he kilt somewhere," Davis said.

"That son of a bitch has some nerve," one of the others in the Citizen's Militia said.

"What are we goin' to do?" Regret asked.

"We're goin' to kill as many as we can," Bellefontaine replied. "That's what we are going to do."

A horse of one of the militiamen, perhaps nervous from the darkness and the tension, whinnied, then turned around. As he did so, one of his hooves struck a metal bucket that was lying on the bank of the river.

Inside the village

In her tipi, Quiet Stream heard the sound and she opened her eyes, not sure if it was something she actually heard, or whether it was something she dreamed. She lay there in the dark for a moment longer, drifting comfortably in that zone between sleep and wake, when she heard another sound. This time it was the sound of shod horses' hooves striking rocks.

None of the villagers' horses were shod.

"Father," she said. "There are white men in the camp."

Big Hand sat up and listened. Like Quiet Stream, he heard the sound of shod hooves on stone. He grabbed his rifle, then stepped through the opening of the tipi.

"Village awake! Village awake!" he called loudly. "White men are in camp!"

"Kill that screaming son of a bitch!" Bellefontaine shouted, and several fired at the same time. Big Hand fell, even as other warriors, heeding his call, were beginning to appear outside.

Bellefontaine's men began shooting at everyone they saw, men, women, and children. When they didn't have a specific target, they fired into the tipis. They also began setting fire to the tipis. They continued their indiscriminate assault for the next half hour, keeping up such a rate of fire that it was impossible for the Crow to marshal any type of organized resistance.

Davis and Regret, in a personal killing frenzy, killed and scalped three women and five children who had surrendered and were screaming for mercy. Following their example, the other members of the militia went on a bloodlust rampage of their own, killing all the wounded they could find before mutilating and scalping the dead, including pregnant women, children and babies. They also started plundering the tipis that had not yet been burned, dividing up the spoils.

As soon as the shooting started, Running Elk ran outside the tipi, and seeing quickly what was happening, he called out in English.

"Wait! Wait! You are making a mistake! These people are innocent! I am the one you want! I was with Mean to His Horses!"

Despite the fact that he was calling attention to himself, Running Elk was not hit, even though the bullets were whistling all around him. But though he was spared, he saw his mother, father, and young sister killed, along with dozens of other villagers.

Running Elk had come out without a weapon, hoping that by doing so he could surrender, and spare the other villagers. Now he realized that his plan would not work, and he started back into the tipi to get his rifle when he saw Quiet Stream go down.

"No!" he shouted, and, forgetting about his weapon, he ran to her.

"Quiet Stream!" he shouted, kneeling beside her. She had been hit by at least three bullets, and there was blood from her shoulders to her waist. "Quiet Stream!" he said again, softer this time, but his voice racked by the agony and anger he was feeling.

"I will never have your children," Quiet Stream said. She gasped a couple of times, then she quit breathing.

Running Elk looked around him, and seeing a war club in the hands of a nearby dead warrior, he grabbed the club then turned to look toward the white men who had come into the village on their killing spree.

"Ahheee!" he yelled as he ran toward one of the invaders. Reaching up, he pulled the white man from his saddle, and crushed his skull with one blow of the heavy war club.

Running Elk leaped into the empty saddle then, and with his war club held high, urged the horse in pursuit of another of the invaders. One blow brought down another invader, and another as well. So far Running Elk had managed to kill three men, and was sending panic through the others.

"Kill that Indian!" Bellefontaine shouted, pointing toward Running Elk. "One hundred dollars to the man who kills him!"

At least five men turned their guns toward Running Elk, and all five fired as one. Though Bellefontaine didn't know if all five rounds struck Running Elk, it didn't matter, because he saw blood, bone, and brain detritus erupt from the Indian's head, and he knew that the wild warrior was dead.

With Running Elk lying dead on the ground, the shooting stopped. For a long moment the mounted white men fought to control their nervous prancing and whinnying horses as they looked around the village, now fairly well lit by the burning tipis. Everywhere they looked they saw dead bodies, bodies of the warriors, bodies of the old men, including High Hawk whom many recognized, as well as bodies of women and children. High Hawk was wrapped in the American flag, perhaps believing that would save him.

Now, with their last resistance eliminated, Bellefontaine's men began to systematically scalp and mutilate the dead.

"Hey!" Lee Regret shouted, holding a small, black tuft of hair over his head. "Ha! Look what I got!"

"Damn, Regret, what the hell are you screamin' about? That's the scrawniest scalp I've ever seen," Davis said.

"That's 'cause it ain't a scalp," Regret said, a broad, evil smile spreading across his face.

"Well, if it ain't a scalp, what is it?"

Regret pointed toward Quiet Stream's now-naked body. There was nothing but blood at the junction of her legs.

"It come from the other end," Regret said, with a high-pitched laugh.

Examining Quiet Stream's body, Davis saw what Regret was talking about. He had made a scalp of her pubic hair.

When the attack was over, as many as 150 Indians lay dead, most of whom were old men, women and children. In the meantime, Bellefontaine lost only four men, three of whom had been killed by Running Elk.

CHAPTER TWENTY-FOUR

Confluence of the Stinking Water and South Fork

Back on the island the next morning, the Indians renewed hostilities. Again, Mean to His Horses sent his men in attacks against Falcon, Coletrain, and the Buffalo soldiers who were defending the island. And again the attack resulted in high cost to the Indians, this time inflicting no additional casualties among the soldiers.

Then, at mid-morning, Mean to His Horses tried a new tactic. He had two of his men bring forth a captive, and they stood just on the bank of the river so the captive could be seen. The captive was clearly a white man, a soldier, because he was in uniform.

"What the hell?" Coletrain said. "What is he doing there?"

"Do you know him?" Falcon asked.

"Yes, sir, I know him. That's Sergeant Depro. But he is supposed to be back at Fort Keogh. I have no idea what he is doing here."

"Buffalo Soldiers!" Mean to His Horses shouted across the water. "Leave your guns and go away. I will let you live and I will send the white-eye soldier with you. If you do not leave your guns and go away, I will kill the white-eye soldier, and his death will not be swift."

"Depro!" Coletrain shouted. "Depro, what are you doing there?"

"Coletrain! Sergeant Coletrain, is that you? Don't let me die, Coletrain! Me an' you is friends, ain't we? We soldiered together! Don't let me die!"

"Is that man a friend of yours?" Falcon asked.

Coletrain shook his head. "He's a long way from being a friend," he said. "But he is a soldier, so it doesn't matter whether he is a friend or not."

"Who is your best shot?"

"Well, sir, I don't mean to brag, none," Coletrain said. "But that would be me."

"All right," Falcon said. He turned to speak to the remaining soldiers, speaking just loudly enough for them to hear him.

"Men, Sergeant Major Coletrain and I are going to take out the two Indians who are holding Depro. I want all of you to pick out one of the other Indians as a target. As soon as we fire, you fire in volley. If we can take down seven or eight of them all at the same time, the rest of them are likely going to pull back, and that will give Depro a chance to come across the river."

The soldiers all nodded, then got into position and each of them picked out a target.

"You take the one on the left, I have the one on the right," Falcon said.

"What about Mean to His Horses?" Coletrain asked.

"He's sitting up on his horse, thinking he is in command," Falcon said. "But I'm shooting a Winchester, and as soon as we kill the two who are holding Depro, I'll re-chamber a round and kill Mean to His Horses."

Coletrain chuckled. "Damn if it ain't worth gettin' shot a couple of times, just so's I can see the expression on ol' Mean to His Horses's face when he realizes what's happened."

"Take aim," Falcon said, raising the rifle to his shoulder. "I'll count to three."

"Get ready, men," Coletrain called to the others, as he raised the carbine to his shoulder.

"One, two, three, fire," Falcon said.

Falcon and Coletrain fired at the same time, their shots followed almost immediately by the rest of the soldiers. The two Indians who were holding Depro fell, as did at least six more Indians. Mean to His Horses was totally shocked, and for just a second, he looked on in disbelief. Then, quickly, he realized what happened and he turned his horse to gallop away, but it was too late. As a coda to the previous volley, one more shot rang out, and Mean to His Horses fell from his saddle.

Depro was as shocked as Mean to His Horses had been, and he was still standing in place.

"Depro, run!" Coletrain said. "Come over here to us!"

Depro started across the water toward the island, and as he did so, the remaining men of Coletrain's platoon fired a second volley to keep the Indians back. As Depro reached the island, Schuler reached up and pulled him down to safety.

"Thank you," Depro said. "Thank you. I thought I was a goner for sure."

"What were you doing with them, Sergeant Depro?" Coletrain said. "I thought you were back at Fort Keogh."

"I had to go back," Depro said. "I couldn't leave the wagon."

"You couldn't leave the wagon? What wagon? Leave it where?"

"Sarge! Someone is comin'!" Schuler yelled.

"Get ready men," Coletrain said.

Once again, the men got into position to repel an attack, then as the body of men grew closer they could be seen riding in column of twos. Also, they saw the red and white guideon fluttering at the head of the column.

"It's Lieutenant Bond and our men!" Schuler shouted excitedly, and all the men stood then, and began cheering and waving.

"It looks like you men had quite a battle here," Cody said, taking in all the dead Indians.

"It kept us from getting bored," Falcon said.

"Damn, I went with the wrong group," Ingraham said. "I should have been here, where the battle was."

Cody chuckled. "Don't worry about it, Prentiss. I'm sure a man with your fertile imagination will be able to compensate."

Ingraham squinted his eyes for a moment, then suddenly saw the possibility in what Cody said, and he laughed out loud.

"You know, Colonel Cody. I do believe you are right," he said.

DeMaris Springs bivouac

The wounded and dead were brought back to the Ninth Cavalry bivouac area. One of the wounded, Private Travis Jackson, had died before they could get him back. The remaining wounded were treated by Dr. Urban, who was brought from town by Benteen, just for that cause.

"Did you have a surgeon in the field with you?" Dr. Urban asked as he looked at Sergeant Major Coletrain's wounds.

"No, sir," Coletrain said.

The doctor examined the wounds closely. "Well, someone took the bullet out."

"Yes, sir, that would be Colonel MacCallister."

Dr. Urban clucked his tongue and shook his head. "Is there nothing that man can't do? He did as good a job as any surgeon I know."

Coletrain smiled. "Yes, sir, seemed like he sort of know'd what he was a' doin', all right."

"Sergeant Major Coletrain?" Schuler said, as Coletrain began packing his shirttail back in.

"Yes, Schuler, what is it?"

"I think maybe you had better take a look at the guns."

"What guns?"

"The guns we picked from back at the island," Schuler said. "The guns the Injuns was usin'."

"What about 'em?"

"I think you had better take a look at 'em," Schuler said.

Benteen was in his command tent having coffee with Falcon, Cody, and Ingraham, when Coletrain stood outside and asked if he could enter.

"Of course you can come in, Sergeant Major," Benteen replied. "Grab a stool and join us. We're having coffee and a discussion about you."

"About me, sir?"

"I'm putting you in for the Medal of Honor," Benteen said.

Coletrain smiled broadly. "Well, sir," he said. "Well, now. Yes, sir, that would be quite an honor. Especially since I don't feel I did anything to earn it."

"Colonel MacCallister does," Benteen said. "And I set quite a store in what he has to say."

"Colonel, I appreciate the kind words," Coletrain said.

Benteen's orderly handed a cup of coffee to Coletrain, and he thanked him, then took a swallow.

"Now then, Sergeant Major, you wanted to see me?"

"Yes, sir," Coletrain said. "Sir, after the fight, several of the men went out onto the battlefield and began gathering up the guns the Indians was usin'. I thought they was all armed awfully well, and now I know why."

"Why?"

"Here are the serial numbers of three of the rifles."

Coletrain pulled a little piece of paper from his pocket, then began reading from it. "410543, 410275, 410221." He stopped reading and looked up at Benteen. "The fact is, Major, every weapon we picked up started with the numbers four one zero. I just read these three because privates Wright, Dunaway, and Karnes recognized them. They are same carbines they were carryin' before we got the new issue, and was told to turn them in. And seein' as I made out all the inventories, I remember that all the carbines started with the numbers four one zero."

"What are you saying, Sergeant Major? Are you suggesting that, somehow, the Indians managed to get their hands on our old weapons?"

"Not, just somehow," Coletrain said. "I know how they got them."

"Depro?"

"Yes, sir."

Benteen nodded, then got up from his stool and walked over to the door. The three soldiers Coletrain had mentioned were standing there, in case they were needed to validate the weapons as having belonged to them. Benteen believed Coletrain, and thus needed no validation. But he did need them for something else.

"Soldiers, find Sergeant Depro and bring him here."

"Yes, sir," Dunaway said.

"Under arrest," Benteen added.

The three soldiers, who had no love lost as to Depro, smiled in anticipation of the assignment.

"In shackles," Major Benteen added.

"I should have listened to you in the beginning, Sergeant Major," Benteen said. "You suspected he had stolen the weapons when they disappeared from the arms room, didn't you?"

"Yes, sir, but all it was, was me thinkin' it. I didn't have any proof."

"Well, we do now," Benteen said.

At that moment, Private Dunaway returned.

"He ain't nowhere around, sir," Dunaway said. "Someone said they seen him leave, goin' toward town."

"Gentlemen," Benteen said to Falcon, Cody, and Ingraham. "Would you like to go into town with me?"

Falcon and the others rode into town for the express purpose of finding and placing under arrest Sergeant Lucas Depro, but when they got the town, the reaction of the townspeople was such that they put Depro aside. The town was in a major celebration mode, with the volunteer firemen's band playing, fireworks exploding, and a general attitude of giddiness.

"What is going on?" Benteen asked someone who was standing on the side of the street, watching all the proceedings

"Ain't you heard? The Injuns has been whupped."

"Are they talking about your fight at the island?" Benteen asked Falcon. "How did they find out so fast?"

"Paper! Paper! Get your paper here!" a paperboy was yelling from the corner. "Extra, read all about it! Injun village wiped out!"

"Indian village?" Falcon asked. He shook his head. "Somehow I don't think they are talking about the island fight."

Ingraham dismounted, then went over to the paperboy and bought four papers, one for each of them.

EXTRA EXTRA EXTRA

BIG INDIAN BATTLE!
Marvelous Victory!

MANY INDIANS KILLED
TO BUT THREE MILITIA MEN KILLED

Our own brave militia conducted a surprise raid against the Crow Village on the Meeteetsee River last night. The results of the attack were so successful that your humble publisher has seen fit to print this, an extra issue, in order to place all the glorious details of the battle before the eyes of the public.

The attack was carried out by the Wyoming Civilian Militia, organized just for this purpose. In a brilliantly conceived tactical operation, Colonel Pierre Bellefontaine led but twenty men in an attack against three hundred or more armed and wily heathens. Striking in the night, the Wyoming Civilian Militia brought terror into the hearts of the selfsame savages who had but so recently brought terror into the hearts of the hapless white people whom they have so cruelly ravaged in their numerous debaucheries against innocent farmers, ranchers, and homesteaders.

Unwilling to surrender, the savages put up a fierce fight. Bullets were whistling through the night air in their deadly transit as they sought their targets. For hours the battle raged, with the Indians' terrible screams and war cries renting the air as if the howls came from all the banshees of hell. But through it all, our brave militia men stood their ground, often fighting hand to hand against numbers far superior to their own. Finally, as dawn broke, the village stood quiet and empty, its inhabitants having either fled or now lying dead on the ground.

Huzzahs for Colonel Bellefontaine and his brave militiamen, and plans are now underway to hold a town dance in their honor. All are invited where, we are told, souvenirs and booty taken from the village will be on display.

ment. The sound of hoofbeats gave him pause. Halting,

CHAPTER TWENTY-FIVE

The Crow village on the Meeteetsee

Falcon, Cody, and Ingraham picked their way through the bodies and residue of the Indian encampment. There were many more women and children than there were warriors. Like the warriors, the women and children had been scalped and mutilated. They found one pregnant woman with her stomach sliced open, with the dead baby half in and half out of her womb.

Cody had been a guest here in this very camp many times, so he knew several of the Indians and identified them for the others, at least those who had not been so badly mutilated that they could not be identified.

"That is Gray Antelope," he said, pointing to a warrior. "And that is Howling Wolf."

He saw a young woman with the top of her head gone. There were two children lying beside her, and the children had also been scalped. "That is White Deer and her children," Cody said. Then, seeing one of the Indians wrapped in an American flag, he pointed.

"And that is High Hawk. Five years ago I introduced him to President Chester Arthur, who gave him that flag."

"I can't believe the people of DeMaris Springs actually regard this as a great victory," Ingraham said. "Why, this was nothing more than a slaughter."

"They know only what they read in the newspaper," Cody said.

"Someone should tell the true story," Ingraham said.

"Well, there is only one of us who is an experienced writer," Falcon suggested.

"Yes, but after what the newspaper published in an extra declaring this to be a great victory, the editor may not be interested in publishing what I would write."

"It depends upon what the owner of the newspaper tells him to publish," Cody said.

"What are you saying? That the newspaper editor doesn't own the paper?"

"He does in a way," Cody said. "I loaned him the money to start the newspaper, with the idea that when my town is built, he would move the paper to Cody. He is one year in arrears in repayment of the loan. I believe that if I would mark the loan as paid in full, he would be most amenable to publishing the truth."

EXTRA   EXTRA   EXTRA

Raid on Crow Village Re-evaulated

NOW CONSIDERED A MASSACRE

Two years previous High Hawk, a sub chief of the Crow, was the guest of Buffalo Bill Cody in New York City. There, High Hawk met the cream of American society,

winning many over by his friendly
demeanor and native intelligence. He was
also taken to Washington and presented
to many high officials of our government,
and he met President Chester Arthur. He
so impressed Mr. Arthur that the President
of the United States honored him with a
flag that had flown over the White House
itself.

The Crow nation, long friends and
allies with white America, have fought
many battles at the side of our soldiers,
including that most devastating of battles,
the one in which Custer and all his gallant
men fell. The Crow were among those
who fell on that fateful day, including
Bloody Knife, High Hawk's own brother.

But Buffalo Bill Cody, Falcon
MacCallister, and Prentiss Ingraham, the
writer of this article, have just returned
from the Crow Village, where we discovered
the truth of the so-called victory of the
Wyoming Civilian Militia. While there,
we saw High Hawk lying dead in the dirt,
wrapped in the same flag given him by
President Arthur. From a view of the site
firsthand, the evidence is clear that it was
not battle between equal belligerents
meeting on a field of honor. Instead, it
was a massacre of the peaceful Indians
at the Crow Village. Since returning
from those terrible scenes, Buffalo Bill,
Falcon MacCallister, and your humble
scribe were approached by a member of
Bellefontaine's Wyoming Civilian Militia
who, sickened by what he witnessed, has
willingly agreed to tell the truth.

Contrary to the report previously published in this newspaper, the recent event cannot be described as a victorious battle, or even as a battle. Our witness tells us that Bellefontaine approached the village in the middle of the night, thus ensuring that all the occupants would be asleep. Then, with no warning, and without offering the Indians a chance to surrender, Bellefontaine ordered his troops to open fire.

The Indians, believing that they were at peace with the white man, watched in surprise as rifle and pistol balls flew through their village. Many of the hapless Indians had gathered under the American flag fluttering above High Hawk's tipi, thinking this would afford them protection. High Hawk drew down the Stars and Stripes and then, wrapping himself in it, raised a white surrender flag on the same pole. Some of the militiamen, seeing the white flag raised, ceased firing, but Bellefontaine ordered them to ignore the surrender flag.

The militiamen used every weapon at their disposal as they continued to slaughter the unfortunate villagers—rifles, pistols and even sabers which they employed with devastating efficiency against the women and children. The Indians ran in horror, but there was no place to hide. The soldiers herded the women and children into groups and murdered them in cold blood.

In one instance a six-year-old girl clutching a white flag was brought down in a hail of bullets—dead before she hit the ground. Babies' brains were dashed out against trees. The Bellefontaine men then performed outrageous depravities to the corpses. Bodies were scalped and ripped open with knives. The final grisly toll was 118 women and children, and forty-six warriors, including Chief High Hawk.

Buffalo Bill and Falcon MacCallister are filing a formal complaint with the United States Marshal's office, as well as the United States Army, charging Pierre Bellefontaine and those who accompanied him with murder. And knowing those two stalwart gentlemen as I do, the readers of this newspaper may rest assured that Bellefontaine and his minions will be brought to justice.

In the same issue there was another story, telling of the real heroes of the recent Indian engagements.

Mean To His Horses Defeated: To Buffalo Soldiers Goes the Glory

While the white man must face the disgrace of the shameful massacre of High Hawk and the innocent and peaceful residents of the Crow Village, we can celebrate the victory of elements of the Ninth Cavalry. But six days previous, Major Benteen dispatched two platoons of his battalion on a reconnaissance in force, one platoon proceeding northeast along the Stinking Water River in the direction of the Big Horn River, and the other proceeding northeast along the Graybull River with the same objective.

The northern platoon was under the command of Sergeant Major Moses Coletrain, he, as are all the brave soldiers of the Ninth, being a Negro. On the second day of their deployment, Sergeant Major Coletrain, with Falcon MacCallister acting as a scout, encountered a large body of Indians. It was suspected that the Indians were renegades led by Mean to His Horses. When the leader of the Indians came under closer observation, the hideous paint of his face, one side red and the other white, bore out the suspicion.

A charge was made by the mounted Indians, but it was most nobly and bravely repulsed. Many of the attacking Indians were killed, falling from their horses, some less than one rod from the defenders. But the soldiers also suffered killed and wounded.

A second charge was made by the Indians, but once more they were prevented from taking their objective. During the darkness, there was a cessation of hostilities, and Sergeant Major Coletrain thought to use the cover of night to dispatch two couriers, but they were discovered by the heathens and forced to turn back.

Although they were completely surrounded, outnumbered, and more than 30 miles from any hope of aid, the brave soldiers did not despair. During the night they much improved their breastworks. So efficiently did they do so that yet another attack by the Indians the next day was, as had been the previous attempts, turned back, this time without a single loss of life to the men of the Ninth.

Then the Indians tried a new tactic. They presented for the defending soldiers to see another soldier, not colored as were they, but a white man previously captured by them. This was Sergeant Lucas Depro. A threat was made to kill Depro if Sergeant Major Coletrain did not surrender his men, but Falcon MacCallister and Sergeant Major Coletrain foiled Mean to His Horses' plan with their excellent marksmanship. With unerring aim, Coletrain and MacCallister killed the two Indians in whose grasp Depro found himself. Then, following quickly with a second shot from his repeating rifle, MacCallister killed Mean to His Horses. A volley from the other defenders killed more Indians and the remaining savages lost all desire to continue the attack.

Subsequent to Lucas Depro's rescue, it was discovered that he has been facilitating the renegade depredations by supplying them with guns and ammunition. Major Benteen issued an order for Depro's arrest, but the villainous sergeant has disappeared.

* * *

Dance to Honor Militia Cancelled

Parade and Picnic to Honor Buffalo Soldiers

The celebration plans have been changed. While it would be unseemly to hold a dance for colored soldiers, there being no colored women in town, Mayor Cravens and the DeMaris Civic Association have agreed to hold a parade and picnic in their honor.

The order of the parade is thus: Mrs. Foley's Grammar School students, DeMaris High School Cadets, the DeMaris Volunteer Fire Brigade Pumper, the Fire Brigade Band, followed by Major Benteen and the mounted troopers of the Ninth Cavalry.

After the parade, there will be food tables featuring fried chicken, baked ham, potato salad, cookies, pies and cakes, all furnished by the ladies of the town. In addition there will be ice cream, provided by the DeMaris Civic Union. Mayor Joe Cravens will give a speech.

Mme. Mouchette's House for Discriminating Gentlemen

Although Madame Mouchette advertised her establishment as a place where gentlemen could "engage in stimulating conversation with well-mannered and attractive young ladies," it was a whorehouse, pure and simple, and everyone in town knew it.

At the moment Sam Davis and Sergeant Lucas Depro were in the lobby of the house, waiting for Lee Regret, who was upstairs with one of the "well-mannered and attractive" young ladies. Both Davis and Depro had already had their "stimulating conversations," and were reading the latest copy of the DeMaris Springs newspaper.

"Hey," Davis said. "Depro, have you read this? They're sayin' what happened out at the village was a massacre of Injuns. Bellefontaine ain't goin' to like this. He ain't goin' to like it that they're callin' it a massacre."

"Well, that's what you done, ain't it?" Depro asked.

"Maybe so, but there ain't no call to put somethin' like that in the newspaper. It's Cody and MacCallister that's causin' all the trouble. What's a minion?"

"What?"

"It says here that Cody and MacCallister are goin' to see to it that Bellefontaine and his minions will be brought to justice. What's a minion?"

"I don't know," Depro said.

"I don't know either, but whatever it is, it probably ain't good." Davis said.

"Sum' bitch!" Depro said. "Davis, did you tell anybody I'm the one sold them guns?"

"No, why would I do that?"

"It says here that they know I'm the one that sold the guns to the Injuns. Only it warn't just me, it was me, you and Regret. And I ain't plannin' on takin' all the blame my ownself."

Upstairs at Mme. Mouchette's

As she poured water into the basin, the girl saw Regret staring at her from the bed. She picked up the basin and started to step behind the dressing screen.

"Where the hell do you think you are goin'?" Regret asked.

"I'm going behind the dressing screen for my ablutions," she answered.

"For your what?"

"To wash myself."

"Why do you have to go behind a screen, just to wash yourself?"

"Because I'll also be washing . . ." she started then stopped in mid-sentence. "Because there are some things that a lady would like to do in private."

"You ain't no lady, you are a whore," Regret said. "I paid five dollars to be with you, that means you ain't got no privacy around me. I want to watch."

"You didn't pay for this," the woman said, stepping behind the screen.

"I said I aim to watch!" Regret said angrily, and getting out of bed, he padded naked over to the dressing screen, then knocked it down.

The girl let out a short shout of fear, then cringed, frightened that he was about to hit her.

"I ain't goin' to hurt you none," Regret said. "I told you, all I want to do is watch. Now, you go on with your—ablutions."

The girl, cringing silently in fear and embarrassment, dipped the cloth in the water and continued to wash herself. There was a loud knock on the door.

"Mabel, is everything all right in there?" Madame Mouchette called.

"Don't you be worryin' none about Mabel," Regret called back. "Me 'n her is gettin' along just fine."

"Mabel?" Madame Mouchette called again.

Regret walked over and jerked open the door. He saw the woman he had conducted the business with last night, the madam of the whorehouse.

"Get on with you now," Regret said. "I told you, there's no need for you to be worryin' none."

"You are naked," Madame Mouchette said. "You should have dressed before you opened the door."

"You tellin' me a woman what runs a whorehouse ain't never seen a naked man before?" Regret asked.

"I want to see Mabel."

"I tole you, there ain't no need for you to be worryin' about Mabel."

"I want Mabel to tell me that," Madame Mouchette insisted.

"Tell her ever'thing's all right," Regret called back over his shoulder.

"I'm fine, Madame Mouchette," Mabel said. "Really, it's like he said. Ever'thing is fine."

"I thought I heard you call out," Madame Mouchette said.

"It's nothing," Mabel said. "I knocked over the pitcher and spilled water on me. That's all."

"All right," Madame Mouchette replied. The tone of her voice indicated that she didn't quite believe what Mabel was telling her, but neither did she want to challenge it any further. "You call me if you need me," she added, and again, the tone of her voice was in direct opposition to the words themselves.

"Yes, ma'am, I will," Mabel replied.

"You satisfied?" Regret asked.

"Yes."

"Good. Now, get on back to doin' whatever you was doin', and let us be. I got to get ready for the big celebration today." Regret smiled broadly. "I'm one of them heroes the newspaper was talkin' about."

When Regret turned around, he saw that Mabel was no longer squatting down over the wash basin.

"What are you doin'?" Regret asked.

"I'm finished," she said.

"You're finished? That's all there is to it?"

Mabel nodded.

"Hell, what was so damn private about that? You didn't do nothin' but splash a little water onto yourself."

"Do you want me to bathe you?" she asked, smiling seductively at Regret, trying to get him back into a less belligerent mood.

"What?" Regret replied, as if surprised by the question. "No! Why the hell would I want that? I don't need me a bath, hell I took me a bath not no more than two, maybe three weeks ago. And I done it all by myself, too. And whenever the time comes in the next two weeks or so that I'll be takin' me another one, why, I'll take that one by myself too."

"Whatever you say," Mabel replied.

CHAPTER TWENTY-SIX

Regret was still packing his shirttail down in his pants as he came down the stairs to join Sam Davis and Lucas Depro, who were both waiting in the lobby. Depro was no longer wearing a uniform.

"Have you heard?" Davis asked.

"Have I heard? Have I heard what?" Regret answered.

"There ain't goin' to be no dance. Instead, they're havin' a parade and a town picnic today."

"Well, hell, that's as good as a dance, I reckon," Regret answered.

"Yeah, well, there's more to it," Davis said. "The picnic ain't for us, it's for the colored soldiers. And the reason they canceled the dance is 'cause the coloreds couldn't come on account of they ain't goin' to let the coloreds dance with the white women. And now, they're plannin' on celebratin' the coloreds killin' Mean to His Horses."

"Well, I don't see why they couldn't have a picnic for the coloreds, and go ahead and have that dance for us," Regret said. "That way, we could go to both of 'em."

Davis shook his head. "Ain't goin' to be nothin' for us—'ceptin' maybe jail if Cody and MacCallister have their way."

"What are you talking about?"

"Read this," Davis said, showing him the paper.

"You know I can't read."

"Yeah, I forgot. All right, what it says is that Cody and MacCallister went out to the Injun village to have a look around, and now they're tellin' the whole country that what we done was just murder a bunch of Injun women and children."

"How can you murder an Injun?" Regret asked. "Ain't that pretty much like steppin' on a bug or somethin'? It ain't like they was white or anything. I ain't never heard of no one gettin' in trouble for murderin' an Injun."

"There's more," Davis said. "They know that me and you and Depro sold the guns to the Injuns."

"Damn!" Regret said. "They know that? How the hell do they know that?"

"I don't know," Davis replied. "But it don't matter none how they know. The point is, they know."

"We need to get out of here," Regret said.

"Won't do no good to run," Depro said. "It won't make no difference where we go. I know both MacCallister and Cody, and believe me, them two can track a fish through water and a bird through the air. If they are alive, they'll find us."

"If they are alive," Davis said.

"What?"

"You said if they are alive," Davis repeated. "Seems to me like you just come up with the answer. If they are alive they'll find us, if they are dead, they won't. So, the smartest thing we can do is to kill them before we leave. That way we can go somewhere else and not worry 'bout being found."

"Yeah, well, killin' 'em ain't goin' to be that easy," Depro said. "Like I said, I know them two."

"Besides which, we ain't got enough money to go anywhere in the first place," Regret said.

"Don't worry about the money, we'll get it," Davis said.

"How we goin' to get any money? You plannin' on robbin' a bank or somethin'? 'Cause I ain't goin' to do that. A man can get hisself kilt, doin' somethin' like that," Depro said.

"We'll get it from Bellefontaine. He owes us," Davis said.

"Maybe he owes the two of you, but he don't owe me nothin'," Depro said.

"Sure he does. When you got them guns from the army, you was doin' that for Bellefontaine."

"Yeah," Depro said. He smiled. "Yeah, I was, wasn't I?"

Bellefontaine's office

"You are mistaken, gentlemen, I don't owe you anything," Bellefontaine said. "If you wish to run, feel free to do so. But I have no intention of leaving. Not now, not when I have everything going just the way I want it to go."

"You ain't got nothin' goin' the way you want it to go," Davis said. "Didn't you hear what I just said? The paper says what we done out at the village was a massacre."

"There are those who said the thing about Chivington at Sand Creek, and about Custer at Washita. But today Chivington is still a respected man in Colorado, and no one is more honored than Custer. I have no intention of letting a negative newspaper article change my plans."

"Yeah, well maybe that works for you," Depro said. "But it's different with Davis, Regret, and me. We sold guns to the Injuns. If they catch us, we're goin' to jail for that."

"Then, gentlemen, I suggest you start running."

"Yeah, that's what we're going to do, as soon as you give us enough money to get out of here."

"And how much do you consider to be enough money?" Bellefeontaine asked.

"I'd say about a thousand dollars apiece," Davis said.

"A thousand dollars apiece?" Bellefontaine laughed. "You must think I'm a fool. Get out of here. You are on your own."

"You can't turn your back on us now, not after all we've done for you," Davis said. He drew his pistol, then pointed toward the safe that sat against the back wall. "Open that safe and take out your money. We would'a been satisfied with a thousand dollars apiece. Now we want all of it."

"You're making a mistake," Bellefontaine said.

"Not as big a mistake as you just made," Davis said. "Now, open that safe like I told you to."

Bellefontaine walked over to the safe. "What makes you think I have that much money in this safe?"

"It don't matter to me how much money you have. However much it is, we're goin' to take it all," Davis replied.

Bellefontaine opened the safe and stuck his hand inside, then, so quickly that he almost got away with it, he spun around with a pistol in his hand.

"You didn't really think I was goin' to let you steal my money, did you?" he shouted.

But, though he was quick, Davis was quicker. He pulled the trigger and the bullet from his gun hit Bellefontaine in the forehead. He fell, dead before he hit the floor.

"See how much money he has, Depro," Davis said.

Depro looked into the safe, smiled broadly, then stuck both hands in and turned back toward the others with both hands filled with money.

"Look at this! There must be ten or twenty thousand dollars here," Depro said.

Davis looked at Bellefontaine's body. "The dumb son of a bitch should have give us the money," he said. "All we was askin' for was a thousand dollars apiece."

Quickly, the three men began taking money out of the safe and stuffing it down into their clothes.

Out on the main street, the air was redolent with the aroma of fried chicken, and freshly baked pies, cookies and cakes. But no one was eating yet, because all the people of the town were lined along both sides of the street to watch the parade. Mayor Joe Cravens had invited Falcon, Cody, and Ingraham to sit on the reviewing stand with him as the elements of the parade marched by.

First came Mrs. Foley's Grammar school, thirty-seven children from the first to the eighth grade. All were excited at being in the parade and they were waving flags they had made as a part of their school projects, ranging from no more than a few marks on a piece of paper the efforts of the first-graders, to genuine works of art among the eighth-graders.

Next came the eleven high school students, the excitement replaced by embarrassment. They were followed by the brand new pumper, consisting of glistening polished brass, the machine being pulled by six uniformed firemen. After the pumper came the Fire Brigade Band, the music of the tuba and the flute being the most noticeable.

Finally came the mounted members of the Ninth Cavalry, riding in a column of twos, led by Major Benteen. The soldiers were perfectly aligned, impeccably uniformed, and staring straight ahead as the sound of the horses' hooves echoed back from the buildings that lined both sides of the street.

"Ladies and gentlemen!" the town auctioneer shouted through the megaphone he was using. "Here are the heroes of the Stinking Water River fight! The officers and men of the Ninth Cavalry!"

The citizens of the town applauded, then gave the soldiers a loud cheer, notwithstanding the fact that they were black.

Very soon after the parade broke up, the word began passing up and down the street, moving with telegraphic speed.

"Pierre Bellefontaine is dead!"

"Bellefontaine kilt himself!"

"He must'a read the newspaper article."

"He didn't kill himself, someone kilt him."

"How do you know?"

"'Cause his safe was open and all his money was took."

"Bellefontaine is dead."

"Wonder who did it."

Eventually, the rumor reached even the reviewing stand, and Falcon, Cody, Ingraham, and Mayor

Cravens wondered about it, as did everyone else. That was when Mayor Cravens asked Buffalo Bill if he might come to his office for a few moments.

"I want to speak to you about your town," Cravens said.

"Are you going to try to talk me out of building it?" Cody asked.

"On the contrary, sir. Especially if it is true that Bellefontaine is dead. I want to examine the possibility of becoming a part of your new enterprise," Cravens said.

"All right," Cody said. "Falcon, would you excuse me for a while?"

"Take your time," Falcon said. "The aroma of all this food has been driving me crazy all morning, and I intend to try some of it out."

Climbing down from the platform, Falcon recognized Juanita Kirby, Gary, and Abby behind one of the tables. Smiling, he walked over to the table and touched the brim of his hat.

"Mrs. Kirby, how nice to see you," he said. He looked at Gary, who still had his arm in a sling.

"How is your arm?" Falcon asked.

"I have shown it to everyone," Gary said. "I'm the only one of my friends who has ever had a broke arm," he added proudly.

"Broken," Mrs. Kirby corrected.

"Yes, ma'am, I'm the only one."

Mrs. Kirby laughed and shrugged her shoulders. "Correcting his grammar is a losing battle," she said. The smile left her face. "Have you heard the rumor about Mr. Bellefontaine? Do you really think he is dead?"

"Generally, when the rumor is that strong, it is true,"

Falcon said. "I'm sure he is dead. The question, of course, is who killed him?"

"It could have been almost anyone," Mrs. Kirby replied. "As I told you before, he was not a man one could easily like. I imagine he had many enemies, and since the story came out of his brutal activity with those poor people in the Crow village, almost anyone could have done it. I'm just glad that my husband had already left Mr. Bellefontaine's employ. We are going back East, tomorrow."

"Well, I wish you all the luck in your move," Falcon said.

"So, did you just drop by the table to visit? Or would you like a piece of fried chicken?"

"I would love a piece of fried chicken."

The first shot rang out, just as Falcon reached for the drumstick.

One year later—excerpt from the now-published *MacCallister and Cody: Heroes of the Western Plains*

Before we come to the conclusion of this factual story of the adventures of Falcon MacCallister and Buffalo Bill Cody, I believe it would serve the reader well if a perfect picture could be summoned from my imperfect words, by which the reader could visualize the appearance of Falcon MacCallister on the day of the events to be here described.

Falcon MacCallister is a plainsman in every sense of the word, yet unlike any other of his class. He is north of six feet in height and looks even taller due to his bearing. He has broad shoulders, well-formed chest and limbs, a face that, though cured by exposure to wind, sun, rain, and cold, is nevertheless considered handsome by every woman who has ever made the observation. Whether mounted or afoot, Falcon MacCallister is one of the most perfect specimens of manhood one might ever see.

Of his courage, there can be no question, for it has been tested far too often for there to be any doubt. His skill in the use of the pistol and rifle is unerring, while his deportment is entirely free from all bluster or bravado. He is anything but a quarrelsome man, yet he has been involved in innumerable conflicts, always instigated by another party, and almost always ending in the death of his adversary.

On the day of the parade and picnic and while celebrating the victory over Mean to His Horses, extensively written about in a previous chapter of this book, Falcon MacCallister was confronted by the desperadoes, Sam Davis, Lee Regret, and Lucas Depro. Without regard to the safety of the innocent men, women, and children of DeMaris Springs, the three brigands began firing at Falcon MacCallister with the intention of killing him.

"MacCallister, you have drawn your last breath!" Davis yelled. "For my friends and I have come to lay you in your grave!"

"It is not I who will die this day, but you, for I am armed with the power of right!" Falcon called back. As he shouted at the villainous three, he drew his pistol and with but three shots, none wasted to put the innocent to danger, killed the men who would have killed him.

And with their demise, this story of Falcon

MacCallister and Buffalo Bill Cody, a factual account more thrilling and exciting than anything I have written of the two of them before, despite that it is true, comes to an end. Buffalo Bill has returned to tour with his Exhibition, and Falcon, though earnestly invited to be a part of the show, declined. As of this writing Falcon MacCallister continues to live in the wind, and his destiny now, as it ever shall be, is danger.

William W. Johnstone

cCallister and Buffalo Bill Cody, a factual
ount more thrilling and exciting than anything

Turn the page for an exciting preview of the
blockbuster new series, America's leading
Western writer captures the most violent
chapter in frontier history—in the saga
of a Yankee with a rifle, an outlaw with a
grudge, and a little slice of hell called . . .

SAVAGE TEXAS

by William W. Johnstone
with J. A. Johnstone

Authors of *The Family Jensen* and
Matt Jensen, *The Last Mountain Man*

Coming in September 2011

Wherever Pinnacle Books are sold

"Texas . . . Texas . . ."
—LAST WORDS OF SAM HOUSTON, SOLDIER,
PATRIOT, AND FOUNDER AND PRESIDENT OF
THE REPUBLIC OF TEXAS

CHAPTER ONE

Some towns play out and fade away. Others die hard.

By midnight Midvale was ablaze. The light of its burning was a fire on a darkling plain.

It was a night in late March 1866. Early spring. The earth was quickening as Midvale was dying.

The well-watered grazing lands of Long Valley in north central Texas supported many widely scattered ranches. Midvale had come into being at a strategic site where key trails came together. The town supplied the needs of local ranchers and farmers for things they couldn't make or grow but couldn't do without.

A cluster of several square blocks of wooden frame buildings, it had a handful of shops and stores, several saloons, a small café, a boardinghouse or two, and a residential neighborhood.

Tonight Midvale had reached its end. Its passing was violent. The killers had come to usher it into extinction. Raiders they were, a band of cutthroats, savage and merciless. They came under cover of darkness and fell on the town like ravening wolves—gun wolves.

The folk of Midvale were no sheep for the slaughter. The Texas frontier is no place for weaklings. For a generation, settlers had fought Comanche, Kiowa and Lipan Apache war parties, Mexican bandits and homegrown outlaws. The battle fury of the recent War Between the States had left this part of Texas untouched, but there was not a family in the valley that hadn't given husbands and sons to the armies of the Confederacy. Few had returned.

The folk of Midvale were not weaklings. Not fools, either. They were undone by treachery, by a vicious attack that struck without warning, like a bolt out of the blue. By the time they knew what hit them it was too late to mount any kind of defense.

Ringing the town, the raiders swooped down on it, shooting, stabbing, and slaying. No fight, this—it was a massacre.

After the killing came the plundering. Then the burning, as Midvale was put to the torch.

The scene was an inferno, as if a vent of hell had opened up, bursting out of the dark ground in a fiery gusher. Shots, shrieks sounded. Hoofbeats drummed through the red night as the killers hunted down the scant few who'd survived the initial onslaught.

All were slain outright, all but the young women and children, boys and girls. Captives are wealth.

The church was the last of Midvale to burn. It stood apart from the rest of the town, a modest distance separating it from worldlier precincts. A handful of townfolk had fled to it, huddling together at the foot of the pulpit.

That's where the raiders found them. Their screams were silenced by hammering gunfire.

The church was set on fire, its bell-tower spire a flaming dagger thrusting into night-black sky. Wooden beams gave, collapsing, sending the church bell tumbling down the shaft into the interior space.

It bounced around, clanging. Dull, heavy, leaden tones tolled Midvale's death-knell.

The marauders rode out, well-satisfied with this night's work. They left behind nearly a hundred dead men, women and children. It was a good start, but riper targets and richer pickings lay ahead.

The war had been over for almost a year, but there was no peace to be found on the Texas frontier. No peace short of the grave.

But for the ravagers and pillagers who scourge this earth, the mysterious and unseen workings of fate sometimes send a nemesis of righteous vengeance. . . .

CHAPTER TWO

From out of the north came a lone rider, trailing southwest across the hill country down into the prairie. A smiling stranger mounted on a tough, scrappy steel-dust stallion.

Man and mount were covered with trail dust from long days and nights of hard riding.

Texas is big and likes bigness. The stranger was no Texan but he was big. He was six feet, two inches tall, raw-boned and long-limbed, his broad shoulders ax-handle wide. A dark brown slouch hat topped a yellow-haired head with the face of a current-day Viking. He wore his hair long, shoulder-length, scout-style, a way of putting warlike Indians on notice that its owner had no fear of losing his scalp to them. A man of many ways, he'd been a scout before and might yet be again. The iciness of his sharp blue eyes was belied by the laugh lines nestled in their corners.

No ordinary gun would do for this yellow-haired wanderer. Strapped to his right hip was a cut-down Winchester repeating rifle with a sawed-off barrel and chopped stock: a "mule's-leg," as such a weapon was popularly known. It had a kick that could knock its recipient from this world clear into the next. It rested in a special long-sheath holster that reached from hip to below mid-thigh.

Bandoliers lined with cartridges for the sawed-off carbine were worn across the stranger's torso in an X-shape. A sixgun was tucked butt-out into his waistband on his left side. A Green River knife with a foot-long blade was sheathed on his left hip.

Some time around midmorning the rider came down off the edge of the Edwards plateau with its wooded hills and twisty ravines. Ahead lay a vast open expanse, the rolling plains of north central Texas.

No marker, no signpost noted that he had crossed a boundary, an invisible line. But indeed he had.

Sam Heller had come to Hangtree County.

CHAPTER THREE

Monday noon, the first day of April 1866. A hot sun
topped the cloudless blue sky. Below lay empty table-
land, vast, covered with the bright green grass of early
spring and broken by sparsely scattered stands of timber.
A line of wooded hills rose some miles to the north.

The flat was divided by a dirt road running east-west.
It ran as straight as if it had been drawn by a ruler. No
other sign of human habitation presented itself as far
as the eye could see.

An antlike blur of motion inched with painful slow-
ness across that wide, sprawling plain. It was a man
alone, afoot on the dirt road. A lurching, ragged scare-
crow of a figure.

Texas is big. Big sky, big land. And no place for a
walking man. Especially if he's only got one leg.

Luke Pettigrew was that man, painfully and painstak-
ingly making his way west along the road to Hangtown.

He was lean, weathered, with long, lank brown hair
and a beard. His young-old face, carved with lines of
suffering, was now stoically expressionless except for a
certain grim determination.

He was dressed in gray, the gray of a soldier of the army of the Confederate States of America. The Confederacy was now defunct a few weeks short of a year ago, since General Robert E. Lee had signed the articles of surrender at Appomatox courthouse. Texas had joined with the South in seceding from the Union, sending its sons to fight in the War Between the States. Many had fallen, never to return.

Luke Pettigrew had returned. Minus his left leg below the knee.

A crooked tree branch served him for a crutch. A stick with a Y-shaped fork at one end, said fork being jammed under his left arm and helping to keep him upright. Strips of shredded rangs were wrapped around the fork to cushion it as best they could. Which wasn't much. A clawlike left hand clutched the rough-barked shaft with a white-knuckled grip.

A battered, shapeless hat covered his head. It was faded to colorlessness by time and the elements. A bullethole showed in the top of the crown and a few nicks marked the brim.

Luke wore his uniform, what was left of it. A gray tunic, unbuttoned and open, revealed a threadbare, sun-faded red flannel shirt beneath it. Baggy gray trousers were held in place by a brown leather belt whose dulled-metal buckle bore the legend: CSA.

Many extra holes had been punched in the belt to coincide with his weight loss. He was thin, half-starved.

His garments had seen much hard use. They were worn, tattered. His left trouser leg was knotted together below the knee, to keep the empty pant leg from getting in his way. His good right foot was shod by a rough, handmade rawhide moccasin.

Luke Pettigrew was unarmed, without rifle, pistol or

knife. And Texas is no place for an unarmed man. But there he was, minus horse, gun—and the lower part of his left leg—doggedly closing in on Hangtown.

The capital of Hangtree County is the town of Hangtree, known far and wide as Hangtown.

From head to toe Luke was powdered with fine dust from the dirt road. Sweat cut sharp lines through the powder covering his face. Grimacing, grunting between clenched teeth, he advanced another step with the crutch.

How many hundreds, thousands of such steps had he taken on his solitary trek? How many more such steps must he take before reaching his destination? He didn't know.

He was without a canteen. He'd been a long time without water under the hot Texas sun. Somewhere beyond the western horizon lay Swift Creek with its fresh, cool waters. On the far side of the creek: Hangtown.

Neither was yet in sight. Luke trudged on ahead. One thing he had plenty of was determination. Grit. The same doggedness that had seen him through battles without number in the war, endless forced marches, hunger, privation. It had kept him alive after the wound that took off the lower half of his left leg while others, far less seriously wounded, gave up the ghost and died.

That said, he sure was almighty sick and tired of walking.

Along came a rider, out of the east.

Absorbed with his own struggles, Luke was unaware of the newcomer's approach until the other was quite near. The sound of hoofbeats gave him pause. Halting, he looked back over his shoulder.

The single rider advanced at an easy lope.

Luke walked in the middle of the road because there the danger of rocks, holes and ditches was less than at the sidelines. A sound caught in his throat, something between a groan and a sigh, in anticipation of spending more of his meager reserves of energy in getting out of the way.

He angled torward the left-hand side of the road. It was a measure of the time and place that he unquestioningly accepted the likelihood of a perfect stranger riding down a crippled war veteran.

The rider was mounted on a chestnut horse. He slowed the animal to an easy walk, drawing abreast of Luke, keeping pace with him. Luke kept going, looking straight ahead, making a show of minding his own business in hopes that the newcomer would do the same.

"Howdy," the rider said, his voice soft-spoken, with a Texas twang.

At least he wasn't no damned Yankee, thought Luke. Not that that made much difference. His fellow Texans had given him plenty of grief lately. Luke grunted, acknowledging that the other had spoken and committing himself to no more than that acknowledgment.

"Long way to town," the rider said. He sounded friendly enough, for whatever that was worth, Luke told himself.

"Room up here for two to ride," the other said.

"I'm getting along, thanks," muttered Luke, not wanting to be beholding to nobody.

The rider laughed, laughter that was free and easy

with no malice in it. Still, the sound of it raced like
wildfire along Luke's strained nerves.

"You always was a hard-headed cuss, Luke Pettigrew," the rider said.

Luke, stung, looked to see who it was that was calling him out of his name. The rider was about his age,
in his early twenties. He still had his youth, though,
what was left of it, unlike Luke, who felt himself prema-
turely aged, one of the oldest men alive.

Luke peered up at him. Something familiar in the
other's tone of voice . . .

A dark, flat-crowned, broad-brimmed hat with a
snakeskin hatband shadowed the rider's face. The sun
was behind him, in Luke's eyes. Luke squinted, peer-
ing, at first unable to make out the other's features.
The rider tilted his head, causing the light to fall on
his face.

"Good gawd!—Johnny Cross!" Luke's outcry was a
croak, his throat being parched from lack of water.

"Long time no see, Luke," Johnny Cross said.

"Well I'll be go to gawd-damned! I never expected
to see you again," said Luke. "Huh! So you made it
through the war."

"Looks like. And you, too."

"Mostly," Luke said, indicating with a tilt of his head
and a sour twist of his mouth his missing lower leg.

"Reckon we're both going in the same direction.
Climb on up," Johnny Cross said. Gripping the sad-
dlehorn with his right hand, he leaned over and down,
extending his left hand.

He was lean and wiry, with strength in him. He took
hold of Luke's right hand in an iron grip and hefted
him up, swinging the other up onto the horse behind
him. It helped that Luke didn't weigh much.

Luke got himself settled. "I want to keep hold of this crutch for now," he said.

"I'll tie it to the saddle, leave you with both hands free," Johnny said. He used a rawhide thong to lash the tree branch in place out of the way. A touch of Johnny's boot heels to the chestnut's flanks started the animal forward.

"Much obliged, Johnny."

"You'd do the same for me."

"What good would that do? I ain't got no horse."

"Man, things must be tough in Hangtree County."

"Like always. Only more so, since the war."

They set out for Hangtown.

Johnny Cross was of medium height, compact, trim, athletic. He had black hair and clean-lined, well-formed features. His hazel eyes varied in color from brown to yellow depending on the light. He had a deep tan and a three-day beard. There was something catlike about him with his restless yellow eyes, self-contained alertness and lithe, easy way of moving.

He wore a sunbleached maroon shirt, black jeans and good boots. A pair of guns were strapped to his hips. Good guns.

Luke noticed several things right off. Johnny Cross had done some long, hard riding. His clothes were trail-worn, dusty; his guns, what Luke could see of them in their holsters, were clean, polished. Their inset dark wooden handles were smooth, well worn with use. A late-model carbine was sheathed in the saddle scabbard.

The chestnut horse was a fine-looking animal. Judging by its lines it was fast and strong, with plenty of endurance. The kind of mount favored by one on the dodge. One thing was sure:

Johnny Cross was returning to Hangtree in better shape than when he left it.

The Cross family had always been dirt-poor, honest but penniless. Throughout his youth up till the time he went off to war, Johnny had worn mostly patched, outgrown clothes and gone shoeless for long periods of time.

Johnny Cross handed the other a canteen. "Here, Luke, cut the dust some."

"Don't mind if I do, thanks." Luke fought to still the trembling in his hands as he took hold of the canteen and fumbled open the cap. The water was as warm as blood. He took a mouthful and held it there, letting the welcome wetness refresh the dust-dry inside of his mouth.

His throat was so dry that at first he had trouble swallowing. He took a couple of mouthfuls, stopping though still thirsty. He didn't want to be a hog or show how great his need was. "Thank you kindly," he said, returning the canteen.

Johnny put it away. "Sorry I don't have something stronger."

"That's plenty fine," Luke said.

"Been back long?"

"Since last fall."

"How's your folks, Luke?"

"Pa got drowned two years ago trying to cross the Liberty River when it was running high at flood time."

"Sorry to hear that. He was a good man," Johnny said.

Luke nodded. "Hardworking and godfearing . . . for all the good it done him."

"Your brothers?"

"Finn joined up with Ben McCullough and got kilt at Pea Ridge. Heck got it in Chicamagua."

"That's a damned shame. They was good ole boys."

"War kilt off a lot of good ole boys."

"Ain't it the truth."

The two were silent for a spell.

"Sue Ellen's married to a fellow over to Dennison way," Luke went on. "Got two young'uns, a boy and a girl. Named the boy after Pa. Ma's living with them."

"Imagine that! Last time I saw Sue Ellen she was a pretty little slip of a thing, and now she's got two young'uns of her own," Johnny said, shaking his head. "Time sure does fly . . ."

"Four years is a long time, Johnny."

"How was your war, Luke?"

"I been around. I was with Hood's Brigade."

"Good outfit."

Luke nodded. "We fought our way all over the South. Reckon we was in just about every big battle there was. I was with 'em right through almost to the finish at the front lines of Richmond, till a cannonball took off the bottom part of my leg."

"That must've hurt some," Johnny said.

"It didn't tickle," Luke deadpanned. "They patched me up in a Yankee prison camp where I set for a few months until after Appomatox in April of '65, when they set us all a-loose. I made my way back here, walking most of the way.

"What about you, Johnny? Seems I heard something about you riding with Bill Anderson."

"Did you? Well, you heard right."

Hard-riding, hard-fighting Bill Anderson had led a band of fellow Texans up into Missouri to join up with William Clarke Quantrill, onetime schoolteacher turned leader of a ferociously effective mounted force of Confederate irregulars in the border states. The fighting there was guerrilla warfare at its worst, an unending series of ambushes, raids, flight, pursuit and counterattack—an ever-escalating spiral of brutalities and atrocities on both sides.

"We was with Quantrill," Johnny Cross said.

"How was it?" Luke asked.

"We gave those Yankees pure hell," Johnny said, smiling with his lips, a self-contained, secretive smile.

His alert yellow-eyed gaze turned momentarily inward, bemused by cascading memories of hard riding and hard fighting. He tossed his head, as if physically shaking off the mood of reverie and returning to the present.

"Didn't work out too well in the end, though," Johnny said at last. "After Bill's sister got killed—she and a bunch of women, children and old folks was being held hostage by the Yanks in a house that collapsed on 'em—Bill went off the deep end. He always had a mean streak but after that he went plumb loco, kill crazy. That's when they started calling him Bloody Bill."

"You at Lawrence?" asked Luke.

Lawrence, Kansas, was a longtime abolitionist center and home base for Jim Lane's Redlegs, a band of Yankee marauders who'd shot, hanged and burned their way through pro-Confederate counties in Missouri. In retaliation Quantrill had led a raid on Lawrence that became one of the bloodiest and most notorious massacres of the war.

"It wasn't good, Luke. I came to kill Yankee soldiers. This business of shooting down unarmed men—and boys—it ain't sporting."

"No more 'n what the Redlegs done to our people."

"I stuck with Quantrill until the end, long after Bill split off from him to lead his own bunch. They're both dead now, shot down by the bluebellies— I'd appreciate it if you'd keep that to yourself," Johnny said, after a pause. "The federals still got a grudge on about Quantrill and ain't too keen on amnestying any of our bunch."

"You one of them pistol-fighters, Johnny?"

Johnny shrugged. "I'm like you, just another Reb looking for a place to light."

"You always was good with a gun. I see you're toting a mighty fine-looking pair of the plow handles in that gun belt," Luke said.

"That's about all I've got after four years of war, some good guns and a horse." Johnny cut an involuntary glance at the empty space below Luke's left knee.

"Not that I'm complaining, mind you," he added quickly.

"Hold on to them guns and keep 'em close. Now that you're back, you're gonna need 'em," Luke said.

"Yanks been throwing their weight around?" Johnny asked.

Luke shook his head. "'T'ain't the Yanks that's the problem. Not yet, anyhow. They's around some but they're stretched kind of thin. There's a company of them in Fort Pardee up in the Breaks."

"They closed that at the start of the war, along with all them forts up and down the frontier line," Johnny said.

"It's up and running now, manned by a company of bluebelly horse soldiers. But that ain't the problem— not that I got any truck with a bunch of damn Yankees," Luke said.

"'Course not."

"What with no cavalry around and most of the menfolk away during the war, no home guard and no

Ranger companies, things have gone to rot and ruin hereabouts. The Indians have run wild, the Comanches and the Kiowas. Comanches, mostly. Wahtonka's been spending pretty much half the year riding the warpaths between Kansas and Mexico. Sometimes as far east as Fort Worth and even Dallas."

"Wahtonka? That ol' devil ain't dead yet?"

Luke shook his head. "Full of piss and vinegar and more ornery than ever. And then there's Red Hand."

"I recollect him. A troublemaker, a real bad 'un. He was just starting to make a name for himself when I went north."

"He's a big noise nowadays, Johnny. Got hisself a following among the young bucks of the tribe. Red Hand's been raising holy hell for the last four years with no Army or Rangers to crack down on him. There's some other smaller fry but them two are the real hellbenders.

"But that's not the least of it. The redskins raid and move on. But the white badmen just set. The county's thick with 'em. Thicker 'n flies swarming a manure pile in a cow pasture on a hot summer day. Deserters from both armies, renegades, outlaws. Comancheros selling guns and whiskey to the Indians. Backshooters, women-killers. The lowest. Bluecoats are too busy chasing the Indians to bother with them. Folks 're so broke that there ain't hardly nothing left worth stealing any more but that don't matter to some hombres. They's up to all kinds of devilments out of pure meanness.

"Hell, I got robbed right here on this road not more than a day ago. In broad daylight. I didn't have nothing worth stealing but they took it anyhow. It'd been different if I'd had me a sixgun. Or a good double-barreled sawed-off."

"Who done it, Luke?"

"Well, I'll tell you. First off, I been living out at the old family place, what's left of it," Luke said. "Somebody put the torch to it while I was away. Burned down the ranch house and barn."

"Yanks?" Johnny asked.

Luke shook his head. "Federals never got to Hangtree County during the war. Probably figured it wasn't worth bothering with. No, the ranch must've been burned by some no-goods, probably just for the hell of it.

"Anyhow I scrounged up enough unburnt planks and shacks to build me a little shack; I been living there since I come back. Place is thick with maverick cattle—the whole range is. Strays that have been gone wild during the war and now there's hundreds, thousands of them running around loose. Every now and then I catch and kill me one for food. I'd've starved without.

"I had me some hides I'd cleaned and cured. I was bringing 'em into town to sell or barter at the general store. Some fishhooks, chaw of tobacco, seeds . . ."

"And whiskey," Johnny said.

"Hell, yes," Luke said. "Had my old rifled musket and mule. Never made it to Hangtown—I got held up along the way. Bunch of no-accounts come up, got the drop on me. Five of them."

"Who?"

"Strangers, I never seed 'em before. But when I see 'em again— Well, never mind about that now. Lot of outsiders horning in around here lately. I ain't forgetting a one of 'em. Led by a mean son name of Monty."

"Monty," Johnny echoed, committing the name to memory.

"That's what they called him, Monty. Big ol' boy with a round fat face and little piggy eyes. Cornsilk hair so fine and pale it was white. Got him a gold front tooth a-shining and a-sparkling away in the middle of his mouth," Luke said. "Him and his crowd gave me a whomping. Busted my musket against a tree. Shot my poor ol' mule dead for the fun of it. Busted my crutch over my head. It hurt, too."

Luke took off his hat, pointing out a big fat lump in the middle of his crown.

"That's some goose egg. Like I said, you always was a hardheaded fellow. Lucky for you," Johnny said.

"Yeh, lucky." Luke put his hat back on, gingerly settling it on his head. "While I was out cold they stole everything I had: my hides, my knife, even my wooden leg. Can you beat that? Stealing a man's wooden leg! Them things don't grow on trees, you know. That's what really hurt. I walked from hell to Texas on that leg. Yes, you could say I was attached to it."

"You could. I wouldn't."

"When I come to, them owlhoots was talking about if'n they should kill me or not. Only reason they didn't gun me down on the spot is 'cause Monty thought it would be funny to leave me alive to go crawling across the countryside."

"Yankees?"

"Hell no, they was Southerners just like us. Texans, some of 'em, from the way they talked," said Luke.

His face set in lines of grim determination. "I'll find 'em, I got time. When I do, I'll even up with 'em. And then some. That gold tooth of Monty's is gonna make me a good watch fob. Once I get me a watch."

He waved a hand dismissively, shooing away the topic as if it were a troublesome insect. "Not that I want to bother you with my troubles. Just giving you the lay of the land, so to speak. And you, Johnny, what're you doing back here?"

Johnny Cross shrugged. "I came home for a little peace and quiet, Luke. That's all."

"You come to the wrong place."

"And to lay low. The border states ain't too healthy for any of Quantrill's crowd."

"You wanted, Johnny?"

"Not in Texas." After a pause, he said, "Not in this part of Texas."

"You could do worse. Hangtree's a big county with lots of room to get lost in. The Yanks are quartered forty miles northwest at Fort Pardee in the Breaks. They don't come to Hangtown much and when they do they's just passing through. They got their hands full chasing Indians."

"They catch any?"

Luke laughed. "From what I hear, they got to look sharp to keep the Indians from catching them."

"Good, that'll keep 'em out of my hair."

"What're your plans, Johnny?"

"One thing I know is horses. Mustangs still running at Wild Horse Gulch?"

"More now than ever, since nobody was rounding 'em up during the war."

"Figured I'd collect a string and sell 'em. Folks always need horses, even in hard times. Maybe I'll sell 'em to those bluebellies at the fort."

Luke was shocked. "You wouldn't!"

"Gold's gold and the Yanks are the ones that got it nowadays," said Johnny Cross.

Something in the air made him look back. A dust cloud showed in the distance east on the road, a brown smudge on the lip of the blue bowl of sky. Johnny reined in, turning the horse to face back the way they came. "Company's coming," he said.

"Generally that means trouble in these parts," Luke said.

"Ain't necessarily so, but that's the way to bet it," he added.

Johnny Cross unfastened the catch of the saddlebag on his right-hand side, reaching in and pulling out a revolver. A big .44 frontloading cap-and-ball sixgun like the ones worn on his hips: new, clean and potent.

"Here," he said, holding it out to Luke. "Take it," he said when the other hesitated.

Luke took it. The gun had a satisfying heft and balance in his hand. "A six-gun! One of them repeating revolvers," Luke marveled.

"Know how to use it?" Johnny asked.

"After four years with Hood's Brigade?" Luke said in disbelief.

"In that case I'd better show you how it works, then. I wouldn't want you shooting me or yourself by accident," Johnny said, straight-faced.

Luke's scowl broke into a twisted grin. "Shucks, you're joshing me," he said.

"I am? That's news to me."

"You're still doing it, dang you."

Johnny Cross flashed him a quick grin, strong white teeth gleaming, laugh lines curling up around the corners of his hazel eyes. A boyish grin, likable somehow, with nothing mean in it.

Sure, Johnny was funning Luke. Hood's Brigade of Texans was one of the hardest-fighting outfits of the Confederacy, whose army had been distinguished by a host of fierce and valiant fighters.

Johnny turned the horse's head, pointing it west, urging it forward into a fast walk.

Luke stuck the pistol into the top of his waistband on his left side, butt-out.

"It's good to have something to fill the hand with. Been feeling half-nekkid without one," he said.

"With what's left of that uniform, you *are* half-nekkid," Johnny said.

"How many more of them ventilators you got tucked in them saddlebags?"

"Never enough."

"You must have been traveling in some fast company, Johnny. I heard Quantrill's men rode into battle with a half-dozen guns or more. That true?"

"And more. Reloading takes time. A fellow wants a gun to hand when he wants it."

Luke was enthusiastic. "Man, what we couldn't have done with a brace of these for every man in the old outfit!"

"If only," Johnny said flatly. His eyes were hard, cold.

A couple of hundred yards farther west, a stand of timber grew on the left side of the road. A grove of cottonwood trees.

East, the brown dust cloud grew. "Fair amount of riders from the dust they're kicking up. Coming pretty fast, too," said Luke, looking back.

"Wouldn't it be something if it was that bunch who cleaned you out?"

"It sure would. Any chance it's somebody on your trail, Johnny?"

"I ain't been back long enough."

Luke laughed. "Don't feel bad about it, hoss," he said. "It's early yet."

Johnny Cross turned the horse left, off the dirt road

into the cottonwood grove. The shade felt good, thin though it was. The Texas sun was plenty fierce even at the start of spring. Sunlight shining through spaces in the canopy of trees dappled the ground with a mosaic of light and shade. A wild hare started, springing across the glade for the cover of tall grass.

Johnny took the horse in deep behind a concealing screen of brush. "We'll just let these rannies have the right of way so we can get a looksee at 'em."

Luke was serious, in dead earnest. "Johnny—if it is that pack that tore into me—Monty is mine."

"Whoa, boy. Don't go getting ahead of yourself, Luke. Even if it is your bunch—especially if it is—don't throw down on 'em without my say-so. They'll get what's coming to 'em, I promise you that. But we'll pick the time and place. Two men shooting off the back of one horse ain't the most advantageous layout for a showdown.

"I know you got a hard head but beware a hot one. It should have cooled some after four years of war," Johnny said.

"Well—it ain't," said Luke.

Johnny grinned. "Me, neither," he said.

The blur at the base of the dust cloud sweeping west along the road resolved itself into a column of riders. About a dozen men or so.

They came in tandem: four pairs in front, then the wagon, then two horsemen bringing up the rear. Hardbitten men doing some hard traveling, as indicated by the trail dust covering them and the sweat-streaked flanks of their horses. They wore civilian clothes, broadbrimmed hats, flannel shirts, denim pants. Each rider was armed with a holstered sidearm and a carbine in a saddle-scabbard.

A team of six horses yoked in tandem drew the wagon. Two men rode up front at the head of the wagon, the driver and a shotgun messenger. A freight wagon with an oblong-shaped hopper, it was ten feet long, four feet wide, and three feet high. A canvas tarpaulin tied down over the top of the hopper concealed its contents. Crates, judging by the shape of them under the tarp.

The column came along at a brisk pace, kicking up plenty of dust. There was the pounding of hoofbeats, the hard breathing of the horses, the creak of saddle leather. Wagon wheels rumbled, clattering.

The driver wore his hat teamster style, with the brim turned up in front. The men of the escort were hard-eyed, grim-faced, wary. They glanced at the cottonwood grove but spotted no sign of the duo on horseback.

On they rode, dragging a plume of brown dirt in their wake. It obscured the scene long after its creators had departed it. Some of the dust drifted into the glade, fine powder falling on Johnny, Luke, and the horse. Some dust got in the chestnut's nostrils and he sneezed.

Luke cleared his throat, hawked up a glob of phlegm and spat. Johnny took a swig from his canteen to wash the dust out out of his mouth and throat, then passed the canteen to Luke. "What do you make of that?" he asked.

"You tell me," Luke said.

"You're the one who's been back for a while."

"I never saw that bunch before. But I don't get into town much."

"I'll tell you this: they was loaded for bear."

"They must've been Yankees."

"How can you tell? They don't wear signs, Luke."

"They looked like they was doing all right. Well-fed, good guns and mounts, clothes that wasn't rags. Only folks getting along in these parts are Yankees and outlaws. They was escorting the wagon, doing a job of work. Outlaws don't work. So they must be Yanks, damn their eyes."

"Could be."

"They got the right idea, though. Nothing gets nowhere in Hangtree less'n it's well guarded," said Luke. "Wonder what was in that wagon?"

"I wonder," Johnny Cross said, thoughtfully stroking his chin. A hard, predatory gleam came to his narrowed eyes as they gazed in the direction where the convoy had gone.